ICE for the ESKIMO

Also by the author

SHADOW KILLS
SLOW DANCER

ICE for the ESKIMO

A J. D. Hawkins Mystery

W. R. Philbrick

BEAUFORT BOOKS
New York

No character in this book is intended to represent any actual person; all the incidents of the story are entirely fictional in nature.

Library of Congress Cataloging-in-Publication Data

Philbrick, W. R. (W. Rodman)
Ice for the Eskimo.

I. Title.
PS3566.H474513 1987 813'.54 86-22290
ISBN 0-8253-0403-2

Published in the United States by Beaufort Books Publishers, New York.

Designed by Irving Perkins Associates

Printed in the U.S.A. *First Edition*

10 9 8 7 6 5 4 3 2 1

FOR LYNN H.,
WITH LOVE.

Acknowledgment

For a clear picture of trial procedures in Boston, the author is indebted to Lawrence F. O'Donnell for having the courage and tenacity to write *DEADLY FORCE: The true story of how a badge can become a license to kill.*

I

THE ABDUCTION

1

I WAS BUSY RUNNING A SMALL WAR ON THE second Thursday of November and as a result didn't see in the paper about Fitzy withdrawing from the lawsuit until that afternoon. By then Lois had come to tell me the children had been snatched and Fitzy was having a breakdown and my gun-battle strategies no longer seemed important.

At the time my old pal Lieutenant Detective Casey had his back to the wall. The wall was cinderblock, part of an abandoned warehouse in Southie, and chips of it had been spattered loose by automatic gunfire. Casey had been hit by a piece of the exploding concrete. Blood poured from a superficial head wound, blinding him. He held his empty .38 in both hands, following the sound of the wounded psychopath he had stalked into the warehouse. The lunatic killer was armed with an Uzi submachine gun, an antique Lüger, and a Colt .38 he had taken off Detective Shannon after leaving him for dead. The killer had been gut-shot by Casey with his last bullet. Now he was crawling toward the blinded cop, dragging himself across the warehouse floor. The sheath knife strapped to his left shin made a scuttling sound. . . .

Casey pivoted, I wrote, *trying to judge the killer's distance, his precise location.*

''Stop right there,'' he warned. ''Or I'll shoot.''

The killer laughed. The sound of it echoed, disorienting the blinded detective.

''What I'm going to do,'' the killer whispered, ''I'm going to get close enough to slice your throat. You won't know I'm there until you feel the cold steel.''

Outside, in the dumpster where he'd been left for dead, Detective Shannon groaned and sat up.

The intercom sounded.

I punched the SAVE key on the word processor and froze the action. As I wheeled away from my desk I wondered how I was going to get Shannon from the dumpster to the warehouse in time to save Casey. Had the killer been counting the shots? Did he know Casey's .38 was empty? Could he have been confused by the echoes in the empty warehouse? Maybe that would give Detective Shannon enough time to stumble in for the rescue. I pulled up to the foyer wall, swiveled my wheelchair sideways, and pressed the intercom.

"Yes?"

"It's Lois, Jack. I need to talk."

Even distorted by the crackling intercom the fear in her voice was audible. I rolled over to the door and went through the drill of undoing the locks and the chains and sat there, waiting to find out what had gone wrong.

Finian Xavier Fitzgerald is my lawyer and my friend, having been the latter a lot longer than the former. We squeaked through Boston Latin together, passing crib notes and glossy magazines of questionable taste. We once kissed the same girl in the same basement of the same church rec hall and did not come to blows, quite. We had our first taste of booze together, our first reefer (mostly catnip), and once shared a grimy, roach-infested flat in Dorchester. When I got married to Marge he was my best man and when he got married to Lois I was his. After my "accident," Fitzy came to the rescue and sued the Boston Police Department and the City of Boston for a whole lot of money and won most of it, enabling me to buy my Beacon Street apartment and pay for the special interior conversions that made day-to-day life easier for a paraplegic.

When Marge and I split, Lois was there to help me through it. Two years later, when Megan Drew came into my life, it was Lois who made me face up to my disability and overcome my fears, so that Meg and I could have a virtually normal relationship.

Lois came through the door shaking.

''It's the twins,'' she said.

Lois has a willowy build, thick dark hair that fans over her shoulders, strong cheekbones, and deep-set blue eyes. For the first time in my experience those eyes were empty.

''They're gone, Jack. They've been taken.''

In the movies zombies walk as if jerked by wires, slightly out of sync, and that was how Lois moved. She put her purse down on the foyer tiles, then picked it up again. She kept bringing her hand up to touch her face and then missing, or changing her mind. She looked at the floor, the ceiling, anywhere rather than make eye contact. After a while I got her to come into the living room, sit down, hold on to a glass of bourbon, and tell as much of it as she knew.

''Yesterday afternoon Fitzy took Sarah and Rory to see this Disney movie at the Sack Cheri, the one over by the Pru. On the way back, he stops at an intersection on Holyoke Street. All of a sudden this van whips around in front. Then it backs up, slams into the bumper of Fitzy's Renault. Next thing happens, two guys leap out of the van.''

In a flat, deadened tone Lois described how her children were stolen. Before Fitzy could push down the lock the two thugs, both wearing pantyhose over their heads, yanked the door open and dragged him into the street. The kids were screaming. Fitzy couldn't see what was happening to them because one of the thugs sat on his back and jammed a gun barrel into his ear. He heard a van door slide shut, then he was jerked to his feet and thrown in the backseat of his Renault. The thug took the gun out of his ear, pressed it against the back of his head, and warned him that if he didn't withdraw from the *Jones vs. City of Boston* trial he would never see the children alive again.

''He doesn't know how long he stayed in the backseat,'' Lois said, her knuckles white around the glass of bourbon. ''Just lying there. They'd thrown the keys in the gutter. It took him awhile to find them. Then I guess what he did, he just drove around for an hour or so. He was scared, Jack, that I'd be mad he'd let the twins get taken. He was right, you know. I *am* mad. What the hell was on his mind, riding around out there, not coming home to tell me?"

"He must have been in shock, Lois."

"Yeah, something like that." She looked up from the glass, meeting my eyes, then gulped the bourbon down like a dose of medicine. "So what happens is, I'm at the house, expecting Fitzy and the kids, no idea anything has happened to them. The phone rings, on Fitzy's private line, this muffled voice says, 'Lady, tell that asshole you married to stay the fuck out of the courthouse or your kids are history. Don't call the cops, just stay by the phone. Do exactly what I say or I'll shoot the little brats in the back of the head.' That's exactly what he said, the voice, I remember it *exactly,* he said, 'he'd shoot the little brats in the back of the head.' "

"Jesus, Lois."

"Then he hangs up. So I run to the front door and, Jack, he's out there, *Fitzy is parked in the street.* He's just sitting there behind the wheel. I go running out, he's got the doors locked, he hides his face when he sees me. I'm his *wife* for god's sake, I been married to the stupid schlep for twelve years now, and he's *hiding?*"

"He was in shock."

"Well, he's *still* in shock. All night we sit there by the phone, he won't move. The only thing he does is he calls up the *Globe* and tells them that his workload is too heavy and he's withdrawing from the case. That way the kidnapers will know he's obeying."

"The whole thing sounds crazy. It doesn't make sense."

"Jack, what do we do now? Fitzy says if I call the cops in, he'll kill me. I think he means it, too."

The newspapers were strewn over the hearth. Using my tongs, I scooped up the front section of the *Globe* and found the notice.

ATTORNEY WITHDRAWS, CITES BURDENS

South End trial lawyer Finian X. Fitzgerald announced today that he is withdrawing from the controversial *Jones vs. City of Boston* lawsuit, scheduled to begin jury selection tomorrow. The suit stems from the accidental shooting of thirteen-year-old Horatio Jones, in Roxbury, by Boston police detective Ernest Edwards. Fitzgerald, acting on behalf of Mrs. Ida Mae Jones, the youth's mother, has filed a $2.5 million wrongful-death suit, charging that the department was negligent in hiring Edwards, who had had numerous disciplinary actions taken against him prior to the Jones shooting.

In a telephone statement Fitzgerald stated that his work load was too heavy and that personal considerations had forced him to withdraw. He had no further comment.

Beacon Hill attorney Milton Pridham, who is assisting in pretrial preparations, could not be reached for comment.

Lois got up suddenly, went to the bar, and returned with the bourbon. She sat back down and left the bottle there on the coffee table. The glass remained empty.

"What's crazy," she said, "what doesn't make sense is Fitzy sitting there in the den. He's there *all night* Jack, smoking cigarettes and staring at the phone. He won't talk to me. This morning we start getting all kinds of calls on the listed line, reporters wanting a confirm. I have to tell them Mr. Fitzgerald isn't taking calls, and finally he insists I unplug that line."

Something clicked and I backtracked. "Wait a minute, the *unlisted* line?"

"That's what they called on, the bastards who have the twins. That's what Fitzy is, I bet, this very minute staring at, the unlisted line, the one supposedly for private calls. The other he has listed under the office number, in case some poor fool decides he just has to talk to the famous lawyer in the middle of the night, which believe me happens all the time. Fitzy, he'll talk to anyone. Except now he won't talk to me. I'm the mother of his children. He thinks it's too late, the kids are already dead. So he just sits there."

"And you haven't called the cops?"

Lois gave me a look, a glance that locked into mine. "I want to, Jack. That's what you do when somebody steals your children, you call the cops, the F.B.I., right? But Fitzy says forget it, that's signing a death warrant, his words. Also, he's convinced the cops did it."

"He thinks the *cops* took the twins?"

"Yeah," she said, laughing with a jagged edge that lacked any trace of mirth. "Crazy, isn't it?"

Although I had myself once been the target of a rogue cop, I couldn't see it in this case, and said so. However much the local constabulary might have it in for Finian X. Fitzgerald (and after losing two very large civil suits to him, and with a third in the offing, they had every reason to loath his name on Berkeley Street), the idea of cops conspiring to kidnap his kids made no sense. Bully him, definitely, ticket his car, certainly. But since new police union ordinances meant that no one on the force could be held at personal financial risk for injuries caused while on duty, the committing of a reprehensible felony like kidnaping made no sense. Why go to that extraordinary risk when the city would ultimately pay, not the cops involved?

I was not sure that Lois knew what I was saying, or cared.

"It doesn't matter who took them," she said. "I just want them back."

Feeling the need to make a physical gesture, I wheeled up close, putting my hands over hers. Beyond a slight stiffening in her wrists, Lois did not respond.

"What I'd like to do," I said, "I'd like to call someone in on this. A guy I heard of. Just for an opinion. Nothing official."

After a while she nodded, keeping her eyes averted.

"All right," she said. "Make the call."

2 FROM THE DECK ON THE BACK ROOF OF MY apartment, overlooking the serpentine traffic on Storrow Drive, the beige waters of the Charles River are usually visible. I pushed open the slider and humped my chair over the tread. Beyond the haze of Cambridge, on the opposite bank, the sky was slate gray and close enough to touch. A crisp November wind chased a solitary sailing dinghy on the river. On the Esplanade the jogging loonies trudged along, wearing designer sweat suits and custom-made shoes and puffing like little locomotives. I wheeled one circuit of the deck, clearing my head, and went back inside to Lois while we waited for the Eskimo.

He arrived in less than twenty minutes.

"I been carrying the beeper around for eight, ten years. Frankly, it's a pain in the ass," he said, shedding his overcoat as he came through the door. "I'm there in my car, watching some guy or some gal or more likely some guy *and* some gal, the thing goes off, screws up the stake. But I'm glad I got it, an emergency situation like this comes up. Come on now, dear, chin up. I'll get those kids back. Promise."

Lew Quinn put his arm around Lois's shoulders and gave her a reassuring squeeze. She did not react.

In the several years I'd been banging out crime novels, I'd never actually met a private investigator. Police detectives, yes, more than I'd ever bargained for. But the private sector guys, who got most of their work running security checks for corporations and administering polygraphs to frightened, resentful employees, these were characters who had never figured in any of my stories. Quinn the Eskimo had come to my attention because a reporter I knew had written a nonfiction account of the Eskimo's career and managed to get a paperback sale and an option for a television movie that was never made. It was obvious why the television moguls hadn't wanted to bother with Quinn. Despite the colorful nickname, stuck on him by an admiring client grateful for his coolness under pressure, Lew was a bland-looking guy in his midfifties with an undistinguished, fleshy face, a spreading paunch, and tinted glasses. He looked and sounded like ten thousand other guys who had been raised in Dorchester and had never been farther west than Jamaica Plain.

"What I'm saying to you, Mrs. Fitzgerald, I been brought in for several other situations similar to this, meaning someone grabs the kid, then makes telephone contact, and in each and every case we got the child back safe and sound. They *don't* call, that's when you worry."

Lew gave Lois another squeeze—obviously he liked to lay on hands—and then looked over at me and winked. It was a cool, professional kind of wink, implying that comforting potential clients was all part of the Lew Quinn service. After declining a beer (beer went through him, he said, and his kidneys were already beat from too many years of sitting behind the wheel on endless stake-outs), he accepted a cup of hot cocoa.

"Two things we got to clear up before I get started," he said, settling into the armchair opposite Lois, whose head swiveled jerkily to keep him in sight. "The first is why you haven't called in the F.B.I., who believe me would have an interest, and why your husband isn't in on this. I want, what I need to get started, I have to have the cooperation of both parents. That is essential."

In a voice that was no longer quite as inanimate as it had been, Lois made her excuses for her husband. Fear, guilt, shock, despair, she fit the words to Fitzy as if she did not really believe what she was saying. For his part, the Eskimo was dubious. He glanced at me, his shaded glasses steamed up from the hot cocoa.

"I gotta talk to the guy," he said. "Can you fix it?"

That was how I happened to get myself seriously in Dutch with my best friend. We went down to the Fitzgerald's South End residence in a parade of vehicles, Lois in the lead, Quinn behind her, and me in the rear in my van. Since the front steps were nonnegotiable, I went around to the back, where they'd installed a ramp, and rolled up to the rear entrance while Lois and Quinn went in the front. I was into the kitchen and pushing hard when Fitzy came at me, his face as discolored and mottled as piddled snow. His heavy-lidded eyes, always protruberant and questing, were clouded with rage as he shook his big fists in my face.

"They get killed, it's *your* fault," he said hoarsely. His breath was sour and vile as he leaned over me. I looked at the fist and he withdrew it. "Something like this happens, you do exactly what they say. Exactly, okay? What the hell do you know about it? You think this is like something out of one of your books, Jack? You think you can twist things around, make it all work out right?"

The Eskimo hung back in the darkened hallway while Lois came into the kitchen and had her say.

"Sit down and shut up and listen," she told him. "This is not a cop. This is not the F.B.I."

Fitzy swung around. Ordinarily he is not a threatening kind of man, despite his considerable size. Under the circumstances—the circumstance being that he looked like he was sleepwalking through a nightmare—he appeared capable of serious mayhem.

"You bring him into our house?" he said, shouting at Lois and gesturing at the investigator, who carefully kept a chair between himself and Fitzy. "What if they're watching the street? They think we're getting smart they'll do just what they said they'd do. The guys shove a gun in my ear, you think I don't believe them?"

"Sit down and listen," Lois said.

"You go running to Jack, what is he, a magician he can get them back? The son of a bitch doesn't *have* any kids. How can he know?"

"Mr. Fitzgerald," Lew Quinn said, "I'm not going to take any course of action unless I get your full approval."

It would be inaccurate to say that Fitzy eventually calmed down.

What he did do was sit at the kitchen table, as Lois demanded, and he kept his mouth shut while the Eskimo made his presentation. This time there was no arms-around-the-shoulders, there was simply a lot of very reasonable talk about the psychology of kidnapers and the importance of keeping calm. Toward the end Lew slipped in a few things about letting the professionals take over, and that was when Fitzy turned and gave me a look that was totally devoid of friendship.

"It was you did this, brought this guy into my house. Anything bad comes of this, Jack, it's on your head."

3 AFTER THE THING HAD GONE DOWN AND I HAD time to reflect on the character of Lew Quinn, investigator, I realized he used his war stories as a kind of tranquilizing agent. Partly, of course, he wanted to inspire confidence in his methods, but more important, he needed to cloud the atmosphere with vaporous tales of successful exploits, like an octopus jetting ink to confuse its prey. Meanwhile, as you expended all your energy trying to separate fact from fiction, he went about his business in precisely the manner he saw fit.

After Fitzy begrudgingly okayed Quinn's plan of action, he and I went back to my apartment to use the phone. Quinn seemed confident that my "contacts," such as they were, at the two Boston dailies would be useful. I wasn't so sure.

"All you gotta do is get the guy on the horn. I'll take it from there. Like the hookers say, I give great phone, okay? For example, one time this major insurance carrier wants to find out if this certain party is actually incapacitated by an injury suffered in collision with a vehicle they covered. I got his wife on the phone, pretended I was a consulting physician—strictly unethical, but it goes with the territory—and from what she says, the poor guy can't even have sex. Most guys would stop there, file for their hours. I took it a step further, got his *girlfriend* on the phone. After ten minutes she's giving me the blow-by-blow, and brother I am not exaggerating. Of course the insurance company can't use any of it in court, but what they do, they contact his attorney, exchange a few pleasantries about what would the wife think of the action the girlfriend is getting, and presto, they get a reduced settlement."

This was in the elevator, waiting for the ancient beast to creak us up to the sixth floor. Quinn had his hands in the pockets of his wrinkled overcoat—his one concession to the uniform of the trade—and rocked back and forth on thick-soled shoes. He had bad feet, which he blamed on a forced march in Korea during his stint in the Marine Corps.

"I can see by your pained expression, Mr. Hawkins, you don't approve of me going after the so-called little guy. The way I see it, ripping off an insurance carrier is no different than holding up the corner grocery, except it's maybe worse, we all have to pay the increased rates."

The doors slid open.

"I didn't say that," I said, rolling out, fishing for my keys.

Quinn laughed. "You didn't need to. Never mind. All I need from you, you get this editor on the phone, let me pull the wool over his eyes."

There were a few awkward moments after I let us into the apartment. Megan Drew, who is now an editor at Standish House, had slipped into bed for a short nap after coming home from work. She had fallen deeply asleep and appeared in the bedroom doorway naked except for a thin T shirt, green eyes blurred with sleep. The Eskimo seemed not the least perturbed, managing to introduce himself without actually leering at her long shapely legs. Meg made a small shriek and backed into the bedroom. I followed, supplying an abbreviated account of what had gone down, while she rubbed her eyes and tried to take it all in.

"Snatched the twins? You mean that big oaf just *let* them take Sarah and Rory?"

Megan had never been one of Finian's fans, so I wasn't really surprised by her immediate reaction. Having myself been held at gunpoint, knowing the spine-chilling fear that can immobilize you, my sympathy was with Fitzy, but it was not an opportune moment to make that point with Meg, who was muttering under her breath as she looked around for her clothes.

In the living room Quinn had taken off his overcoat and was tucking his shirt into the expanded beltline of his double-knit trousers. He then unclipped his clip-on tie, slipped it into the overcoat pocket, and rubbed his hands together, ready for subterfuge. I tried the *Boston Standard* first and got through to Russ White, one of the few reporters who pulled any weight with the chain tabloid publishers there.

"A favor I can do," he said. "Knowing you'll make good."

"I can't promise anything, Russ."

I turned the phone over to Lew Quinn, who paced the carpet as he romanced first Russ White, then the section editor White transferred him to, and finally the compositing foreman, who would have to make the last-minute insertion for the morning edition. The *Globe,* being stuffier, had all sorts of editorial policies that required violating, so it took a lot longer to bring them around. Through it all the Eskimo was brilliant. He moved around the room like an actor on stage, trailing the telephone cord, hands gesturing as he assumed the role. Even his accent had changed, as he spun a thoroughly convincing story in which there was not one thread of truth.

"You ought to be in politics," I said admiringly. "Or selling encyclopedias door to door."

Quinn grinned, obviously pleased with himself and appreciative of an audience. "I did that, selling door to door. But what I'm good at is over the phone. They can't see me, they imagine I look different. I was on this job one time, getting sworn testimony in a boiler-room swindle. They had me take one of the commodity-option broker's jobs so I could get on the inside, make friends. They give me the phone, I sell more phony stocks in a hour than most of the guys do in a month. The big shot in charge, who knows another great liar when he hears one, he wants to cut me in, make me a partner. You should have seen his face when he finally gets in court about two years later. He sees me, assumes I've been nabbed also. The thing is, he's pissed because he thinks I must have gone off and started up a swindle of my own, didn't cut *him* in. What a riot, huh?"

"He do any time, this swindler?"

The Eskimo held his belly and laughed. "Get serious. I mean, you used to be on the cops yourself before you got outfitted with those wheels, right?''

''I was a civilian in the department. A mere tech writer.''

''Yeah, well you must have been around enough to know that any big-time swindler who has enough cash stashed away to hire a good criminal lawyer isn't going to do any time. Not *real* time. Maybe four, five months in the country club, brushing up on his racquetball.''

Megan came in, dressed, her hair brushed, quite intent on ignoring the fact that Mr. Quinn had seen her in the almost altogether.

''Should we go over to stay with Fitzy and Lois? Or would we be in the way?''

I was of the opinion that the two should have some time alone together. Quinn had called and assured the frantic parents that he would do nothing to jeopardize the lives of the children. The newspaper ploy would be merely an alternative means of contact. It had worked before and he had every reason to believe it might be effective again. I had gotten on the line just long enough to tell Fitzy I understood that with what he was going through he should feel and act irrational. He told me to mind my own business and that if I wanted to give psychiatric advice maybe I should go on television. So I was not inclined to intrude any further than I had already done.

With the elements of his scheme in place, Quinn readily accepted a drink—rye and ginger, no ice. Megan, whose idea of a stiff drink is a wine spritzer, made a face as she poured it for him.

''Never a dull moment,'' he said, wheezing slightly as he settled his weight into my best chair. ''I just hope I can pull it off.''

''You mean there's some doubt?'' I said, taken aback. At the hearth, where she was building a small fire, Meg looked suddenly frightened.

''Hey, there's always some doubt. What I'd like, if you could fill me in a little on this *Jones* case, give me a little background.''

''The little boy in Roxbury,'' Meg said, her worried face glowing in the light of the fire.

''Right,'' Quinn said, slurping tentatively at his drink. ''Give me the gory details.''

Fitzy had flatly refused to discuss the upcoming trial, so most of what I knew had been gleaned from the newspaper accounts and from anecdotes Fitzy had been polishing before someone stuck a gun in his ear and stole his children and frightened him into silence. Horatio Jones was a thirteen-year-old boy, rather small for his age, who kept a cage of pigeons on the roof of the Roxbury tenement where he lived with his mother. A Boston police detective, in pursuit of an alleged purse snatcher spotted in the neighborhood, had gone up the fire escape and, for reasons he deemed justifiable, had shot the boy dead when he suddenly appeared around the corner of an air duct, holding the screwdriver he was using to repair his pigeon cages. The detective who fired was one Ernie ''Eyeball'' Edwards, who had previously been cited for violation of the Officers' Firearm Code of Conduct, and his documented instability was the basis for the *Jones* lawsuit against the city.

''Yeah, I heard about this guy Eyeball. He's a roughhouse customer, a shoot-first guy.''

''He shot first, all right,'' Megan said heatedly. ''You really think he has anything to do with taking the twins?''

Quinn wrapped his fingers around his glass and considered the question. ''Stranger things have happened,'' he said. ''But only in the movies. Why would this detective pull a stunt like kidnaping? I mean, what's the purpose? The family involved in the lawsuit, the dead kid's mother, she'll just find herself another lawyer. From the picture I get of this Eyeball guy, he's more the type would personally threaten your friend Fitzgerald. Punch him in the nose, not snatch his kids. No, the cops aren't real smart, in my opinion, but they're not dumb enough to pull a stunt like this."

"Then who?" Meg asked.

Quinn shrugged. "This is a new one on me, some ways. Usually it's one of the parents, stealing from custody, sometimes it's a harebrained scheme to squeeze money. Or you get a crazy enough person, they'll steal a kid just for revenge. This one is different. There's something weird going on here. Maybe we'll never know exactly what happened to trigger off an incident like this. Get the children back safe and sound, that's all I'm in for. Anything else, it's a gift."

He finished the drink, then sighed wearily, rubbing his jowls with the back of his hand. Megan helped him on with his coat and he left, moving gingerly on his bad feet and stiff joints, overweight, in need of a shave, our best hope.

4

I AWOKE ALONE, AWARE OF MEG'S SCENT ON the pillow. I called her name. Got no response. A faint tremor of panic sat me up, and I muscled myself out of bed and into my chair. All the lights are controlled from a central grid mounted at a convenient height on the bedroom wall, so I was able to flood the apartment with light at one throw. No Megan in the bath. No Megan in the kitchen. No note on the cork board explaining how she happened to be spirited off in the middle of the night.

The first bleary light of dawn was starting to put the Cambridge skyline in relief, and the traffic on Storrow was as intermittent as it ever gets. For lack of any other plan of action, I started up the coffee machine and the juicer and waited for the dregs of sleep to clear from my head. The locks on the door began clicking open just when the coffee came sputtering through. By then I'd figured it out.

"First I tried the all-night drug over there on the corner of Exeter," Meg said, holding a rolled-up newspaper like a baton as she shook her thick mop of auburn hair loose from the fur-lined hood of her down jacket. "The girl behind the counter looks like a refugee from the Twilight Zone, I don't think she ever heard of the *Globe*. So I go down Boylston to the subway entrance at the corner of Copley, where that newsdealer sets up. He isn't there yet, I'm freezing. Finally I get out my nail file and break open one of the bundles. Then I got a little spooked, I ran all the way home. Hey," she said, putting the paper down on the counter and reaching for a cup. "How come you're up so early? I was going to wake you. Thought maybe we should go over to Fitzy's first thing and see how Lois is holding up."

"Is it in there?"

Meg nodded, flipping open the paper to the first section. There, set off by thick black borders, was the notice Lew Quinn had contrived to get in on short notice.

WILLING TO NEGOTIATE

Concerning two packages lost November 12, 4:10, p.m., vicinity Holyoke Street. A variety of options for recovery are available. You need not retain packages to ensure obligation. Reply to Lewis Quinn, private investigator. Absolute confidence assured.

''It doesn't seem like much,'' Meg said. ''Creeps like that, that would steal children, I worry they don't read the papers.''

We decided to go over to the Fitzgeralds' without calling, which turned out to be a mistake. Lois saw the van and came tearing out, face wet with tears, thinking we had news of the twins. Fitzy was holed up in his study, sleeping—or trying to—on a couch next to the unlisted phone. He was not inclined, Lois said, to have breakfast with us.

Meg took over, scrambling up eggs, browning toast, keeping up a stream of reassuring chatter. Lois was having none of it. She was not interested in eating, or in casual conversation, and had an ear permanently cocked for the ring of the phone.

''I wonder if they're feeding them,'' she said, looking at the platter of eggs. ''You think they know how to feed a couple of hungry kids?''

''Maybe one of them has a girlfriend, she's babysitting?'' Meg said. ''They turn Rory loose in a kitchen, he can cook for the both of them.''

''If he doesn't burn the place down,'' Lois said woodenly. ''Last week he decided to help me fry up hamburgers, I thought the whole South End was going up in flames.''

The long night had aged her, chiseled new lines, darkened the sockets of her eyes.

"This is what they call a vigil," she said. "Isn't that right, Jack?"

"You have a family doctor?" I asked.

"What, like a nice old guy comes over with his black bag, gives the little lady a sleeping draught? Sorry, Jack. I know you're trying to help—you *are* helping—but I don't want to be tranquilized. I keep thinking, if something happens to them, I'll *know*. I have to be awake to feel it. That may be crazy, but that's the way I feel, okay?"

I said that of course it was okay. Leaving her with Meg, I wheeled into the study.

Fitzy was lying on the couch, smoking a cigarette. His wiry red hair, beginning to thin in front, was matted against his skull. He badly needed a shave. He glanced at me, then returned his attention to the cigarette.

"I'm waiting," he said bitterly. "That's my function around here. I'm the guy who waits by the phone. It's all I'm fit for."

"Finian, it wasn't your fault."

He inhaled, coughed, made a dismissive gesture.

"You tried anything fancy," I said, "someone might have gotten killed."

"Maybe someone has already been killed. You ever think of that?" The shades were down, and in the dim light the end of his cigarette glowed. "Couple of five-year-olds, crying for their mother, the temptation is there, shut them up forever."

The hollowness of his expression reminded me of the look he'd get at B.U. after a couple of days on speed, working up a long overdue paper or preparing for an exam. Even in repose, there, on the couch, his jaw was thrust forward and his lips were set as thin as fine mortar, and as unyielding.

"Why would they do that, Fitz? For that matter, why'd they take them in the first place?"

Fitzy cranked himself up on one elbow, the cigarette jutting from the side of his mouth, eyes quinting from the smoke. "You think I know? Is that what you and Lois have figured out, that I'm an accessory to the abduction of my own children?''

''No, of course I don't think that. It's just none of it makes any sense. They call up asking for money, sure, I'd understand, but demanding you stay out of court for a civil suit . . .''

Fitzy sighed, slumped back down. ''All I know, Jack, they've got Sarah and Rory. So long as they do, I don't say one word about anything. Especially not to a guy like you, even though he's an old friend of the family, he also pals around with every news-horny reporter in town.''

I told him that was fine, I understood, that my only concern was facilitating the release of the twins. Fitzy pulled a big glass ashtray onto his chest, using it to snub out the cigarette.

''Just one thing, Fitz,'' I said. ''The unlisted number. How many people have access to it?''

He smirked. ''Restricted to every down-and-out crook in the city of Boston. The number, as I assumed you already knew, is unlisted only in the sense that it's not printed in the actual telephone book, which doesn't make any difference to most of my clients, since no one has yet found a pay phone inside city limits that has an actual phone book chained to it. That answer your question, Jack old buddy?''

The Eskimo worked out of his house, a triple-decker in a recently yuppyfied neighborhood near Jamacia Pond. He lived on the first floor, using a paneled alcove as his office, and rented out the top two floors.

''I could almost live on the income,'' he said. ''The wife and I split up, she got the house in Brookline, I kept this place. She always hated it over here, the wrong side of the pond she calls it. That's fine, she's got a tax bill now would stop my heart, I had to write out the escrow check. Her new hubby, he pays the bills, and long life to him, the poor sap. He's a dentist over there at Cleveland Circle, he's on the board at the Country Club, the whole bit. Every time I run into him I say, 'Doc, don't it bother you, other people's spit all over your fingers?' I kind of like the guy, but he hates my guts. What can I do.''

Meg, having phoned into Standish House that she was taking emergency medical leave, had elected to stay with Lois at the house in the South End. She had it in mind that Lois needed protection from Fitzy, a loony idea I somehow could find no argument to deflate.

''He'll be okay,'' Quinn said, in reference to Fitzgerald. ''In a situation like this, guys typically have one of two reactions. They either get hold of a gun and go cruising the streets, figuring on pulling a Wild West rescue operation, or else they do what your friend is doing, they freeze up. He's in hibernation. Which is fine, we can get on with our business.''

I asked how long before he expected a reply from the advertisement.

''Any minute, or could be tomorrow. Later than that, say afternoon tomorrow, they don't want to play. Now let me ask you a question, Mr. Hawkins,'' he said, enjoying my discomfort at being so addressed by a man twenty years my senior. ''These fellas suddenly decide to get greedy, ask for cash, how far can we go?''

After a little thought I named a dollar figure.

''You could raise that?''

''Some my own, some from a foundation Fitzy and I administer, the Freedom Wheels Foundation. Figure twenty of that Lois could squeeze out of her family, her sister that married rich. It would be tough, but we could scrape it up before close of business, if it meant we could get the twins back alive.''

''You're what, their godfather, Mrs. Fitzgerald said?''

''That's right. Up to now, all I had to do was bring 'em presents on birthday and Christmas, maybe take them to the Garden, the circus is in town.''

Quinn looked down at my chair, studying the wheels. ''You

must have a hell of a time getting around Boston Garden in that rig.''

I said I'd gotten used to it.

''Yeah,'' he said, ''I guess you have. What was it, an off-duty cop shot you, correct? Lighting off his service revolver in a bar, you caught a ricochet?''

''Something like that.''

''I only ask, I happen to read one of your books last night, one of the Lieutenant Casey stories. I say I happen to read, what I did, I stopped in the drugstore, got a paperback. Just out of curiosity, I'm not big on mysteries, usually they put me to sleep. Funny thing is, in your book there's a very sympathetic picture of the Boston cops. Which is, from my point of view, surprising, you getting shot by a cop, you're not pissed off forever. Some drunk detective fools around and puts a piece of lead in my spine, I'd be very disturbed.''

''Let's just say I've adjusted.''

This was ground that had been covered more times than I cared to remember: the night when I walked into the Shield, a private hangout for cops, and had my way of life permanently altered by a hotdog vice cop named Brad Dorsey, whose idea of livening up the evening was to empty his revolver into the floor. The last slug penetrated the booth where I was sitting, and my legs, as the saying goes, were history. I will never forgive Dorsey for his act of stupidity, but time has evened things out. Poor Brad, never a bright prospect, is now a security guard in a New Hampshire mall. Five bucks an hour and he has to wear support hose to help his aching feet. I wouldn't trade my life for his, no way, no how. With Fitzy's help the city of Boston bought me the time to write the books I'd always talked about in the Shield, and the books led to Megan, and what the hell, I never liked jogging anyway.

One thing about living on wheels—you develop a strong sense of humor or you stew in very bitter juices.

"What I'm hoping," the Eskimo said, "they've got the kids, now reality is setting in. They have to feed the little devils, take 'em to the bathroom. This gets old real soon. They got two options. The one we're pulling for, they'll turn 'em loose, figure they made their point."

"And the second option?"

"This we don't bother discussing. What I do, I always go for the first option. You gotta be an optimist, you do the work I do. Sit around for hours in a car, waiting to catch some sucker coming out of the wrong apartment, or doing backflips when he's supposed to be whiplashed, you don't think positive in a situation like that, you give up and drive home and you never get a big check from a grateful insurance company. Myself, I've got some very large checks."

As I left, Quinn was turning on a game show.

"Waiting," he said, settling into a Barcalounger, remote switch in hand, "one of the things I do best. You hear anything on the grapevine, give me a tingle. I go out on the street for this one, I'd like to be aware."

5 MILTON PRIDHAM DID NOT EXUDE THE ESKIMO'S kind of confidence. Fitzy had described him as a watered-down Boston Brahmin who had been born into the right family and gone to the right schools. And on first sight he did look like someone who might play squash—and lose—to Harold Standish, my publisher and the standard by whom I measured all others of his class. The milky complexion and beardless chin made Milton look even younger than his twenty-five years, and that wasn't going to help in open court. To his credit, he was very aware of his deficiencies, trialwise.

"Trialwise," he said, "we were depending on Mr. Fitzgerald. Mr. Fitzgerald is legendary in front of a jury. That's why I signed on, to get some valuable pointers in this regard. My hope is, he'll change his mind. This afternoon I'm suggesting a motion for delay, on account of Mr. Fitzgerald being indisposed."

This was my first experience of Pridham, whom Fitzy had dubbed "Childe Milton of Louisburg Square," Louisburg Square being the exclusive section of Beacon Hill where the Pridhams resided.

"Milty passed the bar on his second try," Fitzy had said the last time we lunched together. "Now there's nothing wrong with that, except young Milton had more coaches than the New York Yankees. He's not dumb by any means, but he's a lawyer only because it's a family tradition and because you don't get into Boston politics without being in the business. See, Milton's father, bless his little pinched face, has his heart set on Milton being a congressman. I guess when Milton was born the old man hired a consultant, and the consultant hired a cartographer, and the cartographer drew up a map of the kid's life, and on his first birthday they changed his diapers and gave him a compass and said, 'Go forth, Childe Milton, and this world shall be yours. Do not deviate from the blue-veined path, do not smoke pot or sniff glue or stick your weenie into Irish girls, and on your twenty-first birthday you shall be given a charge plate at Brooks Brothers, a trust sufficient to your needs, and the lease of a BMW. As an added bonus we will fix it so you can take a couple of lessons from Finian X. Fitzgerald, a crude fellow with theatrical tendencies who is connected to no particular political faction.' And so Milton went forth.

"He's not a bad kid, Jack, which is why I let him carry my briefcase."

Pridham was clutching his own briefcase, there at the courthouse, in the nonsmoking section of the conference room where Lois had told me he'd be found. On the oak table were three cardboard boxes of transcripts and files, the lifeblood of the *Jones* suit. According to Fitzy, Milton Pridham had signed on as a virtual volunteer, working for bare minimum, aware that if the suit was lost there would be not a penny to share. The family firm of Pridham & Briggs was strictly corporate law, and assisting in the *Jones* suit was about as close to "socially conscious" action as the politically ambitious young man was likely to get on short notice. Now, suddenly, he found himself squinting in the glare of media spotlights, a role previously reserved for Fitzy, who was a showman at heart.

"Mr. Fitzgerald couldn't come to the phone," he said, "so I've had to enter the decision-making process. Mrs. Jones is coming in. I'm going to advise her on the delay, and if Fitzy—ah, Mr. Fitzgerald—remains indisposed to continue, we'll have to seek a new trial attorney. What worries me is the timing here. To be strictly honest, the timing couldn't be worse. When I go before the judge, he's going to want a better explanation than I can supply, since Mr. Fitzgerald hasn't seen fit to take me into his confidence concerning this matter. The reporters started calling me up, I felt awfully silly having to say I had no idea why he decided to withdraw."

Looking silly was not something the Pridhams willingly endured, and as a result Milton was turning as sour as his engrained politeness would allow. He felt he deserved to have the blanks filled in for him—at the very least he wanted a script to read.

"I can't just keep saying that 'personal considerations' have forced him to withdraw. These reporters *know* Fitzy. They keep badgering me, wanting to know what kind of political pressure is being exerted here. Frankly, I feel terribly awkward because it's obvious to everyone I'm not in a position of trust." He hesitated, tapping his slender fingers against the briefcase. "You're a friend of the family, I'm hoping you can intercede, put my case to Mr. Fitzgerald. My father has already made inquiries. It's rather embarrassing. . . ."

"I'll see what I can do. Meanwhile, just stick to your statement. The papers will get bored soon enough and let you alone."

Having myself been a target of the Boston media on a couple of occasions, he had my sympathy. I asked him if he'd been present when Fitzy took sworn testimony from Detective Ernie Edwards. At the mention of Eyeball, Pridham tensed up.

"Yes, I was there. Mr. Fitzgerald asked me to take notes. Said it didn't matter what I wrote down, he just wanted to intimidate the witness. Which I guess I did, because afterward he came up to me, smoking this incredibly smelly cigar, and he blew the smoke right in my face. I have allergies, Mr. Hawkins, and the smoke really bothered me. I tend to break out, which is embarrassing."

"So you think Edwards is capable of violence?"

"He shot that little boy, of course he's capable of violence. He's what I would call a classic hostile witness. Also, he's a terrible liar."

"You think he lied under oath?"

Pridham made a fluting noise through his thin nostrils. "Sure. We've got him in conflict about eight times. Fitzy says the city attorneys tried to rehearse his testimony, but Eyeball's too dumb to remember his lines. They gave him a citation for bravery, you know, the department, after he shot Horatio Jones. Apparently he assumes since he's got the citation, we can't really hurt him.''

''He ever threaten you?''

''Not in so many words. Do you know him personally, Mr. Hawkins?''

I said I'd never had the pleasure.

''Well, he doesn't *need* to threaten, not verbally. They don't call him Eyeball for no reason, Mr. Hawkins. He's got this look that will make your skin crawl.''

Mrs. Jones, mother of the dead boy, was coming in just as I left. Pridham guided her to a seat at the big oak table. As I backed through the door she was clutching her purse to her breast, a tiny woman with coal-black skin and hurting eyes.

Someone followed me from the courthouse.

The mean November wind cutting up through Government Center claimed most of my attention. Fighting it, I concentrated on working up a rhythm, stroking my hands down over the wheel hubs, cursing my stupidity at having forgotten my touring gloves. The wind sputtered, rattling trash cans, creating little whirlwinds at the gutter. My teeth felt like stunted icicles. Turning left onto Cambridge Street, I had to contend with a gradient incline for a block or so, before the parking garage came into view.

That was when I noticed the tail. As I slowed down on the upgrade, footsteps from behind began to gain, then slowed, keeping pace. I thought little enough of it then—the awareness of someone following is simply an instinctive reaction for anyone who gets around a city in a chair. You use your eyes, your ears, and you keep that spray can of potent Mace right there in the side pocket, within easy reach.

There was a time when I had a permit for a gun and carried it, over Megan's objections, until my old friend Sully—Lieutenant Detective Timothy Sullivan—convinced me the weapon itself was a magnet for crime. "They catch a glimpse of the firearm, they'll stake out for you, these street punks, pull an ambush, figure you for an easy target in that chair. Which, no offense, you are. They can get a hundred for that gun, that's enough to fix three, four junkies, reason enough to kill you. Or, God forbid, you'll get rattled, shoot an innocent bystander, they'll sue your ass like you sued ours."

It was Sully who'd given me the police-issue Mace, assuring me that while it would not stop a determined psycho, it would certainly discourage the moonlighting muggers who preyed on the elderly and the handicapped.

With the entrance to the garage in sight, a breather was in order, so I locked the wheels and sat there puffing, eyes stinging from the wind. I had news for T. S. Eliot: April isn't the cruelest month, not in downtown Boston, where the breeze off the harbor can be as mean as a Central American dictator, and a hell of a lot colder.

A shadow loomed. Someone was moving up behind me quickly, footsteps accelerating. I reached into the sidepocket, locked my fingers around the Mace dispenser, and jerked sideways in the chair enough to get a look in back. I saw shoulders turning, the back of a head, and someone—a large someone—walking rapidly away. Setting the Mace on my lap, I unlocked the wheels and swung round, facing the retreating figure.

After eating up twenty yards of pavement he turned to sneak a look. I felt no tingle of recognition—I'd never seen the man. Just another one of a thousand Boston faces, burned by the wind. There was no reason at all for me to think that he walked like a cop—that had to be a leap of imagination, a coincidence that might jibe in one of my books, not in reality.

The kid who'd parked the van wanted to know if I needed help getting back aboard.

"Thanks for the offer, but I got this rig customized," I explained, the adrenaline still sparking from the incident on the street. ''All I gotta do is put in my key here, give her a turn, and voilà.''

The grated platform at the back of the van unfolded with a hydraulic hiss, lowering itself to the pavement. I pushed aboard, turned the key the other way, and was lifted up to the rear-door level. With the key in the third position the door slid open.

''Wow,'' the kid said admiringly. ''What a neat deal. I get some of you wheelchair guys in here, it's a real struggle getting into the vehicle.''

To save time and effort in transfer, I'd had the driver's seat removed. This allows me to roll up to the steering wheel, where two lock-down brackets secure my chair in place. With hand controls at easy access, I'm free to cruise—and cause as much mayhem as any other driver in the city. The van is my escape hatch, and it has proved so useful, so essential to a sense of independence, that fitting out other paraplegics with similar transportation is one of the main functions of Freedom Wheels Foundation, the organization Fitzy and I set up after the Casey books started selling big.

Rather than endure the circle at the Longfellow Bridge, I cut up side streets through Beacon Hill, between the tight rows of brick fronts with the fancy paneled doors and cut-crystal light fixtures. It was on Myrtle that I noticed the gray sedan in the sideview mirror. On impulse I cut around the block again, losing sight of the sedan. It wasn't until I was on Beacon that it appeared again. My mirror and the sedan's windshield were both dirty, and the sedan's driver could not be clearly distinguished. It could have been the same stranger who had followed me from the courthouse—or it could have been anyone.

I slowed at the corner of Clarendon, made sure the turn signal was on, and headed down the ramp to the private garage where I store the van. Behind me the sedan seemed to hesitate, then cruised through the light and on down Beacon.

6

CONVINCED THAT I WAS SUFFERING FROM AN overactive imagination, I entered my building through the lower level, fought with the stubborn elevator for a while, and called the Fitzgeralds as soon as I got into the apartment.

"Nothing doing here," Megan answered, her voice a husky whisper. "We had a little excitement earlier. Your old buddy Russ White from the *Boston Standard* rang the buzzer. I answered, but I don't think he recognized me; I'm out of context over here. He had the usual questions; I repeated the usual lies; finally I had to close the door in his face. He's going to be a problem, Jack, the guy doesn't take no for an answer. . . . Okay, after that I got Lois to lie down—I'm hoping she'll sleep. Oh, almost forgot. Quinn called to say he hadn't heard anything, said he was sitting there reading one of your Casey books. He won't phone again unless he's been contacted."

"Fitzy?"

"Acts like he's in a coma. I brought him some hot cocoa. He said thanks, but he didn't touch it. Maybe he thinks I'm trying to poison him."

"He's freaked out. We get the children back, he'll be as good as new."

I asked if she was going to stay there with Lois.

"For a while. I wish we could do something, Jack. This waiting around, it makes me itch. You think we should get Sully in on this?"

"Later, maybe. For the moment, we'll have to trust Quinn."

Shortly after hanging up I glanced out the window, saw another sedan—not the same one—and realized I hadn't even gotten the license number, a lapse of effort only the most feeble character could get away with in my detective novels. I considered calling Quinn but thought better of it—no need to tie up his line.

More as a distraction than with any hope of writing, I wheeled up to my worktable, turned on the computer, booted up the word-processing program, and loaded the new *Casey* file. The cursor blinked at me, a little green blip begging for instruction. I stared at it for a while and thought about Eyeball Edwards, and a black kid named Horatio Jones, and what connection a rogue cop might have to the abduction of Rory and Sarah Fitzgerald, five years of age.

Waiting can play a funny game with your head. When I was with Quinn his deliberate confidence was infectious. He made it seem certain the twins were alive and would soon be home. Now, staring at the blank screen where I composed my stories, I began to imagine more chilling scenarios: the children abused, the children, like Horatio Jones, extinguished.

I had clicked off the screen and was trying to shake off a swampy sensation of dread when the buzzer rang.

It was Russ White, of the *Boston Standard.*

"Remember me?" he said. "I'm the guy got you that great deal with the McGary chain, they serialized that story of yours? Also, the other day I fixed it so your friend Quinn could place a very odd little notice after deadline."

"We don't want any," I said, pushing the door shut.

Russ did what any good reporter would do. He put his foot in the door.

"Whaddaya mean, we? Your girlfriend is holding the fort over at the Finian X. Fitzgerald residence. You remember Fitzgerald, don't you? Big guy with red hair, likes to wear K mart tropical shirts, frequently seen at the Plough, where he has been known to sign his name in the Guinness with the point of his nose. Lifelong friend of yours?"

"Never heard of him. Never heard of you. Me no speaky English."

"Look, Jack, I'm not going to plead, say you owe me one for getting that notice placed, but the way it is, it's out of my hands. Devlin has a hair up his ass, he's been planning a big splash for this Jones trial, how maybe the mayor will wise up and fire the commissioner, restructure the department. You know the angle. He's got—Devlin has hired a courtroom artist, he's been pulling people off regular assignments, putting together bios of everyone involved in the suit, he's giving it the McGary touch, Devlin is."

"What a sweet guy. Sorry, Russ, but I can't talk about it."

"Fine. Let me in before you crush my foot, maybe there's a few things *I* can tell *you*."

"For instance?"

"For instance I heard that Eyeball Edwards didn't accidently shoot that kid. He did it on purpose."

Russ came into the kitchen, where he helped himself to coffee and a doughnut that was as stale as a Henny Youngman routine.

"You fixed the place up," he said, spotting the new skylight, the ceramic-tile counter tops, the framed prints Meg had picked up on Newbury Street. "Books selling like hotcakes, huh? I heard they were thinking about making Casey into a TV series."

"Well, they thought better of it. They let the option drop."

"Matter of time. They always need a new cop show. What you gotta do, put more fireworks in there, more car chases. And definitely you need to find a romantic interest for Casey. The poor guy does nothing but solve crimes and play his piano and moon about whether he should have stayed with the Jesuits, become a priest. Not enough action for prime time."

"Thanks for the advice, Russ. Now what's this about Eyeball shooting the kid on purpose?"

White was tall and thin with a pockmarked complexion, a sagging lower lip, and active, piercing eyes. Until he'd landed at the *Standard,* which paid him very well indeed, he'd had a distinguished career. Russ started out as an intern at *The New Republic,* then followed with a long stint on an investigative team at *The Washington Post.* A Boston native, he'd finally returned to head the crime desk for the loud, chain-owned tabloid that served as gadfly to the mighty *Globe*.

Devlin, the smarmy young publisher of the *Standard,* called Russ ''the best blood-and-guts guy in the business.'' I knew him to be one of the canniest—and luckiest—reporters in the city. He had an instinct for finding the heartbeat of a story. And unlike most journalists, he did not aspire to writing a syndicated column. He considered column work boring, pretty thin stuff compared to his blood-and-guts beat.

''I was in the Sevens a while back, and who buys me a beer but Larry Sheehan, the very same Sheehan works as a detective out of Homicide for your friend Sullivan. Well, Larry likes the sound of his own voice, and if you keep the whiskey-gingers coming regular he sometimes gets carried away, gives up some deep dark secrets. I say to him, I say, 'Larry, what are you doing on Charles Street, in the Sevens of all places?' I figure, knowing Sheehan, he's chasing tail, or looking to bust somebody for snorting Borax in the john. So the guy surprises me. He says, get this, he says he heard the Sevens was a literary hangout. I'm stunned. I mean, the Sevens is a very pleasant, tarted-up beer joint, but it's not exactly the Algonquin. Dan Wakefield was spotted in there once, he probably dropped in to take a leak, maybe that's where the rumor started. Anyhow, by now Sheehan has a buzz on, he confesses he's thinking of writing a book. He's in the Sevens to soak up atmosphere, inspire himself.''

''Larry Sheehan? Come on.''

''You must have made an impression on him, Jack, using him as a model for the low-brow sidekick in your Casey books. Believe me, Sheehan is now dying to be an author, maybe turn the tables on you. He hasn't written a word, but he's got the title. He's going to call it *Tough Guy: Memoir of a Street-smart Detective.*''

''God help us. Harold Standish hears about it, he'll probably give the little bastard a contract.''

''Never fear. Unless Sheehan figures out how to write his life down on cocktail napkins, it'll never happen. So what I'm coming to, I sprinkle on a few lies, let him think he's got a great story to tell if he only gets the time to write. How he's been on the cops since he crawled out of Chelsea, he must have seen some wild times. Sheehan tells me he's seen and heard stuff would make the hair on the back of my head stand up. 'Do a shift with me, you'll come off looking like a fuckin' porcupine' is how he puts it.

"So then he's obliged to deliver, he's determined to really impress me, what a tough life it is being a homicide dick. I say, I tell him, they're already dead for chrissake, what harm can they do him, these victims he has to investigate? Well, Larry's eyes bug out, by now he's inhaling the whiskey-gingers and he starts really slinging the shit. Under all this flying bullshit is one small item I immediately pick up on, have him elaborate. About how a certain vice cop Sheehan knows, this vice cop was extremely aggravated at a certain black teenager who had been pushing dope, doing things like sugaring the vice cop's gas tank. This certain vice cop decides he's had enough of the little punk, he's going to blow the kid away."

"Horatio Jones was pushing dope?"

"I never said that, lemme finish. So this certain vice cop bides his time, he waits until he gets a call wherein the suspect might be construed to be a certain black teenager who committed the mortal sin of sugaring his gas tank. One day a call comes in on the 911, a mugger more or less fitting the description. The vice cop picks up the dispatch, informs the Turret he is in the area. He goes into the building where he knows the black teenager is always on the roof, which is where the kid deals his dope—he throws the packages down from the roof. The black kid comes around the corner, the vice cop let's him have it. Only two things wrong. He's in the wrong building and he shot the wrong kid. This wrong kid is extremely dead and he has a screwdriver in his hand, not the butterfly knife the pusher always carries that the vice cop was counting on as a reason to fire.''

''So Eyeball shot the wrong boy.''

White shrugged. ''*Sheehan* says Eyeball shot the wrong kid. Maybe Sheehan was just making it up to impress me, the stories he hears.''

''And why are you repeating it to me? You want me to write Sheehan's book for him?''

''Hey, you'd make a great pair. No, what I'm doing, I'm on a fishing expedition. Your girlfriend is over at your buddy's house, slamming the door on working stiffs like me because Finian X. Fitzgerald is backing out of maybe the biggest lawsuit he's ever brought against the city, and everyone assumes he's been pressured or threatened. Face it, the guy loves the limelight, he loves sticking it to the city, loves being the savior of the downtrodden. So why does he suddenly quit, leave the case in the hands of a wet-behind-the-ears attorney who is so nervous he'll have to be wearing rubber pants, he wants to keep his shoes dry while addressing the court? I have to wonder, who is administering the pressure here? Is it out of the mayor's office, one of the staff trying to save the city some money? Is it the cops? Who? All I want is a little nudge in the right direction.''

I nudged Russ White in the direction of the elevator. He took it in good humor.

''I don't suppose you'd tell me what you were up to,'' he said, holding the door back, ''arranging it for a private investigator to place a cryptic ad in the paper, huh?''

''Pure coincidence. You don't believe me, read my books. It happens all the time.''

Russ signed and rolled his eyes. ''Have it your way. Just remember me when the time comes, okay? And if your friend Fitzgerald wants to take on city hall, let me know. I can be in his corner, he wants to fight this.''

I wheeled back inside and turned on my writing machine. It

wasn't in the mood for wordplay. The screen stared back at me, as insolent and empty as an adolescent smack freak. I gave up and poured myself a beer and sat there waiting for the phone to ring.

7

MEGAN CAME BACK LATE, CARRYING A CARDboard box of Chinese takeout.

"Lois is sound asleep," she said. "Fitzy is still in there on his couch. He had his eyes shut, but he could have been faking. I didn't dare get close enough to check it out. Something better happen soon. I don't see how they can stand it much longer, not knowing."

The food was glazed with garlic and cornstarch and did not go down well. A cold beer cut some of it. Meg, vibrant with nervous energy, was obviously exhausted, and I decided to save the incident on Cambridge Street for some other time. The story Russ White had got from Sheehan couldn't wait.

"Good old Larry," Meg said, spearing a piece of twice-cooked chicken. "The guy has to be the model for the original greaseball. That little ducktail of his, and the pointy black shoes? So what do you think, Jack, you believe that stuff about Eyeball shooting Horatio Jones on purpose?"

"It's a possibility."

Meg licked her fingers thoughtfully. "It makes me wonder," she said, "exactly what Fitzy knows about all this."

With sleep a distant prospect, Megan found an Orson Welles movie on one of the cable channels, *Touch of Evil* with Charlton Heston and Janet Leigh. The print was scratchy and the sound was bad. Welles, playing a booze-maddened sheriff, looked like a booze-maddened sheriff. Heston, wearing a black toupé and a stick-on mustache, looked like a man wearing a black toupé and a stick-on mustache. Janet Leigh looked sultry and frightened—maybe she was afraid that Orson would forget his lines and fall on her. None of that really mattered. All we wanted to do was distract ourselves from the emptiness of waiting.

"He's going to plant the evidence and frame Vargas," Megan said, her slender profile washed by the cold light of the screen.

''He's reenacting the murder of his wife. You assume he strangled his wife, only I don't remember if that ever gets resolved. That's why he stole the gun.''

''To murder his wife?''

''No, the wife got hers years before. He steals the gun to frame Vargas because Vargas proved that he, the fat sheriff, stole the dynamite he used to frame the young Mexican, who really *is* guilty, the young Mexican, but it wasn't right that the fat sheriff tampered with the evidence.''

''And that's why Charlton Heston is crawling under the bridge with a radio transmitter?''

''That's the part,'' she said, ''I haven't figured out yet.''

We fell asleep there in front of the tube, Meg curled on the sofa and me slumped in my chair.

When the phone started ringing, Larry Sheehan was on my lap, a little dream demon laughing as his pointed black shoes drummed against my unfeeling legs. Shaking free of the nightmare, I pushed through the darkness to the desk.

''This is Quinn,'' the voice in the phone said. ''I'm in Southie, corner of Dorchester and Emerson. I've got the kids stashed in a safe place.''

''The twins?'' I mumbled. Meg was coming to life on the couch, her expression flickering between fear and hope.

''They been drugged,'' Quinn said. ''I would guess some kind of sleeping pill. Why I'm calling, I got lucky, stumbled on something down here. An ugly situation, except it all makes beautiful sense. I want to take the kids back to the Fitzgerald residence. I think an escort might be in order, get us out of this neighborhood. I'd call the cops, but for some reason I'm just not in the mood.''

Quinn sounded exhilarated. He also sounded frightened. I told him it would take us fifteen minutes.

At four in the morning the streets of Boston are as deserted as they ever get. A cold, fine rain was falling. It made the rutted pavement slick and shiny. We cut around the Common to Tremont, running the lights to Summer Street and across the Fort Point Channel. Confident that I knew a shortcut through the blighted railyards, I made a right turn and was instantly lost in a maze of narrow, cobbled streets.

"Son of a bitch!"

Meg, shivering in the passenger seat, made no comment as I sped the van through freight yards and dead-ends, desperate to find a cutover into the heart of South Boston.

We happened on Dorchester Street just as a couple of cruisers whipped by, lights flashing. At the corner of Emerson three other police cars had set up a barricade. Red flares burned on the wet street. As I pulled the van over to the curb, Meg reached out and squeezed my hand.

The rear door of the van had iced up, and it took a few minutes to free the lift. Meg waited in the street, the fur on her hood wet with the cold rain. Her clear green eyes were as big as saucers.

"I can't see anything," she said. "They won't let me near."

The first cop I recognized was none other than Detective Lawrence Sheehan. He had no way of knowing he had just figured in a nasty little nightmare of mine, or that Russ White had passed on one of his barroom tales. True to form he was bareheaded in the sputtering rain, his thinning black hair scooped back in a duck's ass, wearing an overcoat too decrepit even for Columbo.

"Hey, gee," he said, stalking over on slightly bowed legs, trying to avoid the puddles. "Look what the cat dragged in. And you got the girlfriend with you. What's your name again, honey?"

Megan told him.

"Right," he said. "So let me guess. You're on your way to catch the sun rising over Columbia Point, you saw your old pal Shannon—pardon me, I keep getting confused—Sheehan, you decided to check in, see if I'm as dumb as ever."

Shannon was the name of a certain character in my Casey series, a screw-up sidekick only vaguely based on Larry Sheehan, who did not appreciate his literary notoriety.

''Larry, what happened here?'' I said. Meg was sliding away, trying to get a glimpse through the barricades. The rain and the spiraling gumdrop lights made it hard to focus on what had happened in the cordoned-off intersection.

Sheehan grinned, showing off his snaggle teeth and his hard little chin. ''Gosh, the great armchair—'scuse me, wheelchair—detective, and he can't figure out what happened? I mean, Jack, you got clues up the ass here. For instance there are cop cars all around, so this is a cop-related matter. Then we have the clue of yours truly, who is a homicide detective. Over there, hanging out under that awning, is your hero Lieutenant Sullivan, proving again he's smart enough to stay out of the rain. Sully is presently the head honcho in Homicide, so that's another clue.''

Megan jogged back, ignoring Sheehan.

''Nobody knows anything about any kids,'' she said, her voice rising. ''All I can see, broken glass. The rain—''

''Kids?'' Sheehan looked puzzled. ''What's this about kids?''

I wheeled around Sheehan and headed for the barricade. The flares hissed like maddened snakes. A uniformed cop strolled over to head me off.

''Keep back there,'' he said. ''Police business.''

I made a fool of myself, screaming for Tim Sullivan. Eventually the word got back that a madman in a wheelchair was demanding his attention. Sully came over, shielding his head with a clipboard.

''You'll catch your death of cold,'' he said. ''A successful author like you, you can't afford an umbrella?''

Sully is the kind of guy who carries clear plastic galoshes, and wears them. At his house in Jamaica Plain, where he has lived all his life, he keeps dustcovers on the unused furniture. He has a fit if you don't use the coasters he puts out to keep glasses and cups from putting rings on his late mother's tabletops. A fanatic for detail and not coincidentally one of the best homicide detectives anywhere. Most everyone who knew him or his work assumed he was the model for the tough, intellectual, Jesuit-trained Lieutenant Detective Casey in my crime novels, a fact that now and then strained our friendship.

"Let 'em through," he said. "Morning, Miss Drew. I have some hot coffee over here if you're interested."

Sully made room for us under the awning of a neighborhood candy store. Someone shoved Styrofoam cups of coffee at us. I sipped at it without tasting. Beside me Megan had begun to weep.

Lew Quinn lay in the gutter at our feet. He was on his back, arms sprawled, jaw slack. His blood, diluted by the rain, puddled in the gutter. Smaller pools of blood receded across the street, where he had staggered from a telephone booth. The glass panels of the booth had been shattered by the bullets that killed him.

"He got hit four, five times at point-blank range. I'm amazed he made it this far."

"The children," Meg said. "Where are the children?"

"Children?" Sullivan jabbed me with his clipboard. "Okay, Hawkins, you better fill me in."

Keeping it as brief as possible, I told him who Quinn was, what he was attempting to do for us, and how we happened to be there.

"Quinn, huh? I don't know, for some reason I thought he was retired. Pain in the ass, from what I heard. So he calls you half an hour ago, must have been just before he got shot. He leads you to believe he's recovered the kidnap victims?"

"Rory and Sarah," I said. "Jesus, Sul, you were there at their birthday party last summer. For chrissake, the *twins*!

Sullivan's horn-rims were wet, hiding his pale blue eyes. "Take it easy," he said. "If you're so worried about these kids, you might have called me in."

"There were extenuating circumstances."

"For God's sake don't fight about it now," Meg demanded. "Just *find* them."

Larry Sheehan was hovering there beside Sully, for once keeping his mouth shut. Sullivan tugged at his sleeve and told him to call in enough men to canvas the neighborhood.

"How many?" he said.

"As many as you can get, this hour."

The photographer, cursing the rain, had two uniformed cops shield Quinn's body with a piece of plastic tarpaulin while he took his shots. At each flash of light Quinn's expression seemed to change. I had to force myself to look away.

"What a goddamn shame," Sullivan said. "Now tell me again exactly what he said."

I repeated Quinn's hurried conversation, not at all certain I was remembering it word for word.

"He said 'stashed,' right Jack?" Meg's voice was shaky, but the tears were gone, pushed back for the time being. "That's a funny word for an old guy like Quinn to use."

"You want to go by the odds," Sullivan said. "Whoever shot Quinn has got the twins back again. Changed his mind."

Meg ignored him. "*Stashed,* Jack, it has to mean something. Where would a guy like Quinn hide something valuable, like two children he'd just rescued?"

"An ugly situation," Sullivan said. "This Quinn, an old-style private eye, he says an ugly situation, my guess is he recovered the kids under duress. It got ugly, for some reason."

"They were asleep, Jack, passed out," Meg reminded me, crouching down to bring her face level with mine. "Quinn met the kidnapers, recovered the twins. Then something went wrong and he put them someplace safe while he phoned for help."

"His car?"

Quinn's white Pontiac sedan had been parked in the driveway at his house. The only thing at all remarkable had been the deeply tinted windows, more common down south than up here in New

England. Meg jogged ahead, accompanied by Sully, who was unable to keep his umbrella over her head, though he tried. We circled from the intersection, trying each of the side streets. By now some of the more alert locals, woken by the lights and the convoy of cruisers at the intersection, peered from windows and doorways.

Someone shouted, "Over this way, offi-sah! Cripple in a chair, he's gettin' away!"

Well, I suppose I did have the look of an escaping suspect, wheeling through the streets at maximum speed, hair matted in the rain.

Still, it made me wonder—who had pointed the finger at Quinn?

It was Megan who found the Pontiac. Not one to waste even a moment getting Sully and me to the scene, she stood on the hood and waved her arms. Lights began clicking on along the street. Behind me someone blew a whistle.

When I got there Meg was tugging at the handles, trying to force the door. The windows were too dark to see inside—exactly what Quinn had intended for his stake-outs. Not that I was positive it was his car.

"Hang on there," Sully said, panting. He had to drop the umbrella. I could see him reacting to the touch of cold rain, hating it. "I got the keys from his pocket. Let's see if they fit."

"Sarah!" Meg shouted. "Rory, can you hear me? It's Meg! Auntie Meg!"

The key fit. Sully popped open the door, reached in, and flipped up the latch to the back. Meg scrambled inside, pulling at the seat covers, calling for the children.

Sully coughed and said quietly, "Not a trace. We'll pull men over to this block, go door to door. Try the basements, the alleys."

Meg crawled out of the car, overcome by tears of frustration.

"I was *sure* they'd be in here. I pictured them, wrapped in a blanket."

"It's okay, Meg," I said.

"It's *not* okay."

She stood back, scanning the block, her eyes flashing through the tears and the rain. Standing in for Lois, giving it everything she had.

"Damn!" she cried suddenly. "The trunk! He put them in the trunk."

Sully looked as nonplussed as he ever looks. He fished through the keys, demanded that we stand back while he tried the trunk. Sheehan arrived, thoroughly drenched. He pulled out his firearm as Sully cracked the lid.

The twins were not, as Meg had "pictured," in a blanket. They were wrapped in an old rug. When Sully pulled it loose Sarah was curled up in a fetal position, hugging Rory. For one awful moment we did not know if they were alive or dead.

Then Megan took them both in her strong, thin arms and said, "They're breathing, Jack. They're breathing."

8

AFTER THE TWINS WERE RELEASED FROM Children's Hospital, Fitzy and Lois took them to Disney World. I don't know why that should have astonished me, but it did.

"It makes perfect sense to me," Meg said in Fitzy's defense. "He's still scared someone will snatch them again, so he take the kids out of town. What should they do, hole up in a motel? Take a whitewater tour of the Colorado? He asks Rory what he would most like to do in the world, the kid thinks really hard for about five minutes, announces what he wants more than anything is to talk to Mickey Mouse. So that's what they are going to do, talk to Mickey Mouse."

I was being made to feel like Scrooge, another perfectly respectable literary character who had been Disneyfied into a quacking duck.

"What about Sarah?" I said. "She state any preference?"

"Lois didn't say."

I knew what that meant. That meant Sarah still wasn't talking. After a day of hospital monitoring, Rory had been back to normal—or as normal as the little pirate ever got. Wanting to cling to his mother—a natural reaction to having been deprived of her attention for a very frightening forty-eight hours—and to push the limits of authority with his usual élan. Sarah, normally the more eloquent of the two, given to speaking in complete sentences and capable of sustained flights of fancy she was willing to share with adults, had ceased speaking unless spoken to.

"I know you're worried, Jack," Meg tried to reassure me. "We all are. But the psychologist says its a perfectly normal reaction to trauma. In a week or so she'll probably be back to normal, talking your ear off."

"But meanwhile take her to Disney World, scare her on a bunch of thrill rides, let her get spooked by people walking around in duck suits."

"Jack, she didn't say she *didn't* want to go."

It was none of my business, of course. That's probably why I was reacting so strongly. Maybe if Fitzy had asked me to go along, help cheer the kids up, I'd have been enthusiastic. Put on a pair of mouse ears and wiggled them to tease a smile from Sarah Fitzgerald.

As it was, my old pal Finian X. had had as little to say to me as his frightened daughter. Lois, calling from the airport as they waited for the flight to Orlando, was apologetic.

"He's as much in shock as the children, Jack. He was convinced it was his fault they got taken, that you thought less of him. That I thought less of him, for that matter. Then he decided I was conspiring with you, going over his head to hire poor Lew Quinn."

"That much I understand," I said.

"All we need, love, is time," she said. In the background I could hear the dull roar of a jet throttling up. "Just give us a chance, Jack. We'll send you a postcard from the land of the pink flamingo. And give my love to Meg. She was great. Just great."

One nagging suspicion still lingered. That Fitzy was running away. That Lew Quinn's murder would go unsolved, unrevenged.

Larry Sheehan had the last word on the fate of Lewis Quinn, investigator, which he obligingly shared with the press.

We had taken the twins to Children's Hospital, Sully and Sheehan and I, while Meg drove the van over to Fitzy's after calling them with the good news. While an emergency-room team probed Rory (sleepy and calling for his mother) and Sarah (less sleepy and not crying), Sheehan used the opportunity to poke a few of his custom shivs at me.

"You writers always know how it ends," he had said, the usual filterless Lucky parked in the seam of his mouth. "So tell me, big guy, how's this end?"

Sullivan, on his way to the phone, slowed to say, "You got it coming, Jack, holding out on us. And the Eskimo should have known better, he's supposed to be a professional."

"The Eskimo?" Sheehan said, delighted. "That what they called the poor bastard? Hey, I get it, Quinn the Eskimo, like in the song. Well, Hawkins, thanks to you the Eskimo got iced."

I wheeled away, keeping an eye on the twins, who were not enjoying the lights in the eyes, the hammers on the knees, the doctor tricks that might reveal the extent of physical damage, if any.

"You get it, Hawkins?" Sheehan said, hovering as he followed. "You can use that in your next book, you want."

When one of the doctors asked if I was the father, Sheehan laughed and shook his head, pointedly sucking on the cigarette he'd been asked to extinguish.

"Friend of the family," I said.

"We're taking blood samples, just as a precaution, but all the vital signs are fine. No evidence of barbituate overdose. Whatever they were given, they're coming out of it. We'll want them in for a day or two, just for observation."

By then Rory was bawling and throwing a tantrum. They let me get close enough to take ahold of him. One of his fists hit me a pretty good one in the nose. After a few moments he seemed to recognize me, although it didn't make him happy. He wanted his mother, period. Sarah watched us somberly, sucking her thumb, a habit she'd given up at least a year before. Her thatch of Fitzy-red hair was frazzled and dirty. Her pale-green eyes were wide and unblinking. I smiled at her, but she didn't react.

The *Standard* used it as the front page banner.

ESKIMO GETS ICED

Typical tabloid play. Who was I, as a writer of gory crime fiction, to criticize their gory coverage of an ugly reality? Still, the grainy shot of Quinn lying on his back in a pool of blood doubly imprinted the scene in my memory, and for a while in my dreams.

"This is Quinn," he seemed to say. "I got lucky, stumbled into something. It all makes beautiful sense."

Except that none of it made any sense. The kidnaping hadn't made any sense. The deal Quinn made with the abductors hadn't made sense. And Quinn's murder was yet another senseless act.

"It's an ugly situation," Quinn had said. "I think an escort might be in order, get us out of this neighborhood."

Then he'd added that he was inclined to call in the cops, but for some reason he "just wasn't in the mood." A private eye's irony? Had he wanted all the glory of recovering the children, been unwilling to share it with the police? Or had he been *afraid* of the cops?

"I got lucky," he'd said. And then his luck had turned bad, as bad as luck can get.

It was Sully who told me about the tape he found on Quinn's answering machine.

He had agreed to let me buy him lunch at Victor's, and I knew he would have tuna salad on rye, black tea, and a slice of apple pie. Give his choice that was what he always ordered for lunch. I assumed it was an imperfect substitute for the midday meal his late mother had always served him.

"We pulled a warrant, went through the whole house. The Eskimo, I got to say this about Quinn, he was a neat house-keeper. Everything in its place. Professional filing system, all his invoices, bills, surveillance reports, mileage charts. Only thing, not one scrap of paper on the kidnaping. Just a rough draft of the ad he had you put in the papers. And his answering machine. He's got long-playing tape on the thing, records an hour of con-versation."

"Who called?"

"He got like four crank calls, and this one insurance agent

won't get off the line, wants to sell him another policy. Cute guy. Then he gets two calls from our friendly neighborhood kidnapers, trying to figure if he's for real. Then we got the call that set Quinn up."

After persistent badgering Sully let me have a peek at the transcript.

QUINN: Lew Quinn speaking.
CALLER: Yeah, Quinn, you put an ad in the paper?
QUINN: Yeah, I put an ad in the paper.
CALLER: Funny kind of ad. I was just wondering exactly what kind of packages you're talking, there in the ad.
QUINN: Let me put it this way. If you're the guy I want to talk to, you know the kind of packages.
CALLER: Okay, I heard you were a wiseguy. How about this. I'll tell you the packages got a last name, and you tell me the name.
QUINN: I pull a name out of the hat, the name might be, say, Fitzgerald.

(End of connection)

QUINN: Lew Quinn speaking.
CALLER: Okay, there's been a discussion. You got any bright ideas about the Fitzgerald packages, spill it.
QUINN: My only concern is safe recovery.
CALLER: And that's your idea?
QUINN: The idea is, if you took the packages, you also know certain demands have been made upon the owner of the packages.
CALLER: You got any more ideas?
QUINN: My idea is, without in any way involving the authorities, Mr. Fitzgerald has empowered me to negotiate.
CALLER: What if we're not interested in negotiating?
QUINN: Look, if you asked around about me, you know I'm straight. What I'm saying, you've made your point with Mr. Fitzgerald. You scared the guy out of his wits. He has

no interest in anything but the safety of his, ah, packages. He gets them back safe and sound, it's like you're still holding them, okay? He'll do nothing. He'll pack up, leave town for a while, that's what you want.
CALLER: We'll get back to you. One thing, Mr. Eskimo, you get any bright ideas, trace the call or whatever, the packages go up in smoke.

(End of connection)

QUINN: Lew Quinn speaking.
QUINN: We have a deal?
CALLER: Fitzgerald splits, keeps his face out of the news?
QUINN: Absolutely. My personal guarantee.
CALLER: Leave now, drive to the circle at Columbus Park. Keep going around the circle until someone makes a move. Don't try any funny stuff. We're taking a chance on this. Anything goes bad, you're dead.

Setting his fork on the pie plate, he patted his mouth with his own hankie—not one of Victor's paper napkins, not Sully—and returned the transcript to his briefcase.

"I show you that for one reason only. A dumb romantic like you, you probably think it's your fault Quinn got himself killed."

"The thought never entered my head."

"Yeah? It's right there over your left ear, connected by little balloons, like in the funny papers. Well, forget it. Quinn did what he had to do. He was a ballsy guy and he got those kids back alive, which amazes me, just using that corny stunt, an ad in the paper. And he never even paid any ransom."

"They never asked."

Sullivan shook his head and adjusted his seat so he could look down Commonwealth Avenue. The rain and fog had blown through, bringing clear air unusually warm for late November. The trees on the median, stripped of leaves, looked like pieces of modern sculpture set against a painted sky.

"So the situation I'm in," he said after a pause. "No one wants to talk to me. Fitzgerald takes off to Florida, which I don't blame him, they're his kids and he's taking no chances. You tell me only what Fitzgerald says you can tell me, even though I'm being generous, showing you my files on Quinn. Fitzgerald's sidekick, Milton Pridham, he's got a broom up his ass, starts quoting me the Constitution. All I know is, for some reason it's worth stealing children and gunning down a semiretired private investigator, just to keep Fitzgerald from showing up in court."

"Maybe it's his loud ties, ruins the atmosphere of decorum in there."

"Wonderful. Now he's cracking jokes."

"Look, I gave Fitzy my word, that's true, but I didn't need to because you know as much as I do. Probably more, you let Sheehan chew on your ear."

That straightened him up. He quit fiddling with his empty teacup and raised his rusty eyebrows, wrinkling his high domed forehead. "What have you got on Sheehan?" he asked.

That, I thought, was an odd way to put it.

"Rumor. Not about Sheehan, though. About Ernie Edwards."

Even as I launched into an abbreviated version of what Russ White had related, I could see Sully losing interest.

"Old news," he said dismissively. "Been going around for months. Internal Affairs had half a dozen men assigned. They came up with nothing. Possible that Eyeball started the rumor himself, just bragging."

"Bragging?"

"What can I say? The guy is a Neanderthal. He's not fit to wear the badge. But all the evidence shows him accidentally shooting that boy. They grilled him about five times, the Internal Affairs boys. Eyeball himself even went on the polygraph."

"So what were the results," I said, "on the lie detector?"

Sully shrugged. "Indicates that Eyeball is a lying son of a

bitch, which is no surprise. But that he was convinced Horatio Jones was carrying a weapon and intended to use it.''

''So they gave him a citation for bravery.''

Sully pushed his glasses up over the bump on his nose.

''For some actions in this department,'' he said, ''I have no explanation.''

9

IF MILTON PRIDHAM HAD NO PRACTICE AS YET, he did have an office. It was a small, expensively appointed suite in the same building on Milk Street where his father's firm occupied three floors. It had walnut wainscoting, burnished brass fixtures, a wall of lawbooks, an antique Oriental carpet, and a part-time secretary-receptionist who came with the lease.

"I'll see if Mr. Pridham is engaged," is what she said. A trim, coiffeured blonde with an arch accent who looked a bit startled at having a potential client come in without an appointment.

Mr. Pridham's office door was open. He was obviously not engaged, at least not with a living person. He got up and came into the reception area.

"Thanks, Babs," he said. "This is J. D. Hawkins, the writer Mr. Fitzgerald was talking about. He writes mysteries."

Babs looked wary, as if I might demand that she read one.

"So how is it going?" I said, putting parallel creases in the carpet as I wheeled into the inner sanctum. "Any hope for Mrs. Jones?"

Milton sat down in his upholstered chair and tried not to be nervous. Behind him a small paned window looked out onto the financial district. In the dim street below conservatively dressed men and women glided by on ticktock legs. Very little sunlight penetrated here, in the shadow of the new banking towers.

"This has not been an easy time for Mrs. Jones," he said.

On his big, shiny desk was the life and death of Horatio Jones, divided into files and depositions and ballistics reports. There were a number of photographs of the boy. Posing next to a Christmas tree, standing with his mother at the zoo. School photographs. Others showed him lying on a roof, his limbs twisted, shirt sticking to his body. There was a head shot taken on the mortuary slab, with his eyes as blank as an unwritten book and his black skin turned a pale and bloodless shade of gray.

"Mrs. Jones has developed a sincere attachment to Mr. Fitzgerald. She is, as a consequence, highly resistant to appointing new counsel. Don't get me wrong, she is a sweet lady, but she has a real stubborn streak."

I transferred my attention to Milton Pridham, who was choosing his words as carefully as he had chosen his button-down shirt, his office, and Babs the secretary. "What's your opinion?" I said. "Any chance Fitzy will change his mind, come back in on this?"

Pridham made a steeple of his hands. The pink-tinted horn-rims made his expression almost as blank as that of the dead boy on his desk. He had a way of licking his lips with the point of his tongue that reminded me of something I'd seen at the Aquarium. Maybe I'd picked up Fitzy's prejudice against overbred Brahmins. Maybe it was just the alligator on his tie that turned me off.

"I wish I knew," he said. "I was hoping perhaps you'd have some sense of what's going on with Finian. I understand, with his children being abducted, what a horrible fear that must be. If he'd seen fit to confide in me, well, I'd have done anything in my power. My father's firm, they have a big security organization on retainer, I could have made inquiries."

"Quinn got them back. On his own."

Pridham flexed his fingers, tilting his head. From behind the tinted glasses his eyes surveyed me. "Oh, yes," he said, "the private eye. Is that what happened? I got the impression, from the newspapers, that the police found the children."

"Don't believe everything you read in the papers."

"No, I suppose I shouldn't, at that. Do the police have any idea who took the children? Or why?"

I told him they were working on it, doing a door-to-door in the area between the Columbus Park circle and the block in South Boston where Quinn had been killed. It was a rough neighborhood, or rather a series of rough neighborhoods, whose citizens were not necessarily inclined to cooperate with a police investigation, so it was proceeding slowly.

"There's a pretty good chance they'll eventually find where the twins were hidden. All we know from the kids, they were locked in a dirty bathroom by two men wearing ski masks. Rory said the toilet didn't work, so the thinking is it was a tenement somewhere. He and Sarah were given a box of Dunkin' doughnuts to eat, and later two cups of hot cocoa, apparently dosed with sleeping pills."

"And that's all they know? Can they get in a sketch artist, make a composite of the two men?"

"The abductors never took off their masks. From the way Rory describes their voices, the way they talked, they were fairly young men. From what we can piece together, things Rory overheard, it's likely they're street punks, hired to do the job. Not equipped to keep two children for an extended time, and not quite willing to kill them."

"This is the most bizarre thing," Pridham said. "I can't imagine who would want to do such a thing. Or why."

"No? I came in here thinking maybe you *did* know."

For a moment Pridham lost his composure. Then he remembered who and where he was, and what his ancestors expected of him. He closed his gaping mouth and moved his flighty eyebrows into line.

"What are you implying, Mr. Hawkins?"

"I'm not *implying* anything. I wouldn't dream of implying anything to a lawyer. Last time I tried to imply anything to Fitzy, he buried me in an avalanche of legal mumbo jumbo that took my breath away. What I'm *inferring* is that since you've handled a lot of the paperwork for this case, you may have heard a certain rumor about Detective Edwards and his real motive for shooting Horatio Jones."

Pridham appeared to be stunned.

"How can you possibly know about that?" he said. "Fitzy

said I was to tell no one. And I didn't. I haven't let the deposition out of my sight."

It must have been my imagination, my tendency toward novelistic melodrama, that convinced me Milton Pridham was on the verge of tears.

"I heard it on the street," I said, letting him off the hook. "It's apparently common knowledge among Eyeball's peers that he confided to his cronies that he was intending to gun down a different black teenager, a dope dealer he'd had trouble with."

Pridham relaxed. A little color returned to his translucent complexion.

"Mr. Fitzgerald was adamant," he said, "that I not circulate that rumor. He said it was unsubstantiated, that it would actually work against our case if it came out in court. This is not a criminal trial. We are attempting to prove negligence, culpability. If it looked like we were trying to slander Edwards, it might go against us. I'm not really clear on why Mr. Fitzgerald felt so strongly about that, but he was very firm. He said we could not lose focus."

I remembered Fitzy using that very same phrase when he was handling my suit against the city. What he meant was that it was all very well playing up to the jury, but if he used any questionable tactics, such as wrongly impugning the character of a witness, it would show up on the transcripts of the trial and might be used as a means to reverse the findings. Fitzy tended to trust his juries, once he'd seduced them—he never trusted the legal establishment or the court system.

"What bothers me," I said, "is how everyone wants to ignore Eyeball Edwards. Here's a guy going around bars and social clubs, bragging about how he accidentally-on-purpose killed the wrong kid. This is after Internal Affairs has been dogging his ass for months, so we can safely conclude that Eyeball Edwards is not playing with a full deck. Then Fitzy hears about it and he says it's not pertinent to the case. Well, maybe. The two of you are lawyers, you're supposed to know. The way I see it, this guy is a trigger-happy rogue cop with a history of roughing up suspects, and he's got everyone too scared to think straight. Internal Affairs do their thing, and typically conclude there is nothing to conclude, so they give Eyeball a citation for bravery and he goes back on duty. The man is still a vice cop, which means he's at large in the toughest part of the city. He has dealings with street punks and petty criminals and stoolies, all part of the job. So for some reason, as the suit comes to trial, he gets a little antsy and he decides to put the fear of Eyeball into Finian X. Fitzgerald, who prior to this hasn't been afraid of much of anyone, certainly not the Boston cops."

"You mean Eyeball kidnaped Fitzy's children?" Milton said.

"I mean he is capable of arranging to have the kids snatched. And the son of a bitch has already proved himself willing to take an innocent life. Gunning down Lew Quinn would just be target practice."

"This is all very interesting, Mr. Hawkins. I know you have friends in the police department. I suggest you discuss it with them."

Pridham stood up, shrugging his blue blazer into place. The message was clear enough. He was a very busy young man, and while my wild theories were entertaining, he had work to do.

"Anything I can do for the Fitzgeralds, let me know. If you talk to Finian, tell him we need him here."

Babs stood up as I wheeled by her desk, as if witnessing a parade.

"I'd like to do that," I told Pridham. "But Fitzy is in Disney World. If he's talking to anybody these days, it's Mickey Mouse. Or maybe Donald Duck."

I stopped the elevator on the way down to take a gander at the firm of Briggs & Pridham. Their logo was imprinted on a pair of massive bronze-sheathed doors. As seen through ports of leaded glass, the effect was severely modern. Row upon row of open cubicles formed a maze that receded into a cool pastel distance. Corporate law on a grand scale, interior design by Hieronymus Bosch.

From where I was squinting, it looked a giant, monogramed bank vault.

Standish House occupies a large Federalist bow front on the Beacon Hill end of Beacon Street, overlooking the Common. I think the chinless gargoyles on the roof corners are modeled after Harold Standish III, who inherited the company.

Mary Kean insists it was Harold who was modeled after the gargoyles, and she's in a position to know, having been an editor there for almost thirty years.

"Harold has his good points," she likes to say. "For instance, he hardly ever comes in to work. He is very serious about playing squash, and that's a nice thing in a man. From all reports he is extremely kind to horses, out there at the Myopia. And they tell me he brakes for small animals, when it's convenient."

I've been told the interior of Standish House is perfectly maintained, furnished with period pieces and crystal chandeliers. Harold Standish has an anecdote about Henry James stopping in to exchange insults with the original Harold Standish on his last visit to Boston and being served tea on the very same silver tea service displayed in the foyer there to this day. Other people tell me Henry James couldn't distinguish Standish from a hole in the ground, and that he loathed tea, but it makes a nice story.

Although Mary Kean has now published half a dozen of my Casey novels, I've never been inside the place. The entrance is set atop a pyramid of granite steps. I could be carried up, of course. Until such a time as I decide it's worth suffering the indignity, I will continue to meet my editor in more accessible places, like Jake Wirth's.

There are a couple of steps up into Jake's, which I'm able to hump over with my knobby touring tires while one of the white-aproned waiters holds the door. Mary and I meet in the dining room, under the cartoon of loyal waiters who have gone on to Valhalla, where we can spread proofs out on the table and drink beer and be rude if it suits us.

"You look awful, Jack" is how Mary greeted me.

"Thanks," I said. "Is that a stretch mark I see under your third chin?"

"I'm serious. You look like you haven't slept in days. You sure you feel like going over this stuff now? We can easily put it off for a week. The deadline isn't until the first of January, for the summer list."

If anyone is to blame for my corpse-strewn novels it is Mary Kean. I had been working for the Boston Police Department as a civil service tech writer, churning out such masterpieces as *The Care and Cleaning of the Regulation Holster,* before Brad Dorsey got drunk and fired off his revolver and changed my career for me.

After the accident, during the lengthy and tedious convalescence, I wrote an autobiographical novel that was little more than one long list of complaints. Mary read it and came to see me—an unusual house call from an editor who happened to live within walking distance—and we have been friends ever since.

"If I published this manuscript," she told me then, "I'd lose my job and you would be embarrassed for the rest of your life. What I'd like you to do, if you're interested, is make up a story about some of the cops you know. Murder one of them in the first chapter and figure out who did it before the last page, and if I'm still reading it by then we'll print it."

That was how I started killing people for a living. The discipline of learning how to write a police procedural gave me the focus I had always lacked as a writer, and a structure to build a story around. The character Lieutenant Detective Casey, of the Boston Homicide Unit, was originally based on Tim Sullivan, who held the identical rank, but after six novels and dozens of corpses found and criminals apprehended, Casey was me. He was my legs, my eye over the city, my habits, my conscience.

For instance, Casey, unlike the abstemious Tim Sullivan, frequents Jake Wirth's, where he stands at the bar and has a dark beer and a shot of Jameson and smokes a small cigar. As he watches the smoke curl up he does his best thinking, putting the clues together and solving his cases. From the dining room I can look down to the bar and imagine him there, as I drink my dark and sip my whiskey and stink up the place with a small, fetid cigar.

I skipped the cigar when I was with Mary Kean, who had had to go cold turkey off her four packs a day after a heart attack that damn near killed her. All her life she had been a large, bulky woman, a dark-eyed Armenian Buddha who carried her weight with beautiful grace. Having to lose nearly a hundred pounds had been more of a trial than giving up the cigarettes. She could no longer enjoy the rich German chocolate desserts at Jake's, or have a second beer.

"The doctor says, you want a beer, have just the one," she complained after getting a quick update on the status of Fitzy and Lois and the children. "I never in my life had just one beer. Did Nero Wolfe ever have just one beer? He did not. Never less than three."

"Nero Wolfe didn't have to work for a living. He just did weird things to orchids and ate a lot of food and sent Archie out on errands."

"I thought you admired Rex Stout."

"I do. I just want you to follow the doctor's advice, keep off the butts and the Bavarian pastries. If you don't keep off the butts and the Bavarian pastries you might have another heart attack and have to retire—or worse—and then I'd get a new editor."

"You might like a new editor."

"I promise you, I would not."

Mary showed me a stat of the cover art for *Casey and the Black Seal,* which was still in manuscript, due out the following summer. It was a caper story, more lighthearted than previous Casey adventures, about a seal stolen from the aquarium. I thought the artist had made the seal look too menacing—in the story it was a friendly pup, an aquatic shaggy dog—but Mary insisted this was intentional, meant to be eye-catching.

"Jack, I like the new one, it's a departure for you and Casey, but the fact is, no one gets killed. There's no homicide. So we have to convince your readers they're still buying a suspenseful tale. Which, I think, it genuinely is. It's not too late, though, if you want to insert a chapter and kill someone off."

"I think not," I said, laughing. "I promise you, Mary, this next one, there'll be blood spattered on every page."

That was when Mary dropped her little bombshell. Maybe it was time, she suggested, to give Casey a rest.

"Now don't look that way, Jack. Hear me out. You've written seven *Casey* books in a little more than five years, counting the one we're copy-editing now. You've got stuff going into reprint for the next two years, which will keep the series out there in front of the public. This last one, the aquarium thing, I liked it, the writing carried the story. I'm picking up, though, a definite feeling that you're bored with Casey. You're going through the motions."

This was so unexpected, I didn't know how to react or what I felt about it. Bored with Casey?

"So what do you suggest, I write the Great American Novel?" I said, making no effort to conceal the sarcasm.

Mary smiled and finished her beer. She had the look of someone who has a secret and intends to keep it. "Sure," she said. "Why not give it a try?"

I mentioned the possibility that sudden dieting destroyed certain crucial brain cells.

"Just do me a favor, lover. Think it over."

With that said she broke training and ordered another beer. What the hell, I lit up a cigar and blew smoke at my shrinking Buddha.

10

THE *GLOBE* HAD DROPPED *ANDY CAPP* FROM its funnies, so I had got in the habit of reading the *Standard.* It told me that Milton Pridham had successfully petitioned the court for a ten-day postponement of the *Jones* suit. A police spokesman, responding to criticism that the department was responsible for losing several millions of the city's money in similar negligence and brutality suits, again stated that the officer cited in the case had been cleared by Internal Affairs. Without actually saying so, he implied that black teenagers living in high-crime districts ought not to frequent rooftops, or make sudden movements when confronted by out-of-uniform detectives, lest they find themselves not only quick, but dead.

"Face it, it's a jungle out there," the spokesman was quoted as saying.

The councilman from Roxbury had a fine time with that one.

"The department insists this was not a racial incident," the councilman was quoted as saying. "But when you have a six-foot-two-inch white male who feels it is necessary to shoot down a five-foot-one-inch black boy who has been guilty of nothing more serious than keeping pigeons on a roof, then I conclude we have a racial incident. Maybe we could save this city a lot of money if we just issued bulletproof vests to every black male at birth."

The *Standard,* true to form, never missed an opportunity to reprint a vividly cropped photo of the limp body of Horatio Jones. Eyeball Edwards never appeared on its pages, however, as a matter of editorial policy, since he was a police officer currently working undercover, and as such was awarded gladiator status by the McGary chain.

Seven days after Quinn was killed I got a postcard from Disney World, signed by Rory. Sarah's name had been filled in by Lois, which I found worrisome.

"It will take time, Jack," Megan said. "The poor little girl needs to heal. It's probably the best thing in the world for her, all the sunshine down there. All those other kids raising hell."

What nagged at me was the feeling that Sarah had heard or seen something crucial to the case, something too awful for a five-year-old to comprehend or retain.

Sully was his usual phlegmatic self.

"Something will break," he insisted. "Kidnaping is a stupid crime, therefore the people who do it are too dumb to stay out of jail. We don't pick them up on this, one of these guys is bound to get grabbed for something else. If that happens, he'll decide to sing us a little song. All we have to do is be ready to listen."

According to his wishes, Lew Quinn, much decorated Korean War veteran, was to be buried in Arlington National Cemetery, under one of the white crosses that blur the landscape there. The interment would have to be delayed until the file on his murder was closed. Until then the body was being kept in storage at the city morgue. I found that out by calling up his ex-wife, the one now married to the Brookline dentist Quinn had loved to bait.

"Lew had his good points," she told me. "He always earned a living. He just never knew when to quit. A hundred times I told him, get out, retire, it's a young man's game you're playing. But Lew, he always had some smart-aleck remark. He thought he was a tough guy."

"He *was* a tough guy, Mrs. Slovovitz."

"Well, now he's a dead guy, so that's what he got for acting tough. Which is really a sad thing. He was a nice man, Lew. If we'd had kids maybe we'd still be married. He'd be glad to know they're okay, those two brats who got him killed."

I put the postcard from Disney World on the refrigerator door and couldn't decide which book it was I wasn't writing. Another *Casey* story or the novel Mary Kean was trying to psych me into doing. Maybe, I thought, I should write about a black boy who raised white birds and set them free.

They found the kidnapers' van at the airport, where it had been abandoned.

''Do me a favor,'' Sullivan said, calling from the stationhouse. ''Meet me over there. Apparently some items of clothing survived the fire, maybe you could make an I.D., being the godfather and all.''

''What fire?''

''Meet me,'' he said, and told me which level of the garage.

The drive to Logan takes strong nerves, or a disregard for human life. The cabdrivers careening through the Callahan Tunnel exhibit both qualities, coupled with a fondness for the sounding of horns. I never go through the tunnel without thinking that one of these days the harbor is going to find a way inside, that the tiled walls will someday be scarred with barnacles, and the only commuters will be the kind with fins.

From the tunnel you get on the airport circuit, where you try to avoid permanently merging with buses and limousines. The secret is to select a trajectory and stick with it, and if you miss your turn-off, keep bearing left and it will eventually come at you again, like a full-scale arcade game.

Sully, who had the use of his flashing blues, beat me to the garage opposite the international terminal. The van, charred and covered with damping-foam, had been towed into an open area. The windshield was cracked, blackened with smoke. Wafts of steam came from the rear door, where a fireman in black rubber boots kept watch, an extinguisher strapped to his back.

''Strictly amateur,'' Sully said as I wheeled to his cruiser. ''Soaked the front seats with gasoline, then tossed a cigarette through the vent window. What happened, they must have seen a lot of smoke, thought the whole thing was going to pop. Only it just kept smoldering, never got all the way to the back.''

Sullivan looked happy. He had a number of items sealed in

clear plastic evidence bags, which he lined up on the front fender of his unmarked cruiser.

"This is an example of how police work is supposed to go, only usually it doesn't. We had notified the airport detail, report all vans fitting this description. They didn't spot the van, there must be a couple hundred in here like it, some left for weeks, but what they *did* do, they made the match when the fire squad reported a torched vehicle. Then, to make things especially nice, the fireman who sprays down the vehicle, he's been told to collect evidence for the Arson Unit, the insurance carriers are going bananas, all the cars get torched out here. So this alert fireman bags the items there in the bed of the van before he soaks the interior with his chemicals. I'm going to write this guy up. Maybe he'll get a promotion if the bureaucrats don't screw it up."

In one of the plastic bags was a flattened popcorn box and a cotton scarf that looked like one I'd given Sarah. Purple with a pattern of red seahorses. In another bag was the hood of a small jacket. I didn't recognize it, but the size was about right.

The clincher, and the reason Sully had been called immediately to the scene, was an embossed plastic bracelet. The clasp had been torn and the heat of the fire had twisted it a bit, but most of the lettering was still clearly visible: MY NAME IS RORY FITZGERALD AND I LIVE AT:

"Can you imagine leaving that in the back there, even if you *are* going to torch the vehicle? I can only conclude, Jack, that we are not dealing with criminal masterminds here. We're going to impound the vehicle, and have Forensic do the deluxe dust job." He grinned, shoving his glasses back into place. "The animals did this, they probably don't know how to wipe their fannies, never mind cleaning up fingerprints."

Seeing the children's clothing locked in evidence bags gave me a cold feeling in the pit of my stomach.

"Why now?" I asked. "It's been a week."

''My guess, they parked it over here right after they stashed the kids. Then their dim little brains remember they never cleaned out the back of the van. So they have to wait until one of them gets up enough nerve to come over here with a tin of gas. Maybe they're afraid we've located the vehicle, staked it out. They're amateurs, remember. These are the same guys that go to all the trouble of pulling a snatch, then they give the kids back because it's too much trouble taking care of them. Or because they're afraid. So blowing a simple torch job, it doesn't surprise me.''

''But why the airport?''

Sullivan shrugged, then gathered up the evidence bags.

''You're the mystery writer,'' he said. ''This happened in one of your books, what would be the reason?''

''They fled to another country. Took the money and ran.''

Sully grinned and paused to huff on his glasses, polishing the lenses with the clean white hankie he kept for that purpose.

''Only thing is,'' he said, ''no money changed hands that we know of. If I was this detective of yours, Casey, I would conclude the kidnapers dropped the van here because the place is so anonymous. Automatic tickets. And you can leave a vehicle here for a couple of weeks before it gets towed. The other factor, everyone on the street knows this is where the torches bring vehicles for flame-outs, the ones that get reported stolen about an hour after they go up in smoke. Very popular spot, the Logan garage.''

An airliner hung suspended in the leaden sky over us, looming and silent as it slowly gained altitude. Only after it was gone did the roar of its engines jelly the air.

''Except you're not Casey!'' I shouted.

Sully shook his head and pointed to his ears.

I know damn well he heard me.

Mrs. Ida Mae Jones was waiting inside the vestibule of a drugstore on a corner of Washington Street. An iron grate covered the plate-glass windows and there was a carefully lettered sign above the entrance: CASH SECURED. ARMED GUARDS ON DUTY.

In the center of the sign was something that looked a lot like a bullet hole. Dingy red graffiti had been sprayed through the grates, dribbling down the windows. The whole place looked like it was bleeding.

I found a spot at the curb to pull the van up and left the engine idling as I beeped the horn. A tight group of young men, all black, all wearing caps and posturing tough, looked at the van and at me inside it. One of them pointed and made a hooting noise. His friends laughed.

I honked the horn again. The young gentlemen of Roxbury were not amused. When I'd called Mrs. Jones she'd offered to meet me in town, but I wanted to see where Horatio Jones had lived and died. Without any real enthusiasm she said she would meet me at the corner drugstore and guide me from there to her apartment.

"How'm I gonna know it's you?" she had asked.

"I'll have a paperback book. My picture is on the back."

I tooted again. A short, slightly built black woman darted out of the drugstore. It was bitterly cold and her head was uncovered. As she looked through the side window I held up the paperback.

She nodded and mouthed the word "okay."

Waiting until she had cleared the front of the van before releasing the passenger-door lock, I was amazed at the speed with which she opened the door, slipped inside, and threw the lock down again.

"Mister, you crazy coming down here, you know that?"

I was busy studying the mirror, looking for a break in traffic so we could pull out into Washington Street. The young men moved in. Someone slapped the side of the van and shouted, "Hey, momma! Who you belong to?"

"You better take off quick," Ida Mae Jones said. "One of these trash, he's going to pick up a rock, break this windshield."

A lanky kid in a floppy leather hat climbed up on the bumper and pressed his face to the window. He winked at me. As winks go, it was not the least bit friendly.

"Just go," Ida Mae Jones said heatedly. "That boy, he'll get off. He quick enough to jump off a moving train, the look of him. Mister White Man, you don't get this thing in gear we both in trouble."

Knuckles were rapping on the windows and fists beating the sides of the van as I gunned it. The tall skinny kid on the bumper did a pirouette worthy of Baryshnikov, skipping through the air to the sidewalk as I melded the van into the stream of traffic.

Mrs. Jones leaned back in her seat and sighed, folding her mittens across her breast. "I gotta be crazy, doing this. First thing I get a chance, I'm gonna have my head examined."

"You think we were in real danger?"

"Hey, is the Pope Irish?"

"No," I said uncertainly.

Mrs. Jones laughed. She was having me on. "No? I be darned. You live in this city, you get the impression the Pope, he *must* be Irish."

My first impression of Mrs. Jones, after glimpsing her with Milton Pridham in the courthouse, was of meekness and uncertainty. In the course of an hour on her own turf she erased that impression, replacing it with one that included gutsy, quick-witted, and highly determined.

"I think I better find a different drugstore," she said. "Those trash form the impression I'm doing tricks for white men, they never let up on me."

"Sorry," I said.

"Don't apologize for what trash think. Just take the next left. You smart, you don't let this automobile stall."

Stripped carcases of abandoned or stolen vehicles lay tipped and overturned on rutted sidewalks. Between yellow-brick tenement buildings was a patch of bare ground that had once been a children's park. Just the framework of the swing set remained, and a chipped concrete form suggestive of a dinosaur.

"Look like a war zone, don't it?"

I said it did indeed.

"Pull over here. You wait, keep it idling. I'm going inside and get Missy's boy. He'll watch the van, you give him a dollar." She opened the side door and slipped out. "Give him the dollar *after*, okay. Not before."

The youngster she returned with looked about eight years old. He had a ring in the lobe of his left ear and a comb shoved in his hair. He whistled when he saw me.

"Man, you in a wheelchair!" he said.

I tried to look surprised.

"Damn, and I thought it was a Mercedes Benz."

"Hey," he said, leaping into the passenger seat, "you okay."

"What will you do if someone wants to steal this thing?"

"I scream real loud," he said proudly. "It a very unpleasant sound."

Mrs. Jones was waiting behind the van as I lowered myself to the pavement.

"Pretty slick," she said. "This like a delivery truck, only you the package."

I followed her into an apartment building. It was made of gray brick and steel and was not as battle-scarred as others on the street.

"We in luck today, the elevator working."

Working or not, it was slow to answer. A low-watt bulb, protected by a wire cage, threw faint illumination from the stairwell. Layer upon layer of graffiti covered every square inch of the foyer's concrete walls.

Mrs. Jones glanced at the cover of the *Casey* book while we waited. "Funny thing, that what the boys who spray this paint all over call theyselves. Writers. Like you. They say they artists, spraying that trash. These boys steal from they momma, buy paint cans. Spray a name on the wall, five minutes later, some other boy spray it out.''

The elevator door opened. We got on. It too was covered with multiple layers of sprayed paint.

''My son never once steal from his momma,'' she said. She looked again at the cover of the paperback. ''You have children, Mr. J. D. Hawkins? Or shouldn't I ask, you in that chair?''

''You can ask,'' I said. ''No, I don't have any kids.''

The apartment consisted of two small bedrooms and a kitchenette. A large color television was perched on the dining table. Near the window was an empty aquarium on a cheap, wrought-iron stand.

''That was before Horatio got interested in birds. After it happened, I just let the fish die. I had no interest in those fish no more. You want coffee? I got a beer in there, you want it.''

''Coffee will be fine.''

With her winter jacket off, Ida Mae Jones was small all over. Just a little higher than me sitting down, which meant she did not break five feet. Soaking wet and after a full meal she might have weighed a hundred pounds. Her wrists, as she poured the instant coffee, looked as delicate as fine black porcelain.

''You got a scheme to get Mr. Fitzy Fitzgerald back on my side, I'm all ears.''

''Like I said over the phone, I'll try. The threat to his children has passed and the police seem confident of picking up the kidnapers. I think Fitzy will come around. He's never been a quitter.''

I asked her if she minded revealing how she had happened to choose Fitzy to represent her.

''I saw him there,'' she said, indicating the blank television screen. ''This great big Irish face lookin' at me. What he sayin', he mouthin' off at the police, how they beat up a client of his, and how he was goin' to sue they butts. That's how he say it, sue they butts.''

That was Fitzy all right. He'd won the case, too.

''I already been to a bunch of lawyers. Some hotshot black lawyers here in Roxbury, some Jewish lawyers downtown, they all say the same two things. We terribly sorry, momma, and have you got any money? They say suing the city very risky, they need money upfront, to cover expenses. So I think, why not try me an Irish lawyer? This an Irish town, right? Mayor's Irish, most of the cops. Use one of their own, make those bastards wish they never shot down my little boy. He only a little bigger than me, Horatio. He not exactly the Hulk, you know.''

I asked her if she had ever seen Detective Edwards around the neighborhood before her son was killed.

''Mr. Eyeball? He be around now and then, throwing some trash up against a building, cuffing they hands. Banging they heads off the ground, too. He have a thing going with the junkies, that man.''

''Thing?''

''Yeah, you know, he *play* with that trash. He run 'em around, bust 'em sometimes, break him some heads. Mostly he play, like with toys, you see, having himself a good time. Then he decide he have to shoot somebody, improve his big bad reputation, so he come up here on the roof. Bang, bang, bang. Three times he fire into the heart, just to make sure he dead. Little boy so small he could carry him in his pocket.''

To try and steer the subject away from the actual incident, obviously still very painful for her, I asked how Horatio had gotten interested in raising pigeons.

''School,'' she said. ''Same thing with the fish. He forever curious about little animals. In this neighborhood, it very precious in a boy, he find something besides dope and girls to interest him.''

Since the elevator did not go as high as the roof landing, I formed a picture from Ida Mae's description. A lunar landscape of gravel and tar and decrepit shacks. An ancient set of pigeon coops, newly cleaned out and refurbished by a serious youngster who loved school and dreamed of being a scientist.

From the window I could see across a vacant, junk-strewn lot to another street, another row of tenements. There was a sameness about that pattern of charred turf and smog-scarred tenements, continuing block after block, that might easily have confused a bad-tempered vice cop with a record of careless behavior.

"I assume Horatio had a lot of friends?"

Mrs. Jones folded her arms across her chest and gazed out the window. She was as small and delicate as, well, a bird.

"He have some friends, I guess. Mostly he keep to his self. For a while he join up at the mission boys' club, so he can go on the field trips to all the museums."

She explained that while her son was not Catholic, he had been encouraged to attend the Roxbury Boys' Mission, sponsored by the Boston archdiocese.

"It a mission okay, anyway you look at it. Not many black Catholics here in Roxbury, 'cept a few Haitians, and they keeps to themselves. But that club got itself a black priest—he come from Barbados, some place like that—and a white priest. I assume he there to keep an eye on the black priest, make sure he don't go native, take up with the rest of the Baptist. Horatio, he very excited, every Saturday they take trips to a different museum. Then one time he decide he don't want to go no more."

Had he given her a reason for his sudden loss of interest?

"Horatio a quiet one. He have his own secrets, and I know from experience, better not to push him. He wants to quit hanging out with the Catholics, that fine by me."

Mrs. Jones came down to the street with me, to collect Missy's boy. He was bouncing in the passenger seat, listening to the tape deck. With the ring in his ear and the big comb jammed in his hair he looked like a miniature version of one of the young men who had accosted us at the drugstore. He was a bright, peppy kid, full of personality. I hoped he was strong enough to find a way out, when the time came.

"Hey, my man," he said, "you got some great tunes here. Herbie Hancock, Freddie Hubbard, Hubert Laws."

Positioning my chair behind the wheel and locking it down, I remarked at my surprise that he was familiar with that kind of jazz.

"You serious, man?" The little imp was making faces as I pulled out my wallet. "They oldtimers, but they still famous on the street. Bah-da-da-deet!" He made a horn sound into his cupped hands.

I gave him five bucks. Ida Mae, grabbing hold of the little boy, frowned at me. The kid was giggling and squirming as he fought to stuff the bills down his pants. "You spoil this boy, pay him that much to sit here and listen to music."

"As soon as Fitzy gets back," I said, "we'll talk."

"You just say one thing to that man. Remind him what he promise me in his office, the first time we talk."

With the little kid on her narrow hip, she turned and darted back into her building. I circled the block. From the next street over I could see the roof where Horatio Jones had kept his pigeons, and the birds that still roosted there, flying in tight, nervous patterns against the bleak winter sky.

11

THE GRANITE EDIFICE SQUATS UNDER THE shadow of the John Hancock Tower, a throwback to another age, when the architecture of public buildings was based on quarried stone rather than spires of costume jewelry. I talked my way through the security checkpoint at the rear entrance, got on the elevator to the main floor, and wheeled through the halls looking for Sully's office.

In my years as a civilian writer for Informational Services, I'd jumped at any chance to make a trip to the Berkeley Street Headquarters. For a would-be novelist, the old building had a heady atmosphere, the chief factor being the smell. In the maze of dim odors you can distinguish the faint pong of sweat, cigars, leather, and fear. It is that special cop scent, I think, rather than the billy club, that makes suspects want to confess to crimes they have not committed.

Marilyn, boss of the clerical staff for the Homicide Unit, took a pencil from behind her ear and pointed at Sullivan's office.

"The lieutenant detective," she said, "is waiting."

Behind her work station was a Red Sox team poster. Marilyn firmly believes that, were she to be named manager, the club would never again lose a pennant. What the team lacks, she says, is discipline.

"What you gotta remember, these are just kids on the ball team. They need guidance. They need their butts kicked."

Marilyn, who has been with Sully for most of his career and who raised four children on her own, gives the impression that she would be very good at butt kicking. With her steel-blue hair and hawklike profile, Marilyn bears a remarkable resemblance to Mary Lou, who runs the office for Casey in my novels, a familiarity she seems willing to endure so long as I give her free hardcover copies.

Sullivan was perched on his desk, reading a file. He was wearing a gray tweed suit and a silk tie with a small check pattern. Tim Sullivan may well be the only police detective in Boston, or the world, who bothers to use a Windsor knot. If he could get away with spats, he'd wear them—unlike Casey, who cares little for his wardrobe and usually has spots of dried egg on his vest.

"This guy," he said, rustling the file, "is so dumb, you'd have to keep him after school about three years just to explain the difference between his ass and his elbow. Not that he ever spent much time in school."

"This is the guy who stole the van?"

"Let me put it this way. This is the guy, Kerrigan, who reported the van stolen. He is also, undoubtedly, the guy who stole the van from himself. He is also, most probably, the guy who stole the plates off his brother-in-law's Chevy Nova and put them on his stolen van, so no alert officer would chance to pull him over and come to the conclusion that he was driving the same vehicle he had already reported as stolen. Do you follow the logic?"

"Is that a trick question?"

"The trick," Sully said, "is understanding the extreme simplicity of Kerrigan's mind. He is hired to do a job. Part of the job is that he secure, for limited use, a motor vehicle that cannot be traced to himself. Now the average criminal, he would probably just find a car and steal it. Wrongway has a different angle on things. If he steals a motor vehicle belonging to someone else, there is a danger he may get caught, and with all his prior convictions for drug possession, assault and battery, attempted rape, and so on, he may find himself sharing a very small cell with some very large Negroes. This is a living arrangement he wishes to avoid. Therefore he concludes that he will do the job using his own van, which he will report stolen so as not to be connected to the crime he has agreed to commit. Having heard that it is highly suspicious to report a vehicle stolen after it has been used in the commission of a felony, Kerrigan decides to report it stolen well before engaging in said felonious act, thus clearing himself of suspicion. Only trouble, what if he gets pulled over, they check out the plate number? Kerrigan thinks long and deep, pondering the possibilities.

"What he comes up with, to baffle the authorities, Kerrigan decides he will use his brother-in-law's license plates. The fact that his brother-in-law is assisting him in commission of the felony and will be leaving his thumbprints all over the inside of the glove compartment, does not trouble Mr. Kerrigan, whose technique for avoiding arrest is to be such a big pain in the ass the cops will let him go."

"You mean he's already confessed to kidnaping the twins?"

Sully smirked as closed the file. "Kerrigan, relying on his pain-in-the-ass technique of arrest avoidance, has declined to converse in anything other than hypothetical situations. To Kerrigan, this is extremely clever. Hypothetically, he suggests, what if his brother-in-law, whose criminal record is almost as long and tedious as Kerrigan's, what if this brother-in-law stole Kerrigan's van, put his own license plates on it, and then used it in the commission of the alleged crime? Would that hypothetical situation not match the facts? Or, to quote Wrongway, 'Would I be dumb enough to use my own fucking van?' Unquote."

"What does the brother-in-law have to say?"

The suspect, Sully said, had not yet been apprehended. Sheehan was out looking for him at that very moment, combing the taverns and social clubs of South Boston.

"What I asked you to come in for, I'd like you to take a peek at Kerrigan. There's just the chance he may be the guy followed you from the courthouse the other day."

As he threaded down the long corridor to the interrogation rooms, Sully explained that Kerrigan had not yet been charged, and that, after his initial statements and the implied accusation of his missing brother-in-law, he had clammed up and was waiting to consult a lawyer.

"From what Sheehan told me," Sully said, "he may have a

long wait. Young Kerrigan has a habit of writing checks on accounts that do not actually exist. He has done this to a number of defense attorneys. If he wants a public defender, which is probably all he'll get, he has to wait until the arraignment. Public defenders are not exactly jumping up and down to get the court's attention in order to have the privilege of defending Kerrigan. This may have something to do with the fact that Wrongway smeared excrement on the windshield of a car belonging to the last public defender who stood up for him, because said P.D. failed to get Kerrigan off. As a rule, public defenders don't like getting their wipers clogged with excrement.''

In Sullivan's summation, the suspect was a ''bad actor,'' a phrase that had nothing to do with theatrical ambition.

''I've never actually read your books,'' Sully said. ''But Sheehan, a real fan of yours, tells me you always have your detective observing suspects through a two-way mirror. So this is going to be a disappointment.''

Sullivan pushed open a door. Inside it smelled strongly of disinfectant. A thick wire screen divided a small, windowless cubicle. On one side a bored uniformed cop sat on a wooden swivel chair, reading a magazine. He looked up from the magazine just long enough to nod at Sullivan. On the other side of the screen was a card table and two chairs.

On one of the chairs, sound asleep and snoring loudly, was Wrongway Kerrigan. He looked to be in his mid-twenties. His bare arms were scarred with puncture marks. He was not wearing shoes—a security precaution of some sort—and there were almost as many holes in his socks as in his arms. With his weak chin and jug ears, not even his mother could have described him as handsome.

''No way,'' I said. ''The guy following me was big. In his mid- to late thirties. Wide shoulders. And he didn't move like a junkie. I told you, Tim, he walked like a cop.''

We backed out of the interrogation room. ''Yeah, so you said.

How exactly does a cop walk different than anyone else? Do I walk like a cop?"

"No," I said. "You're an exception to the rule. You walk like a schoolteacher."

In the books Casey walks like a priest. Very soft pedal. He wears tennis shoes because his feet hurt all the time. That's one of Casey's major concerns, the condition of his feet.

I was reasonably certain, from comments Sullivan had let slip over the years, that he had read most of the Casey novels, and that he took secret pride in having been the model for a fictional character, although he continued to pretend ignorance. I wondered if he knew anything about *Tough Guy,* the memoir Sheehan was threatening to write, and how he would fare if that project, however unlikely, came to fruition.

The would-be author caught up with us in the snack shop, where Sully ordered coffee and a corned-beef sandwich. Sergeant Detective Larry Sheehan looked very pleased with himself. For some reason, possibly because the snack shop was crowded with other cops, he decided to be civil with me.

"Hey, hey, waddaya say."

Before I could flinch he fixed his patented handshake on me, his fingers gripping all the way up to my wrist.

He had not yet, he informed Sully, located Mutt, as Kerrigan's brother-in-law was known.

"What I did find is almost as good. We got the hole they stashed the Fitzgerald kids in, Lieutenant. And guess what, someone tried to torch it."

Lew Quinn had agreed to make contact with the kidnapers at the Columbus Park circle, and he was killed on the corner of Emerson Street, so it was no surprise that the children had been hidden somewhere in between those two points. The somewhere, it turned out, was in an abandoned building a block from Broadway.

"The alarm got answered yesterday, 5:25 a.m. They sent out

a pumper and a follow-up vehicle. The fire was restricted to the hallway area, and it was obviously arson. Bunch of oily rags. It didn't go up only because they partially wrecked the building a couple of years ago and the roof is wide open over the hallway, so the whole area is soaked.''

Sully caved in and allowed me to follow them to the Broadway location. Maybe he knew that, given the condition of the building, I would be unable to interfere. While he entered the scorched front of the building, Sheehan elected to stay behind and sketch in the scene for me.

''I been checking every arson call in the neighborhood, since we found the van flamed out at the airport. Also Mutt Dawson is a known torch, so it figures he'd set fire to the place, just out of habit.''

I kept waiting for the sneer to manifest itself on Sheehan's face. This cooperative approach was completely out of character. It made me uneasy, wondering what game he was playing.

''I go down there, that smelly basement, we find what used to be the super's apartment, only most of it has been torn out. In one corner is a lavatory. It has a brand-new lock on the door. A sliding bolt. Inside is a toilet, a tub, doughnut bags on the floor. In the tub is a pillow. I remember the little boy saying he slept on a pillow inside a bathtub, so it begins to look good, this is the place. Then we find a Barbie doll, which the mother said the little girl had with her when she went to the movies, and which never showed up in the van. Then, and this is so unbelievably stupid it had to be Kerrigan and Mutt in on it, we find Kerrigan's number plates thrown in a dumpster about ten feet from the back of the building. My conclusion is, you want to fuck up a perfectly straightforward crime like kidnaping, get Wrongway Kerrigan and Mutt Dawson to do it.''

Sheehan had every right to be pleased with himself. It was a piece of textbook policework. The recovery of the number plates tied it up very neatly.

"So why did they shoot Quinn?" I asked, when Sullivan was safely out of range. "That's the part doesn't make sense."

Sheehan cupped his hands around a match and leaned in with his filterless Lucky. It was disturbing to realize that his creased, hollow face would look appropriate on a dust jacket. *Tough Guy*. As titles went, it wasn't bad.

"Kerrigan and Mutt are junkies," he said. "They both got the shakes more or less all the time, except when nodded out. Neither of them ever been busted on a firearms violation, although Kerrigan once tried to crush some guy's head with a tire iron that was missing his weekly payments to his friendly neighborhood loan shark."

"So you think someone else shot Quinn?"

Sheehan humped his shoulders and took a deep drag of the cigarette. "I don't think anything, regarding that, except you can draw your own conclusion. Your buddy Quinn got it five times in the chest. I don't know if you ever tried shooting a target, but getting five pops in an area as bit as a grapefruit, that's mighty fine shooting, partner. Now remember that these two bozos that grabbed the kids can't even figure out how to burn a building down, they got all the time in the world. And Quinn is carrying a weapon and he never even gets it out of the clip?"

"So whoever shot Quinn was a professional?"

"Like I said, you draw your own conclusions, okay?" He fussed with the lapels of his overcoat, dusting off the ash that had dropped from his cigarette. "And maybe next time you write one of those books, you keep in mind that just because certain cops talk the way they do, which is a habit of a lifetime, they are not totally stupid, okay?"

So that was it. Larry Sheehan wanted his fictional counterpart to have a little more integrity.

"This cop Shannon in your books, how about he gets a promotion? He stays all the time at the same rank, the reader loses interest. Do I have a point?"

"It's a suggestion, Larry. I'll think about."

"Okay," he said, giving me a sharp little punch in the shoulder. "You do that."

Megan thought I was meddling, and said so.

"You go to see the mother of the little boy they shot," she said over a pasta dinner I'd picked up at one of those trendy yuppie delis on Charles Street. "That I understand. The poor woman has gotten a raw deal, maybe you can get Fitzy to help her again. Any word when they're coming back from Florida?"

"No. Milton Pridham hasn't heard. I think Fitzy left a number with him, for the motel they're at, but he won't divulge it."

"What worries me is you messing around with Sheehan. This guy is bad news. The last time you had anything to do with Larry Sheehan, you ended up in Boston Harbor, trying to breathe all that dirty water."

"And Sheehan helped pull me out."

"Uh-huh," Megan said, amused. "It was the other one dove in and pulled you out. Sheehan just stood by, directing the rescue. So now suddenly he's a good guy, a great cop? This is what worries me."

"So how is it going at work? Henry James been in to tea lately?"

Rather than spoil a perfectly ordinary pesto sauce, we agreed to disagree. I would continue to play wheelchair detective, and Meg would continue to tell me it was a bad idea. Which did not discourage me from trying to get in the last word.

"The odd thing about Sheehan's behavior today," I said, pushing my paper plate forward as Meg dished out the last of the cannelloni, "is I got the distinct impression he wanted me to think about Eyeball Edwards. He never said the name, but that was his message, the implication that an expert marksman shot Quinn."

"I have an idea," Meg said. "Let's invite good old Larry over for dinner, see what's really on his mind."

"You're very sexy when you're being sarcastic."

"It's just, Jack, sometimes the clash of male egos is deafening. Fitzy just about has a nervous breakdown because he thinks his manhood failed him when he didn't singlehandedly fight off two armed kidnapers. Lew Quinn decides to go in alone, prove he's a hero. And now you start nosing around, making such a pest of yourself that a psycho like Eyeball Edwards is bound to notice, and maybe takes a shot at you, he's such a fabulous marksman."

"Only a silver bullet could kill me. Or possibly the garlic on your breath."

"Men," Megan said. "No wonder they're an endangered species."

12

RUSS WHITE HAD THE STORY FOR BREAKfast. In true *Standard* style, a crisp shot of the basement bathroom was splashed over the entire front page, with a white circle around the Barbie doll, barely discernible, and an X in the bathtub, where it was alleged that Rory had slept.

COPS LOCATE KIDNAP LAIR
Suspect in custody

I was reading his detailed, and for the most part accurate recap of the abduction of the Fitzgerald twins, their retrieval, and the murder of private investigator Lew Quinn when Milton Pridham called.

''Sorry to disturb you, Mr. Hawkins. I read somewhere that you write in the morning, so I'm probably interrupting your latest novel.''

Without exactly agreeing, I let him think so.

''Mrs. Jones is with me now. We have been going over the options. Whether to seek another continuance, or whether to proceed without the counsel of Mr. Fitzgerald. I hope I'm not breaking a confidence, but Mrs. Jones mentioned that you visited her and that you made statements to the effect that you intended to persuade Mr. Fitzgerald to return here and take up, as it were, the gauntlet.''

Giving Milton a taste of his own legalese, I agree that, substantially, her verbal deposition was true.

''What I've done, Milton, is I've written Fitzy a letter, made two copies, and sent one care of his home address and one care of his office. I don't know if he left forwarding instructions. It may be the letters are just sitting there. My intention, Milton, was to call Fitzy up in Florida, but the telephone number down there seems to be privileged information.''

There was a silence on the other end of the line. I sipped at my tea and reached over to swipe an uneaten croissant from the plate Megan had left, and listened to Milton Pridham breathe in my ear.

''I'm in a very difficult position,'' he said eventually. ''As you have guessed, I've been in touch with Finian. More with his wife, really, since he doesn't seem to want to come to the phone. I have endeavored to keep him apprised of events, and he has, through Lois, given me sound advice as to how best to delay the process—I mean file motions for delay. Even that has been like pulling teeth, since he is determined to follow the instructions made by the men who kidnaped his children.''

''And who now,'' I said, ''are in custody. That's the point I want to make to Fitzy, if only I can talk to him—that the twins are no longer in danger. Or if he's still afraid, and I don't really blame him, he can leave the kids down there in Florida with Lois and come back here and take over the case. Sully tells me—that's Lieutenant Sullivan—that the department will provide him with armed bodyguards. Or if Fitzy doesn't want any cops involved, which I also can understand, considering Eyeball Edwards is still out of his cage, we can hire a private security firm.''

I could hear Pridham cover the receiver, and the muffled sound as he conferred with Ida Mae Jones. It seemed odd that he would call me with a client in the room, unless he was trying to impress her with his willingness to make every effort.

''Mrs. Jones appreciates the gravity of the situation,'' he said. ''As do we all. At her suggestion I am going to call the number Mr. Fitzgerald entrusted to me. I will tell him—or his wife—that you wish to converse, and suggest that they call you. Are you amenable to that?''

''Jesus, Milton, I've been trying to get you to do that for the last three days. Of course I'm amenable.''

When Pridham got off the line I returned to the *Standard*, concentrating on the comic pages. Life made a hell of a lot more sense when it was contained in four panels. What would *Judge Parker* make of Pridham's maneuvering? Was the Beacon Hill lad trying to horn in on the very generous settlement that a favorable ruling would give to Mrs. Jones? Fitzy would be down for his usual one-third—conservative by trial-lawyer standards, most of whom took half—and I wondered what provision had been made for Pridham, as the very junior counsel. It was possible that he could cut his own deal if he lined up a new law firm for the *Jones* suit.

In my novels the rich always aspire to more wealth. Money is the motive for almost every underhanded deal, the fuel for the fires of criminal passion. Milton hadn't impressed me as the greedy type, there in his own little office, plotting a long-term career in politics. He hadn't impressed me at all. A closed, secretive young man, burdened by the social prestige of his own family, it seemed unlikely that he would dare to commit any impropriety that might be called to the attention of the bar. Scandal, for his kind, was a slow and certain death.

Childe Milton of Louisburg Square, Fitzy had called him. And yet Finian, no mean judge of character, had taken him on, entrusted the case files to him. By all appearances he now trusted Pridham more than he trusted me.

Is that what was getting my goat? That the man who was my closest friend no longer saw fit to confide in me?

Expecting that I would have to hang around the apartment all day waiting for the return call, I burned off nervous energy by tidying up my desk. A short outline for a Casey adventure looked thin and anemic. I was beginning to understand the motive for Arthur Conan Doyle's decision to push Holmes over the falls. Not that my Casey would ever be as famous as Conan Doyle's cocaine-shooting character.

Without knowing quite how I had arrived there, I was beginning to agree with Mary Kean. I needed to give the series a rest. I needed to write a different kind of book. Maybe a nonfiction account of, say, a notorious civil suit brought against a major city police department. A department that gave cops a license to kill, so long as the victims were poor, black, and defenseless. A department that knowingly harbored a detective with sociopathic tendencies, who had resorted to violence on numerous occasions, and who even now was allowed to operate as a lone wolf, answering to no one, out of a Vice unit that had been riddled with corruption.

I was making notes on a yellow legal pad when Lois called.

"Hi, handsome. Is it cold up there?"

"I can't see the outside thermometer from here, it's covered with ice."

"Then you'll be happy to know it's raining in Orlando."

"You call up to discuss the weather, Lois? So how are the twins?"

"No, I didn't call up to discuss the weather. The twins are fine. They both send you love. Sarah is coming around. I drove her out to the beach yesterday. We had a nice time discussing all the icky things that wash up along the shore."

"She's talking, then?"

"In fits and starts, Jack."

"How about Fitzy?"

Silence.

"Are you going to put him on or what?"

"You're making this tough, Jack. Milton says you've been in touch. Fitzy doesn't want him to give out the number or where we're staying, and I know that sounds silly. All I can tell you, Fitzy has his reasons. It has nothing to do with you. It's . . . well . . ."

"What, the people I know? The cops?"

More silence.

"Lois, there is no way this line is tapped, if that's what Fitzy is worried about. And as to the two thugs who grabbed the twins, Sully has one in custody and the other is going to get picked up any minute, he stays true to form. Which I'm sure you know, if you talked to Milty.''

Her sigh was deep and heartfelt. When she continued her voice was thick, as if she was near to tears.

''Jack, all I can tell you is nothing has changed.''

''Let me ask you this, Lois, and then I'll let you go. I think someone is still scaring you, making threats. Am I right, Lois? Just tell me this, who's the son of a bitch who's got you frightened?''

Lois mumbled goodbye and hung up.

I rolled over to the desk and looked at the notes I'd been making. One name kept popping out at me. Detective Ernie Edwards. He'd freely admitted taking one innocent life. What other mischief was he involved in? And why was Sheehan, a fellow cop, pointing me in his direction?

The idea of the Catholic Church operating a storefront mission seemed out of character in staunchly Catholic Boston. But then the mission was in the staunchly black section of Roxbury, located a few blocks from the somewhat blurred color line. As Father Napoleon Duvall explained, it had been conceived as a mission in the original sense of the word.

''We are flag bearers for the glory of God. We are a voice that speaks in the wilderness. And, my friend, look around. This is indeed the wilderness.''

The storefront windows had been boarded up with plywood, so it was impossible to do as he suggested. Unless the weather had changed in the last ten minutes, snow was settling over the gray buildings, condensing to slush. Miserable enough weather to discourage, I hoped, the young vandals who roamed the neighborhood, to whom the smashing of windshields and the prying off of hubcabs was simply a reflex.

''The most important thing we do here, or *attempt* to do, is keep the white devil out of these boys.''

Father Duvall explained that the white devil was heroin. The boys were any black young men under the age of sixteen who could be induced to enter the mission. Inside there was a ping-pong table, a library of tattered paperbacks, and a picnic table where a chessboard lay open, the pieces in place. The walls were bare, save for a velvet painting of the Sacred Heart of Jesus. The rendering of Jesus was vague enough so that he might be white or black, or any shade in between. That morning the mission was empty.

"We must endure many days of discouragement," Duvall said apologetically. "The boys tend to come in packs. A boy with a following may bring us a dozen souls. If he leaves, most follow. Today we are in a low swing of the cycle. Tomorrow, perhaps, there will be many."

Father Duvall was not a physically attractive man. He had a face like a barbecued frog. His eyes were pickled eggs, widely spaced. One shoulder was markedly higher than the other, suggestive of a bone disorder. His voice, however, was magnificent. A deep, mellifluous baritone, with a pleasant undertone of his native West Indies French. It was a voice and manner born for radio, or the pulpit, and I wondered by what celestial logic he had been assigned to this small, dismal storefront.

"So it is," he continued, "one day follows the next. The idea of this club, this mission, belongs to Father Sydney. He has left us for the time being, an unfortunate problem with his health. But I have embraced his dream wholeheartedly. I do my best to serve in his stead. If we can save one boy from the needle, if we can interest even one soul in the service of God, it will have been worth all the days of discouragement."

Having finished his set piece, Father Duvall relaxed.

"If we only had a pool table," he said. "With a pool table, there might be some hope of making this all work."

"Mrs. Jones mentioned a science club her son belonged to."

Sitting down opposite me, Father Duvall nodded. "Again, that was Father Sydney's idea. He had some university training in science, I think, and he took the interested ones on field trips to the local museums. Horatio Jones was one of the interested. A very brainy child. I say child, Mr. Hawkins, because the boy was still very much an innocent at thirteen. That is, to say the least, unusual here, where the boys tend to grow up very fast or not at all. Horatio had his passions. For books, for museums, for his fish and his birds. He focused all of his attention on such things, and willfully ignored the evil around him. There were those, I am afraid, who misinterpreted his air of innocence. Who thought it intentional. Who attempted to take advantage.''

It was disconcerting, knowing that such a large, superbly controlled voice emanated from such a slightly built body. Duvall fished in the pocket of his black shirt—he wore no collar—and withdrew a pack of cigarettes.

''I have two vices at present,'' he said, lighting up. ''This filthy habit, and the pleasure I take at hearing myself talk. Lately, I'm afraid, I've had to talk to myself. Our recruits, our potential soldiers, have deserted to another camp. Some, I very much fear, have given themselves up to the white devil. Do you know anything about heroin addiction, Mr. Hawkins?''

''Very little.''

Father Duvall inhaled, shuddering slightly as his narrow chest filled. ''I said I have two vices. Really it is three. The third is hatred. I indulge myself in the hatred of heroin. It is not the addiction, the ruination of the body, that I loathe. It is the insidious malignancy it brings to the soul. Under the influence of heroin the most vile part of the personality takes hold. The vileness grows, until it dominates. The vileness lies, the vileness steals. In the end the vileness dies, and with it the body. And—oh, this is the true evil of the white devil—the soul *loves* the addiction, the soul takes great pleasure in its season in hell.''

''Are you suggesting that Horatio Jones was tempted by heroin? By your white devil?''

Father Duvall was startled. His poached eyes bulged as a fit of coughing doubled him over. "Pardon me," he wheezed. "The stupid cigarettes." After catching his breath, and his composure, he continued. "No, if Horatio had been chipping, I'd have known it. He was frightened off by certain other events. Principally the evil presence of Spenser Eames. Speedy. I tried to warn Father Sydney. But Father Sydney shut his eyes to the truth, and the consequence was that Speedy Eames infected the mission."

Who, I asked, was Speedy Eames?

Father Duvall's black face darkened markedly. His diction became clipped and angry. "Who was Speedy Eames? I am convinced Speedy Eames was a demon in a small package. Exactly as heroin is a demon in a small package. To see the boy, well, it was hard to believe what harm he could do. Not much bigger than Horatio in size. But in experience—oh, I fear there was not much on this earth that Speedy had not experienced. Father Sydney was taken in by that innocent, impish face. The poor man simply refused to see the meanness in the boy."

When I asked what the boy called Speedy had done to frighten Horatio Jones away from the science club at the mission, Father Duvall was reluctant to engage in specifics.

"It was part of my job to know each of the boys, their likes and dislikes, their problems, their fears. Horatio was not one to so unburden himself. There seemed little need, at the time. He was by far the best student. Many of the boys, like Speedy, had little schooling. Truants. Reading disabilities. Very desperate home situations. We had great hopes for Horatio. Father Sydney and I had already lined up several scholarships. There was no doubt he'd have gotten into one of the better universities."

It was becoming obvious that Father Duvall had such a great love for the truth that he was unwilling to part with it. I asked again what Speedy had done to frighten Horatio from the mission.

White smoke curled out from the priest's wide black nostrils.

He studied me with his swollen eyes before saying, "I do not know, precisely. At first the two seemed inclined to be friends. This frightened me. Speedy had great powers of persuasion for one so young. He had great charm, when he chose to use it. Of course, in some ways he was a thousand years old. As old as temptation. A little black succubus with a giggle that would send a chill down your spine, Mr. Hawkins. Of course he brought drugs into the club. Angel dust. Crack. He sold such things on the street, running for older drug dealers, and he brought it inside here—at first, I think, to give to the other boys. They call it 'tasting.' It is one way for a dealer to develop a clientele."

"And Speedy was dealing?"

"Undoubtedly."

"Father, tell me, did you ever hear that Speedy had something going from a rooftop? That he sold his stuff from there? Or that he taunted a cop named Edwards, the same cop who shot Horatio Jones?"

Duvall put a hand to his brow, shielding his eyes, as if anxious to conceal the pain showing there.

"About the roof. Yes, I heard. I heard the little bastard—pardon me, I mean the little so-and-so—bragging about how he had a tin can tied to a string, and he'd let the string down to the street. His clients put the money in the can and Speedy pulled it up and took it out and dropped down the packets of heroin, or whatever he was selling. He called it 'going fishing.' "

"And about the cop? Speedy and Detective Edwards?"

He shook his head. "No, I didn't hear that. Certainly Speedy had problems with the police. And taunting them, that was definitely in character."

"So it is possible that Speedy had involved Horatio in his schemes? Dealing from the rooftops?"

Father Duvall's dry, leathery lips worked intently on the cigarette. "No, I do not think that," he said after some consideration. "Heroin was not the only evil personified in Spenser Eames."

I asked him what, exactly, he meant by that. He sighed and looked away. "There are some subjects I am simply unwilling to discuss. Crimes against nature, against God. Suffice it to say that Speedy was capable of infecting others with his habits, his habits of drugs . . . and otherwise." He snubbed the cigarette out, grinding it angrily. "My faith does not allow me to celebrate the death of any but Christ, Mr. Hawkins. Yet there is a part of faith that deals with seeking balance. It is as if the fates of those two young men became interwined and confused, although in the end it was the same."

"Fate? You mean Horatio getting shot?"

"Yes. Because that was the fate one would have expected for Spenser Eames. To be shot by a policeman. Instead, by some horrible accident of chance, it was the quiet, obedient Horatio who caught the bullet. And now Speedy has become a victim of the fate of the innocent. Run down on his bicycle and left to die."

"He's *dead?*"

Father Duvall looked surprised. "Yes, of course. It happened a couple of weeks ago. I thought you knew. A little more than a year after Horatio died. And only a block away."

A skinny black kid held the door for me as I wheeled out. He had a bruise over one eye and an expression that dared me to notice. Father Duvall's gentle baritone rumbled in the background, making him welcome. Outside, under a thin blanket of fluffy snow, Roxbury looked like something out of a fairy tale. It gave me hope that the little man inside the boarded-up storefront would be able to work an urban miracle or two.

13

IN MEGAN'S OPINION, GOING AFTER EYEball Edwards was a crazy, dangerous stunt. On reflection, I'm inclined to agree. All I can say is, at the time it seemed like a great idea.

I left the Roxbury Boy's Mission elated, convinced I'd put the pieces of the puzzle together. The confusion between two similarly built black boys of the same age, both of whom flew their dreams from the rooftops of the ghetto. The first a studious, well-behaved youth, the second a worldly apprentice-conman who distributed small packets of death, for a price. And now both of them gone, taken out of the picture by a careless, violent cop who considered himself immune to prosecution.

According to Father Duvall, Spenser Eames had been run down a few weeks ago. It was reasonable to assume that the I.A.D. boys were aware of the circumstances of the teenage pusher's death, and that they had chosen to ignore the coincidence—not untypical of cops assigned to investigate their own. Therefore it seemed pointless to present the police with the case I was building against Detective Edwards. They would either laugh me out of the building, or put me in an interrogation room to confront Eyeball himself on his own territory, a situation any wise person would seek to avoid.

That left one avenue open to a civilian like me.

"I'll be damned." Russ White looked up from his work station as I pushed into his office. "Hey, Jack, you look like you've seen a ghost."

"It's a little like that, now you mention it."

When the McGary Media Corporation bought the old *Boston Standard,* the first thing they did was move the editorial offices out of Causeway Street, adjacent to the since-demolished North Station, and cross the tracks to glitzy new digs across from Government Center. The sportswriters didn't like the new address because they were no longer able to fall out of their desks and into the press box at Boston Garden.

The second thing the new owners did, after sacking anyone on the editorial staff who dared to use the term "journalistic integrity" with a straight face, was turn up the volume. Loud banner headlines became larger and louder still. It was a rare edition that did not feature a blazing fire or a bloodied corpse on the front page. Devlin, the new publisher, a business school wunderkind who was so smooth he looked like he'd been pureed in a Cuisinart, made Russ White supervisor of the crime beat and gave him four reporters with deadened nerves and cast-iron stomachs, all of them more than willing to intrude on the private lives of victims and survivors.

It was not a classy organization, the new *Standard,* but it did not hesitate to stir up trouble, or name names.

"This juvenile dope dealer who supposedly sugared Eyeball's gas tank. Was his name Spenser Eames, street name Speedy?"

"First thing," Russ White said, "let's check the morgue."

He meant of course the newspaper's files of published stories, not the pathology laboratory. Father Duvall hadn't been specific about what day Speedy Eames had been run down, so Russ had to screen his files. When he found the item, he whistled.

"Get a load of the date," he said. "Three days before the Fitzgerald kids were abducted. Either there is a connection or it's one hell of a coincidence."

BODY FOUND

A Roxbury druggist, setting out his trash for early-morning pickup, made a gruesome discovery in the alley adjacent to his business. Police, alerted to the presence of a blood-spattered body, investigated.

"At this point we're assuming the victim was struck by a car," said Sergeant Alex Bullock of the Area D stationhouse. ''He was apparently riding a bicycle, which was found at the scene.''

Preliminary forensic reports indicate the victim, identified as Spenser David Eames, 15, of Roxbury, died of massive injuries to head and torso.

''Looks like a hit-and-run situation,'' Sergeant Bullock reported. ''We'll be turning it over to the Homicide Unit. That's standard procedure in a vehicle-induced death.''

I asked Russ if there had been any follow-up stories. He punched a command into his word processor and waited, watching as machine code blurred the screen. Nothing showed up.

''Let me scroll back,'' he said. ''Maybe it got filed under the wrong heading.''

He scanned every crime and accident item filed since the initial report. Nothing further on the sudden death of Speedy Eames.

''Nothing unusual,'' he said. ''You got a kid hit by a car. This is not big news, not in Roxbury. We get a kid hit by a car in Newton, we might expect a follow-up. Danger on suburban streets, school zones, that kind of thing.''

''It's comforting to know that the *Standard* strives for such balance.''

''What we strive for here,'' Russ said, deadpan, ''is to sell ever more copies.''

I patrolled his cubicle, trying to contain an excess of energy without actually crashing through the thin partition walls, while he glued his ear to the phone. Like most good reporters, and at least one private investigator I had known, Russ White had a genius for extracting information over the telephone. He also had a connection at the Homicide Unit.

''Well,'' he said, after a thirty-minute stint of being switched from one department to the next, ''the reason we didn't do a follow-up is there was nothing to follow up. The Area D boys turned it over to Homicide. Homicide looked at the report. Someone over there scrawled I.P. on it, Investigation Pending, and slipped it back in the file. Before you conclude this is part of a vast cop conspiracy, take it from Russell, your hotdogging bloodhound: This is standard procedure. This is the way a hit-and-run report gets treated, unless a witness comes forward. Without a witness they have nothing to work with, nowhere to start. Area D, doing their thing, detailed two uniformed officers to interview door to door in the area of the accident. Nobody heard nothing. Therefore the case is left open, pending an investigation that will remain pending unless one of the bosses gets hot over it for some reason, assigns it to one or more of his overworked detectives. What we've got here, Jack, is your typical bureaucratic logjam.''

I asked if he had anything else on Spenser ''Speedy'' Eames. Arrest reports, court dockets, anything.

White grinned, tipping back in his seat. ''You forget, the kid was a juvy. No names filed in juvenile court. Even with my special friend over there in Files, I can't get a look at that stuff.''

''Can we get through to Edwards, see if he'll make a statement?''

The chair squeaked like a rabid mouse as Russ plunked his feet back to the floor. ''Gee, now I'm really insulted. Obviously you didn't read my court update story yesterday. If you'd read it, you'd know that Edwards has been given a thirty-day leave, with pay, to prepare for testimony in the *Jones* suit. Which has again been granted temporary delay by Judge Skittles. That's why Eyeball doesn't give a shit about the trial. He gets a paid vacation out of it. You count the paid vacation they gave him when he shot Horatio Jones, he's making out pretty good. He gets the extra time off, there's that many more rent evictions he can serve.''

"He's moonlighting?"

"Sort of. Little known fact: Ernest D. Edwards, D/B/A Putnam Rental Associates, serves more eviction notices than any other single-owner property in Cambridge. That's right, folks, Eyeball owns rental property. A lot of it. A big apartment complex on Putnam Ave. Rents mostly to college students of the female gender, and he apparently gets off on serving eviction notices, the rent gets behind or he doesn't like the tenant. Numerous complaints about harassment from the landlord, namely Eyeball, which is how I came across the information.

"What happened is, I get a call two weeks ago, from this gal currently enrolled in grad school at Harvard. She has been to the Cambridge cops and she has been to Legal Aid and nobody wants to do anything about this creepy landlord of hers, who lives in the building and likes to ring her bell about four in the morning, try to catch her with her negligee on—or off, probably. She is not the only young lady in the building who gets this special attention and she figures the *Standard* ought to do something about it. The switchboard sends her through to me, seeing as how this is a major crime, negligee peeping. Well, I'm always polite with outraged citizens, you never know when you'll figure an angle for a good story. This one was going nowhere until she tells me the name of this ogre who's been bothering her. Ernest Edwards. He's always flashing this cop shield at her, trying to impress. She figures he bought it in a hawk shop.

"Well, when I hear the name a little light goes on over my head. Can this be the same Ernest Edwards we all know and love? I figure, maybe he's just prowling the halls over there, pretending to own the place, which would be in character. Just for giggles I go down to the deed office, look up the buildings on Putnam Ave. See, it turns out to be *three* buildings, not one, and there it is on the title, Ernest D. Edwards. I figure there may be more than one Ernest Edwards, so I get a snapshot of our favorite detective and I take it up to this young lady who phoned me, and bingo. She makes him.''

I asked if he still had the snapshot. Russ fished through his desk, then handed me a still that had been taken the year before, when Edwards was temporarily suspended following the Jones shoot.

''I can't be sure, since I only caught a glimpse of the guy. But it's possible that this is the man who followed me from the courthouse and then took off when I pulled out my can of Mace.''

''That sounds in character. Figured a guy in a wheelchair would be easy to intimidate. So what I did after the irate female confirms it's Detective Edwards who's been giving her a hard time, I check with the Cambridge cops. They assure me they have investigated said complaints and found no basis for legal action. What it all boils down to, no way are they going to proceed against a brother cop. End of story. Well, not quite end of story. I check with the Cambridge assessor. The building complex Eyeball owns is valued for tax purposes at a little over two million.''

I whistled. Russ nodded in agreement.

''Right,'' he said. ''So how does it happen that a vice detective, who makes about what a midlevel copy editor does here, how's he finance a major real estate investment like that? He doesn't do it moonlighting as a bouncer at the local bistro, or vending dogs at Fenway Park.''

''The son of a bitch. He's got a scam going.''

''I been thinking along similar lines. All I need, to make this story fly, is something to tie it together. Which this Speedy kid getting squashed under mysterious circumstances just might do.''

White shut down the screen, pushing himself away from the work station. He shrugged on a suit jacket, draped a plaid scarf around his neck, and grabbed a lined overcoat from a hook on the wall.

''So whaddaya say, Jack, shall we take a little trip across the river? The Plough is only a couple of blocks west of Putnam. If we don't find Eyeball looking up skirts, we can always stop in for a pint of Guinness.''

I lost Russ somewhere on Mass. Ave. His Escort had been there in my rearview as we crossed the Longfellow Bridge into Cambridge. The next time I looked he was gone. Mass Ave. is crazy in the late afternoon anyway, and the extra traffic created by the Christmas shopping frenzy made it that much worse, so it was not surprising we got separated.

Contrary to what Megan later assumed, it wasn't bullheadedness or dumb courage that made me get out of the van and start looking for Eyeball on my own. When I pulled up to the triad of apartment buildings on Putnam Ave., I truly believed Russ White would be along any minute.

The rental office was in the center building. Neat brick masonry blending into a densely populated residential neighborhood. Bare ivy vines clung to the brick, which is probably a zoning requirement in Cambridge. The walk had been salted, so traction over the wet concrete was no problem.

I hadn't the slightest idea what I was going to say to Ernie Edwards if I found him. I figured on doing some reconnoitering, leaving the hard part to Russ, who could at least run like hell if Eyeball took umbrage at his questions.

The entrance to the building had only one low step. A piece of cake to negotiate. The door was a little more difficult, having a hydraulic closer that kept pinning it against my chair. In the foyer I took a minute to rub the circulation back into my hands while checking out the door buzzer situation.

I rang the super's button and got no response. Finally I tried the old trick of ringing every apartment in the building. I kept that up until one of the college girls, who should have known better, buzzed me in.

Inside the lobby it was warm and quiet. The door to the rental office was locked. A quick perusal of the apartment directory, set on the wall behind a glass panel, revealed that each of the three buildings housed sixteen units. A little arithmetic showed that Eyeball was getting a good deal, if the property was assessed at a mere two million. But then, he was the kind of guy who would know how to fix things with the tax assessor.

Good old Eyeball. Smart enough to invest his money, and too dumb to keep his name off the deed. I wondered how he would explain acquiring such a lucrative piece of real estate. Saved his pennies? Won it at the track?

Forty-eight units of tasty Cambridge real estate. Had to be worth four million, easy, with the current boom and the housing shortage. Way, way beyond the means of a vice cop. Unless he had something very large going on the side.

There were a number of possibilities. A vice cop who knows the streets and the sources, and who had sufficient nerve and a lack of conscience, could, for instance, wholesale heroin. Or cocaine. Or angel dust. Big money in drugs.

Yup, I reckoned, drugs would fit right in there. Explain why a vice cop, whose beat was downtown, spent a lot of his time busting heads in Roxbury. Staking out his turf. It might even explain why he allowed himself to get into a beef with a fourteen-year-old pusher. A pusher whom he had almost burned a year before, who had lain low and stayed alive these last twelve months until he had somehow attracted Eyeball's attention just before the trial came to jury.

Horatio Jones had been an accident, more or less, a case of mistaken identity. But Speedy Eames was murder. No way to brazen it out if the hit-and-run was tied to him. End of career as freewheeling, lone-wolf cop. Turn in shield and go to jail. Goodbye, Eyeball, and have fun in Walpole. Just be careful in the showers, in case you run into any old street punks who bear a grudge.

Edwards had been running his mouth about wanting to take out Speedy. If he'd finally done it, run the boy down, it might explain why he was suddenly panicked about the civil suit. Oh, yes, there was ample motive for not wanting a cunning, cop-baiting lawyer to put you in the witness stand. Where he might, skilled cross examiner that he was, delve a little too deeply into the real circumstances behind the death of Horatio Jones. Reason enough to come up with a last-minute scheme to scare him out of the trial, off the case. Take your chances with a young, inexperienced attorney, one unlikely to intimidate you in the box, or reveal whatever nasty business has made your rich.

My wet wheels squeaked on the linoleum as I cruised the lobby, trying to think of an angle, a way to pry the truth out of Detective Ernest D. Edwards. What was keeping Russ White? Had I misunderstood him? Had he stopped at the Plough on the way over? Was he waiting for his Guinness to clear, assuming I would meet him there? I was about to go out and check the street when a young women exited the elevator.

She wore an ankle-length down coat, earth color. Tufts of fine blond hair protruded from under a knit cap. She had a stack of textbooks in a clear plastic satchel. Striding by she gave me a sidelong glance. Who the hell was this guy in the wheelchair hanging around her lobby?

A minute later she came back inside, minus the books.

"Excuse me, are you the person ringing all the buzzers?"

I admitted as much.

"You looking for someone? Or are you just getting in out of the cold?"

"I'm here," I said, "to see the landlord."

That was the wrong thing to say. The young woman's attitude changed abruptly. Her eyes sparked. She put a suede-gloved hand on her cocked hip and said, "You're another of his creepy friends, the jerk who owns this place? Well, if you think you're going to hang around the lobby and make obscene suggestions to the women in this building, why I'll . . . I'll call the cops right now."

She looked like she was about ready to swing. I backed up my chair.

"Take it easy, lady. I don't know Edwards from a hole in the ground. I just need to ask him a couple of questions. Believe me, Eyeball is no friend of mine."

She looked doubtful. "Is that what they call him? Well, I guess it fits. I don't know why any civilized person would want to converse with that creep. But you want him, try the basement. He's got a rock he lives under down there."

Figuring that the next woman into the lobby might strike first and ask questions never, I let the elevator deposit me in the basement. I wheeled out cautiously, wondering what the hell I would say to Eyeball Edwards if he suddenly loomed out of the shadows.

"Pardon me, Detective Edwards, is it true you murdered two teenage boys, and while we're asking, where did you get the money to go into Cambridge real estate?"

"You caught me fair and square, Mr. Hawkins, sir. You want me to go downtown and make a full confession?"

Fat chance. Where the hell was Russ White? This was *his* idea, seeking out Edwards on his own turf.

The rough breathing I heard turned out to be the furnace. The squat shape of it filled one dark corner, an iron-jacketed beast with stunted copper arms extending upwards. In contrast to the arid lobby above, this place was warm and damp, almost tropical. I followed a green shag carpet that formed a runner between wire cages that had been divided off as storage space for the tenants.

Novelists have no business in dark basements. They suffer from an excess of imagination. Breathing furnaces, tropical snakes slithering in the carpet, cardboard beasts in wire cages. Pale catlike eyes glowing.

"Jesus," I croaked, sucking in my breath as a real cat, not an

imagined one, sprang into a pool of light, hissed, and was gone.

When I got there, the door to the super's apartment was wide open. From inside came the smooth sound of an FM announcer. A Mozart string concerto followed, at low volume.

Somehow it was tough imagining Eyeball Edwards tuning in to Mozart. Maybe the gal in the lobby had been wrong. Thus encouraged, I rolled right up to the open door, rapped on the jamb, and called out, "Hey, anybody home?"

No one but us sprightly violins.

"Detective Edwards?"

With the door open, I figured it couldn't be trespassing.

My first impression was that *Playboy* had finally figured out how to put a staple-free, pop-up bachelor pad in the magazine. Open the page and, voilà, an interior that you could only fully appreciate while wearing a velvet smoking jacket and silk pajamas with little rabbits on them. The layout was squeezed too close together and the styles didn't quite match, but the elements were all in place. The home entertainment center with the big video console. The Altec Lansing stereo speakers, out of which Mozart modulated. An upholstered bar with all the right brands in neat little bottle racks. A silver-plated cocktail shaker in the form of a penguin—very cool indeed. On the walls, still in their original shrink packs, air-brushed renditions of various body parts, much larger than life, and representing both genders. Meat-market art.

There were more pictures of similar body parts strewn over a smoked-glass table. David Hamilton's *Private Collection* of female nymphets. A stack of hardcore photo magazines, some with titles like *Teenage Leather Boys* and *Hot Buns* and an especially lurid number called *Chickenhawk,* which, I discovered at a single glance, was not about our feathered friends. No siree. If this was indeed Eyeball's little love nest, then he had kinks that were not the subject of discussion in detective locker rooms.

The kitchen area was outfitted with all the latest gizmos—

choppers and dicers and squeezers and a high-tech espresso machine that looked ready for a space launch. That put a smile on my face, the image of a tough cop like Edwards with a demitasse between his fingers.

Beyond the kitchen was the bedroom. Beaded Art Deco curtains glittered over the doorway, catching the light from within. I waited there in the kitchen, listening. My heartbeat. Mozart.

Wheeling up, I maneuvered my chair sideways to the curtains and tried to peek through the membrane of beads. The glitter came from a revolving mirrored lamp. Under it, out of focus through the glass beads, was the shape of a bed.

As I pushed the chair through the curtain the strings of beads slithered over me, cool and slippery, like tendrils. The revolving lamp made sparkles of light waltz through the bedroom, over the walls and the rumpled bedding.

Eyeball Edwards, vice cop and bon vivant, was sitting up in bed. He was naked, but in a paroxysm of modesty he'd covered his private parts with both hands. On the bed was a shoulder holster, empty. On the pillow beside him was a pistol. Any mystery writer worth his salt could identify it as a .38 Colt Detective Special. Eyeball was staring at me with his left eye. The revolving lights made it look like he was winking. Very devil-may-care. *You caught me with my pants down.* A glop of blood had coagulated where his right eye had been.

You caught me with my brains blown out, see if I care.

Behind me Russ White said, "Darn it all, Hawkins, how could you shoot a guy who owns a first edition of *Teenage Leather Boys*?"

14

SULLY HAD LARRY SHEEHAN INTERROgate me. That was my punishment for playing detective, interfering in their investigation.

"Last guy I know working the private sector got himself shot," Sully said, huffing at his horn-rim glasses, polishing the lenses with a linen handkerchief. "Guy by the name of Lew Quinn. Ever heard of him? We got his remains in a drawer around here somewhere. You wanna check, see if he looks familiar?"

"Sully, I went in there to talk to Edwards, that's all."

"Yeah," he said, slipping the glasses on and squinting at me. "Well, tell it to Detective Sheehan. He's a good listener, if he ever takes the finger out of his nose."

Sheehan, unperturbed, examined the finger that had been probing his left nostril. With deliberate nonchalance he wiped it on his trouser leg. Sully made a face and headed for the door.

"That'll get him out of the room every time," Sheehan said with satisfaction. "The Lieutenant is probably the smartest cop I know, but he's got a real delicate stomach. He don't mind stiffs, but gee, pick your nose and he turns green."

Sully was headed to an adjacent conference cubicle, where he would be questioning Russ White. Not that we had anything to hide. It was just that Sullivan had this idea that citizens, especially journalists, can't be trusted to leave things undisturbed at a crime scene. It was true we'd gone through Eyeball's belongings, being careful not to smear fingerprints. Also that Russ had made an inventory of Eyeball's extensive collection of porno cassettes. Also that while we were waiting for the Cambridge cops to respond he'd gone back to his car for a camera and snapped a couple of rolls of film, most of it starring the late Detective Edwards.

We certainly wouldn't have been so nosy if Edwards had objected. As it was he put up a slight stink, but didn't have a word to say.

Gallows humor. You catch it from cops and undertakers.

"So tell me again," Sheehan said. "You and this reporter, White, you were going over to interview the deceased, is that right? But White got stuck in traffic and you went in alone?"

"He ran out of gas. On Mass. Ave. at rush hour."

"So you go down there, the basement apartment, and you bust in the door."

"The door was open, Larry. Wide open, like your fly."

He looked down, then smiled his crocodile smile. "You got me, Hawkins. I had no idea you was such a funny guy. You heard the one about the Eskimo?"

"Yeah, I heard it."

"Your buddy White put it in there, the *Standard*. He even spelled my name right. For a reporter he's not a bad guy. Couple of times he even bought me drinks. I'm trying to remember, I don't think you ever bought me a drink, Hawkins."

"Call room service. Whatever you want, put it on my bill."

"Hey, I could use a beer and a chaser. The Lieutenant would have a bird, huh? Only thing worse than picking your nose, taking a drink."

"Aren't you going to turn the tape recorder on?"

Sheehan tapped the end of a cigarette on the back of his hand, frowning at the tape machine. "This is a waste of time. You think I don't know that? You don't know shit. And if you did you wouldn't tell me, because you think I'm a dumb fuck. You think because I grew up in Chelsea and talk like I got rocks in my mouth, I'm not on the same level as you."

It was reassuring to know that Sheehan and I had returned to our former adversarial relationship. That I could handle. It was when he tried to get cozy that he threw me. But he was wrong about me thinking he was dumb. I didn't think Larry Sheehan was dumb at all. It was Shannon, his fictional equivalent in the

Casey books, who was as dumb as a boot. In the books Shannon also grew up in Chelsea and talked like he had rocks in his mouth, but that didn't mean he was supposed to be an exact replica of Sheehan.

"So what you're saying," Sheehan said, "this was entirely coincidental, you and the reporter going over there to make a social call on Detective Edwards. This idea the Lieutenant has, that maybe someone called you up, told you Edwards had been croaked, and rather than call us you went over there yourself to poke around, this theory is without merit?"

"Larry, it's a good theory, as theories go. It just happens not to be true. We went over there to talk to the guy. We had no idea he'd been murdered."

"You went over there to talk, huh? Football, I guess. You want to know does he think the Pats got a chance in the play-offs."

"More along the line, did he happen to run over a black kid a while back. And who did he steal money from, to own a forty-eight-apartment complex in Cambridge. Questions like that."

Sheehan shook his head, favoring me with one of his hard-guy looks. "You serious? You were going to ask him that? Then you're lucky he was already dead, pal. I know Eyeball, he'd have tipped you out of that chair, then eaten it, spoke by spoke. That was one of his tricks, eating things normal humans don't usually eat. Like glasses at a bar."

"He was a chomper?"

"Yeah. What he liked to do, he'd grab a glass, take a bite out of it, grind it up with his back teeth. This made him very popular in certain bars, they got nothing better to do than watch some-body eat the crockery."

"Sounds like the life of the party. So, Larry, can you tell me why everyone is so excited about this, they immediately assume it was murder? It was his own gun right there on the pillow beside him. Maybe Eyeball got depressed and shot himself."

Sheehan snorted, waving his hand at his cigarette smoke. ''All I can say is, you didn't know him. Ernie liked to shoot *other* people. He just wasn't the type to swallow his piece. Forensic will test his hands for cordite traces, but I'm betting it wasn't self-inflicted. What happened, someone caught up with him.''

''Or maybe they just didn't like the look in his eye.''

''You're too much, you know that? Hey, you listening? Pay attention.''

I was busy. A small, mean idea had just elbowed itself into my mind. What if Eyeball's kink for underage sex had gone beyond a fondness for mere pornography? What if his interest in Speedy Eames, whom Father Duvall had described as a little black succubus, was physical? Mind-boggling. Was it possible that a glass-chomping macho man like Ernest Edwards was something more than just another bent cop?

Did Eyeball have an eye for the boys?

That would explain a lot of things. A tough-talking cop like Edwards would have done anything to prevent testimony identifying him as a defiler of teenage boys. Ample motive for kidnapping the twins, for eliminating Lew Quinn, and for running down Speedy Eames.

In his fear of being exposed, had Detective Ernest Edwards become a one-man crime wave? There was just one thing the theory didn't explain.

Who had silenced Eyeball, and why?

II

THE LEPER COLONY

1 THE BIG WIND BLEW IN FROM DISNEY WORLD, smelling of cocoa butter and Irish whiskey. He wore baggy chinos and a short-sleeve shirt. There were purple flowers on the shirt, big ones. The chinos were tucked into Bean boots, his only concession to the weather. It was snowing, and had been for an hour. Below my deck the Charles was barely visible, a gray smear blurred by white static.

"I brought you a souvenir," Fitzy said.

"I'd love a shot," I said, eyeing the bottle of Jameson he'd put on the table.

"Yeah, sure. Help yourself. I think my little buddy here could use a drink, too."

Fitzy had cupped his hands over the table. Now he opened them and out walked Donald Duck. He tottered from side to side, dragging his webbed feet. His beak opened and closed. He made quacking noises.

"Isn't that great?" Fitzy said. "I just put a new battery in the little guy, he'll be good for hours."

Finian X. Fitzgerald is not by nature a nervous person. He was nervous now and it didn't suit him. The nervous stuff was catching. I reached for the bottle.

"You got a hell of a tan there, Fitz."

"Yeah? Thanks."

"That red blister on your nose, it looks good."

"Call me Rudolph."

He tapped Donald Duck on the head. Donald stopped quacking.

"You don't look surprised, Jack. I thought you'd be surprised, I show up at your door with booze and a fowl joke. That's f-o-w-l."

"I got it, Fitz. Also I got a call from Ida Mae Jones. She was very excited, her white knight was coming back, gonna kick him some butts in court."

"You talked to her, huh?"

"Briefly. She's under the mistaken impression that I somehow prevailed upon you. Which I was unable to do, as you had some kind of ear infection, couldn't come to the phone."

Fitzy got a water glass from the cabinet and sat down. He put his feet up on the table. Donald Duck tipped over and started kicking his plastic feet. Fitzy switched him off, then filled the glass with the Jameson. He'd already made a dent in the bottle.

"Jack, old buddy, I am very, very sorry about that. A certain party had me scared shitless. Now that the certain party is no longer with us, I feel much better."

"Eyeball?"

Fitzy put a finger to his lips. "Sssh. Let us not even mention the bastard's name. Let us just be thankful someone had the guts to put out his lights."

As the whiskey seeped into his blood, Fitzy began to unwind. He told me about the telephone calls that had resumed those last few days in Florida. The muffled voice that he could not quite identify.

"What he liked, he liked to get Lois. He liked to tell her exactly what would happen to the kids next time. Very graphic descriptions. Very specific about what kind of abuse he would personally administer. Jack, this was a sick mind. He *knew* I wasn't going to make a move. He just liked making the calls. Always concentrating on what he would do to the kids the next time."

"And you're sure it was Eyeball?"

"It was either him or someone he put up to it. Some sicko he hired. Or maybe the guy did it for free, just to get his rocks off."

"Fitzy, how the hell did he get your number in Florida?"

He ran both hands through his wiry red hair, his eyes popping wide, that old Fitzy look I knew so well. "That was the real scary part, Jack. He got to Milton. Now Milty is just in this for a little positive exposure, help his political aspirations. He wasn't ready for any rough stuff. What happened, he got jumped coming out of this office. Big guy wearing a ski mask sticks a gun to the side of his head. I assume Milton wet his pants immediately, if not worse. I know *I* did when they had me crouch in the backseat of my car. I figured this was it, goodbye Finian. So whoever it is, he wants only one thing from Milton. The telephone number. Naturally Milton gives it to him."

"Naturally."

"Try it sometime, Jack. Someone puts a gun to your head, you tend to babble. You are very eager to do exactly what the guy with the gun wants you to do. You'll say *anything*. Giving up a telephone number, that's a pleasure, it's so easy."

Fitzy was right. That didn't make me think better of Milton Pridham. I remembered how he'd looked sitting behind that big desk in the office leased with his father's money, the smug expression on his face.

"Understand, I didn't know about the other kid getting killed. Spenser Eames. That's I guess what set Edwards off, trying to mess up the trial. But when I first started taking sworn depositions from Eyeball, after I filed the formal complaint and got the lawsuit rolling, he could have cared less. I was suing the city, not him personally. The I.A.D. had cleared him in the shoot, that's all that matters to him. He's still on the cops, doing whatever he does to get his kicks. I am a mild irritant. He doesn't care about me or the lawsuit. When those two creeps jumped out of the van and took the kids, I had no idea who was behind it. I was blank. Then we start getting the phone calls, I'm supposed to stay out of the case, naturally I start thinking about Eyeball. He's a dangerous man. He's about half-crazed, which any normal person would pick up on about thirty seconds after meeting him.

From a legal viewpoint, it still wouldn't have made any real sense even if I *had* known about Spenser Eames suddenly getting wiped across the pavement, if I had been smart enough to make the connection to Horatio and Eyeball."

"Which you would have."

"Yeah, maybe. Or maybe not. Why would Eyeball risk killing Speedy? 'Cause the little criminal had something on him, some vice-related thing? Makes sense, but you need more than supposition to bring it up in court. Also it's not pertinent to the complaint I filed, which is against the city for being so lax in their hiring practices they let a known screw-up stay on the force until he finally kills a innocent kid, namely Horatio Jones. I try to introduce new charges against Eyeball, Judge Skittles is liable to fire one of his torpedos, sink the whole case."

"But Eyeball didn't know that."

"I guess not."

"He sees his chance to erase Speedy, then he gets spooked at what might come out of a trial, so he goes after you."

Fitzy stood the little plastic duck up on its feet. His face was flushed. Beads of sweat had formed along his hairline. I'd had enough of the Jameson that it looked like Fitzy was slowly melting.

"Yeah, he went after me. He went after the kids. He went after Lois. He went after Childe Milton. Then I guess what he did, he went after someone else. Oops, picked on the wrong guy and bang bang, the Eyeball is history."

I poured a tot more in my glass. The printed flowers on Fitzy's shirt looked ready to spring free of the fabric.

"So Fitz," I said. "Any ideas? I mean on who this wrong guy might be, was able to shoot Eyeball with his own gun?"

Fitzy pushed the duck's head. It started walking across the table, quacking.

"I dunno," he said. "Why don't we ask our little buddy?"

The toy butted up against my glass, feet ticktocking, beak open.

"Who'd have believed it," Fitzy said. "Good old Donald a dipsomaniac."

I woke up when someone threw cold water on me. I was not pleased. It took a moment for my head to clear enough to remember going into the bathroom, drunk enough to have the whirlies. I had undressed and slid onto the seat in the shower stall, figuring on a nice warm shower to sober me up.

The nice warm shower put me to sleep. Megan had come home, found me doing my unconscious prune imitation, and turned on the cold.

"I just wanted to get your attention," she said, throwing a big towel over my shoulders. "Sorry."

"Fitzy came home. We were celebrating."

"I saw the empty bottle. Also I noticed this whale passed out on the couch. The whale is wearing a shirt so loud he could be arrested for disturbing the peace."

"Christ, that was dumb. I could have drowned in there."

"I think the big danger was erosion. Your fingers look like something Vincent Price feeds to his pet piranha."

After helping me dress, Megan put a blanket over Fitzy.

"Much better," she said. "He was clashing with the drapes."

I stayed in the kitchen, drinking coffee diluted with milk. My stomach wasn't happy where it was, it wanted to go elsewhere. Meg fixed herself supper and tried not to look amused.

"Miss wine spritzer. Miss Perrier-on-the rocks."

"If you'd waited till I got home, maybe I'd have gotten drunk with you."

"Promises, promises. You call Lois?"

"Yes. She says make sure he doesn't drive home. Wanted to know how the two of you were getting along. I told her I didn't see any blood."

''We're fine.''

''You want some yogurt? Might help your stomach.''

''Only thing yogurt ever helped was bacteria.''

Fitzy was out cold, snoring fitfully. We went to bed early and watched the tube. Meg got up a couple of times to check on him and reported no discernible signs of life.

''Maybe we should get him upholstered,'' she said.

''He's been through hell. Trite but true.''

''You don't look so good yourself.''

''I appreciate your candor. Now shut up. And do not tickle me, Miss Drew. I do not respond to such stimulation.''

''That looks like a response to me. You want the light on or off?''

''Up to you.''

''I think,'' she said, ''off.''

Two significant things happened the next day, three if you count the Patriots beating the Rams. The first was that after fourteen hours, the great trial lawyer rose from the dead.

His first words were as prophetic as we have come to expect from great trial lawyers.

''What's for breakfast?'' he said. ''I could eat a horse.''

''Fresh out of horses. We have already had breakfast and are thinking about lunch. As in going out for lunch.''

''What day is it?''

''This is Sunday, Fitz. There are sixteen shopping days until Christmas. You want to start out with breakfast, even though it is well past the hour when decent people eat breakfast, there is sausage in the larder. Also eggs, toast, juice. Some parboiled 'taters could be converted to home-fries.''

''Hurry,'' he said. ''This is an emergency.''

I rustled up the grub while he showered.

''He's singing in the shower,'' Meg reported. ''That's a good sign.''

Freshly scrubbed and bubbling with more energy than seemed possible for a man who had challenged John Jameson and lost, Fitzy ate ravenously.

"Sunday," he said. "What a great invention. What I'm going to do, I'm going to leave you two lovebirds alone, go home to my wife and kids. I will go into my den, turn on the TV. I will watch football and drink imported beer. I will go to bed at a reasonable hour. Then tomorrow I'll go into court and kick me some butts."

Meg said, "Welcome home, Fitzy."

He grinned around a piece of toast.

The second thing that happened was in the *Sunday Standard*. I didn't get around to reading it until we came back from a late afternoon lunch at Legal Seafood. The excuse was that a dose of the grilled swordfish would help replace the brain cells I'd destroyed the night before. Megan, who sometimes likes to pretend she is living in an age before the invention of central heating, built a fire and was contentedly feeding it split birch logs that had cost about a buck a piece. I perused the comics and eventually read Russ White's feature on the late and unlamented Ernest D. Edwards.

"I'll be damned."

"It's not too late for church," Megan said, "if you want to catch the evening service."

"The Bay Village boys. The Steam Bath Scandals."

"You're talking in headlines again, Jack."

Bay Village is a predominantly gay neighborhood. This fact is not appreciated by many of the straight residents who still live there and and who object to the quantity of male prostitutes cruising the area. Complaints to the Vice Unit and the Liquor Commission and the Metropolitan Health Authority are common. The general sentiment is, bust the cruisers, shut down the bars, close the steam baths. Naturally the main enforcement agency is Vice. Liquor inspectors refrain from entering the leather-boy bars unless accompanied by Vice cops. Health inspectors find the steamy atmosphere of the bathhouses unhealthy. They too require police escorts.

The special vice squad assigned to such tasks is the Male Prostitute Undercover Detail, or the M.P.U.D., also known as MUD or, to fellow cops, as the dick patrol. Since no one in the Vice Unit wanted to be permanently associated with the dick patrol, assignments were on a revolving basis.

What Russ White had turned up, by careful examination of departmental records, was that Detective Ernest Edwards had been assigned to the dick patrol when the squad made its biggest, most controversial bust, which had led to the Steam Bath Scandals.

"Sounds familiar," Meg said, reading over my shoulder. "Was that the one where that guy Karkis got arrested?"

It was indeed. The operation had centered on Lester Karkis, a Bay Village businessman who owned several clubs and one of the more popular bathhouses. Karkis had for a time published a broadside called *Gay Village Banner*. As a club owner and gay rights activist he was well known in the community. What was not well known before the bathhouse bust was that he was also a hardcore kiddy-porn distributor with mob connections. Another of his less publicized business ventures involved the private parties he organized in his steamy club. Members only.

"He's the one had the teenage boys. The runaways."

Some of the boys had been no more than twelve years of age when Karkis took them from the streets. In the spirit of brotherhood Karkis had found a loft for the boys to stay in. He provided them with food, clothing, and drugs. Pot, angel dust, poppers. In return the boys posed for photographs and did special favors for preferred customers in Karkis's bathhouse.

In San Francisco that is called having a party. In Boston it is called conspiracy to contribute to the delinquency of minors, statutory rape, pedophilia, prostitution, and crossing state lines with pornographic material, all felonies that Karkis was eventually charged with.

The dick patrol, in their enthusiasm, had alerted the media before staging the bust. A number of prominent Bostonians got their picture in the paper and on the tube. Some of them had their shirts pulled over their faces. Some of them were not wearing shirts. Some of them were wrapped only in rather thin bath towels. None of them were happy.

In Boston, where books get banned even to this day, sodomizing children is not socially acceptable. Not if it gets in the papers. Especially not if it gets on TV. Lester Karkis was indicted. He was scheduled to go on trial.

Then in the privacy of his own home, Lester Karkis pled guilty. He shot himself.

"He's the one who left the note," Meg said. "The one with the bad spelling."

Leave it to an editor to remember that. Before swallowing a pistol Lester Karkis had typed a short note: I PLEAD GUILTY. SORRY FOR ALL THE MIZERY I HAVE CAUSED.

There were those who claimed that Lester Karkis, college graduate and publisher of the *Gay Village Banner,* would not have spelled misery with a "z," no matter how miserable he was. It was suggested that perhaps Lester Karkis had help with his note. That possibly someone who spelled misery with a "z" had helped Lester put the pistol in his mouth and pull the trigger.

"They said it was mob-related," Meg said. "He was in Dutch with the Mafia."

"You're mixing your ethnic stereotypes, Megan. Or is it metaphors? But, yes, that was the theory. A mob killing. Not your typical mob killing, since the mob doesn't usually bother to leave suicide notes. In any case, Homicide didn't buy the bad-spelling theory. They filed it as a self-inflected gunshot wound."

Megan leaned on my back, reaching over my shoulder to turn

the tabloid page. ''Funny thing isn't it?'' she said. ''Every time you learn something new about Eyeball Edwards, there seems to be somebody in it who got shot.''

''Yeah,'' I said. ''Funny thing.''

2 FITZY WAS SCHEDULED TO START JURY SELECTION in the afternoon, a show I didn't want to miss. In the morning I got the van out, took it to a car wash to have the salt rinsed off, and headed over to Roxbury to tilt lances with Father Napoleon Duvall.

The cold snap had passed through, pulling after it a front of unseasonably warm air. There was not a trace of snow left. Sunlight poured over the city. Winter-fat robins celebrated along Comm. Ave., strutting their stuff on bare branches. Jogging fools loped by in T-shirts and shorts. No doubt there is a graduate student somewhere working on the thesis that the phenomenon of late-twentieth-century self-torture in the hope of attaining long life is directly related to similar perversions practiced by the flagellants of fourteenth-century Spain, who cut and flayed themselves in a quest for eternal salvation. The angry god of Nike, versus the Martyr of Toledo. Good for a doctorate any day.

I slipped into a chink in the traffic on Mass. Ave. and rode the dragon to Washington Street. Around me the neighborhoods began to decay like time-lapse photography, transporting me into a bleak future.

The Roxbury Boys' Mission had supplicants this day. From inside came the noise of a hotly contested ping-pong match. With the exception of a few common expletives, the language they used was foreign to me. I wondered if Berlitz offered a crash course for honky muffocks like me. How did Father Duvall, a man of precise and thoughtful eloquence, communicate with these angry young men? Did his blackness allow him to transcend the cultural barrier of having been raised in the French West Indies?

The barrage of competitive voices ceased as I pushed into the mission. Two boys with paddles froze over the table. The tight cluster of spectators turned as one, focusing a neutral blankness at me. Caravaggio could have painted the intensity of that scene:

the dark young faces, the faded green of the table, the upraised paddles, and, lying by the net like a white punctuation mark, the tiny ping-pong ball.

Duvall saw me and glided over the warped floorboards of the storefront. He murmured a few words as he passed through his flock. Slowly the tableau unfroze. Someone picked up the ball and let it bounce. The bantering voices resumed at reduced volume.

The priest's manner was reserved, even more cautious than on our first encounter.

"Shall we adjourn to my office?" He indicated the entrance to a back room, what had once been a storage area. As he made the gesture I noted his hands for the first time. Long, slender digits, finely formed. The hands of an artist or a musician.

"I saw your picture in the paper the other day," Duvall said, planting himself on a folding wooden chair. "I hadn't realized you were so actively involved. You're working for Horatio's mother?"

He tapped a cigarette from one of several packs scattered around the storeroom. The moist frog eyes regarded me intently. The Grand Inquisitor began, I suspected, with just such deflective questioning.

"I'm a private citizen, Father. Helping out another private citizen. Looking for truth."

Behind the gray shroud of smoke a white smile glinted briefly.

"Ah, yes, I see. You search for truth, justice, and the American way."

"You could put it like that. But as you can see I am presently unable to leap tall buildings with a single bound."

Father Duvall laughed. The rich baritone warmed the small room. Behind him, rusted metal shelving sagged under the weight of cardboard file boxes. Even in this small outpost there was paperwork to be done, forms to fill out. For no particular reason I thought of Gogol's dead souls, the list of dead serfs used as collateral for a loan.

''You described yourself as a writer, Mr. Hawkins. I didn't think to inquire what sort of writer. But of mysteries. Ah! We have great regard for mysteries in our church. It is an article of our faith that mysteries, our sacred mysteries, I mean, need not be solved. Indeed, can never be. But that does not prevent my superior, Monsignor McCue, from being a great fan of that genre. Of novels, I mean. He would be delighted to know that we have received such a distinguished author here in our humble mission.''

''Father, there was another priest here when Horatio Jones was a member. A Father Sydney.''

''Yes. This mission was his project originally. I should say his dream.''

''And it was Father Sydney who took Horatio around to the museums?''

''Yes.'' Duvall eyed me warily. ''Along with a number of other boys.''

''Where might I find Father Sydney?''

The long dark artist's fingers cupped his chin as he held the cigarette away with his other hand.

''Father Sydney has been ill. Too ill to receive visitors.''

''Is he in a hospital here in the city?''

''Father Sydney is not available for interviews, Mr. Hawkins. He is being healed. More than that it is not my place to say.''

''He's on a retreat of some sort?''

Father Duvall blinked slowly. A black frog on an asphalt lily pad.

''When I saw you come in this morning, I thought perhaps an attack of conscience had brought you back. That you had found a sympathy for this mission.''

''I did bring my checkbook, if that's what you mean.'' I pulled an envelope from my jacket pocket. ''I'd appreciate a receipt, for Uncle Sam.''

Duvall put his cigarette on the edge of a foil ashtray and withdrew the check from the envelope. ''This is most generous,'' he said.

''You shop around, you can pick up a good used pool table for that.''

He nodded, slipping the check back into the envelope. ''Most generous. You were hoping to find Father Sydney. The check was to be in payment for that information?''

''I just gave you the check, Father. You don't look like a man who would take a bribe. Not even in a good cause.''

''It wouldn't be a good cause,'' he said, ''if it required taking bribes. I thank you. A pool table will be an attraction.''

From the storefront came screaming laughter, the sound of palms slapping.

''So you think I should try Monsignor McCue?''

''I didn't say that,'' Duvall said. He looked amused.

''No,'' I said. ''You didn't.''

Courthouses are designed with certain criteria in mind. A proper courthouse intimidates the accused, awes the jury, and puffs up the importance of the judges and their attendant squires, the attorneys. The ceilings are very high, the seats are very low. In courtroom no. 4 of the Boston federal district court there are windows on one side. The windows are far up enough so only the sky is visible. As if God is looking in, seeing that there are no thumbs on the scales of justice.

Not that thumbs ever cheat the scales. Money does that, and power.

The jury selection process had already begun when I got there. The clerk of court, a dapper little man with a crimson bow tie and black suspenders showing outside his vest, drew names from a cask. The cask looked as though it might once have held a gallon of Kentucky bourbon. The clerk, with his strawberry nose, looked as if he had imbibed hundreds of such gallons over the course of a lifetime.

"Mr. Metcalf," he bellowed. "Number thirty-four."

The prospective juror made his way into the box. He smiled shyly, as if he had just won a school prize.

Fitzy, seated at the plaintiff's table, raised an eyebrow when he saw me. Beside him Milton Pridham, looking young but very lawyerlike, was taking notes. Both of them were wearing bow ties. I'd never seen Fitzy wear a bow tie. For some reason it made him look like a large Irish version of a Cheshire cat. Then I noticed that Judge Skittles, who couldn't have been more than two hundred years old, also wore a bow tie. The clerk of courts, Milton, Fitzy, and the judge—more bow ties than had ever been gathered in one place outside of the Somerset Club. To which Otis Skittles, as I recalled, belonged.

Very Brahmin was courtroom no. 4, or trying to look that way.

Fitzy winked and stroked the wings of his tie.

"Mrs. Escovitz," the clerk said, holding a slip of paper aloft. "Number sixteen."

Mrs. Escovitz required help into the box, on account of her high heels. She had a lot of black hair and all of it was piled on top and lacquered in place. She wore bifocals with rhinestone frames and carried a bag of knitting. I liked Mrs. Escovitz.

Mrs. Ida Mae Jones sat alone, in the first row, directly behind the plaintiff's table. There was plenty of room—not more than a dozen spectators were there, and no reporters I recognized. The media would get into the act when the trial got underway. For them jury selection in a civil suit was routine and, because of restrictions on the attorneys, uncontroversial.

At the defense table, representing the city law department, was Chief Counsel Thomas T. Dennet. Tom had been assistant to the chief when Fitzy sued the city on my behalf. He'd lost that one badly. This time out he looked sleek and confident. He wasn't wearing a bow tie. As he scanned the plaintiff's table he looked like he was thinking, "Fuck these bow ties, they want to play kiss ass the judge."

"Mr. O'Dwyer," the clerk announced. "Number forty-one."

They picked eight prospective jurors. Two would be alternates. Six would decide the case and award damages if Fitzy won them over. Since neither side was allowed to address the prospective jurors during the selection process, Judge Skittles read questions to each juror. The idea is to determine if the potential juror has long-standing prejudices that would influence his or her opinion in the case.

Fitzy pays attention to every answer.

"I assume every juror is prejudiced," he says. "What I prefer, they're prejudiced in my favor. I like mothers and cabdrivers. I don't like firemen, not if they work for the city. A firemen is always worried, if I get damages from the city, will it come out of his pay."

Two mothers were among those selected to decide the case of *Jones vs. City of Boston.* There were no firemen. There were no blacks.

"Would have been nice to get a black grandmother," Fitzy said after the session was dismissed. "But they go by demographics, the federal court. Only four blacks in the pool, so the odds were against it. And no black grandmothers, even if we'd pulled one of the four."

Ida Mae Jones, looking very small and black in the big white courtroom, said, "What you want, you want a Aunt Jemima?"

"That would have been nice," Fitzy said. "We get 'em sequestered, have her make pancakes."

Mrs. Jones looked tense and frightened, not the same woman who had brazened her way through a gang of neighborhood punks and welcomed me into her apartment. "What's yo 'pinion, honey?" she said, addressing Milton Pridham. "These white folk gonna give white people's money to a po black woman, lived half her life on welfare?''

Milton's bow tie bobbed as he swallowed. He looked at Fitzy.

''Just remember, Ida Mae,'' Fitzy said. ''You may be black and the jury may be white, but money is always green.''

That made her smile.

3 MONSIGNOR MCCUE WAS A HARD MAN TO SEE. As chancellor for the archdiocese he answered only to the archbishop, and to God. His secretary informed me that his appointment book was full and would undoubtedly remain so. When I told her my business was in relation to a Father Sydney, formerly of the Roxbury Boy's Mission, there was a pregnant pause. She put me on hold. I listened to a thin version of Vivaldi's "Four Seasons." Overplayed, but far better than the average "on hold" Muzak. After spring had sprung, the secretary returned to the line with the information that the monsignor would make every effort to accommodate me.

"Wednesday at 10:15, Mr. Hawkins. May I ask how you are acquainted with Father Sydney?"

"A mutual friend."

"Would that be Father Duvall?"

"I was thinking more of Horatio Jones."

The secretary did not reply to that. Her silence was immaculate. I was pretty sure the good monsignor would have something to think about before we met.

Tim Sullivan had Mutt in custody. It happened this way. Wrongway Kerrigan had raised bail and been released. Sheehan tailed him from the Charles Street Jail, where he had been held, to the Shamrock Tavern on E Street in South Boston. Sheehan waited outside, slouched down in his beat-up Plymouth. Inside the bar, according to what Sheehan was able to discern later, Kerrigan had four beers. Schlitz. Then he dropped a quarter and called up Mutt, his brother-in-law and accomplice, who had been hiding out with Kerrigan's former girlfriend. Mutt sauntered into the

Shamrock about fifteen minutes later. His ass had barely hit the stool when Sheehan arrested him.

"You went in there alone?" I asked Sheehan. We were in Sully's office at police headquarters. Sullivan was out conferring with Marilyn, getting files pulled, and the door was open.

"Sure I did," Sheehan said, grinning around his cigarette. "You expect me to call in the National Guard?"

"What did Kerrigan do when you arrested Mutt?"

"He started whining about how he hadn't set him up. Which Mutt didn't for a second believe. I get the cuffs on Mutt, he lunges forward and tries to take a bite out of Kerrigan's nose."

I laughed.

"Right," Sheehan said. "You saw that nose. You wanna fasten your teeth on that scabby thing?"

Sully came back carrying a stack of files.

"Detective Sheehan is getting recommended for a citation," he said. "He tell you about that?"

"No."

"Well, he's a shy kind of guy," Sully said. "That was a beautiful collar. And Mutt is singing like a little birdy."

"Kerrigan's in too, with some lawyer he dug up. Now he wants to turn state's evidence, rat on Mutt."

"It's a game they're playing," Sully said. "Pin the tail on your brother-in-law."

Their two versions of the kidnaping jibed at a number of points, although each accused the other of being the mastermind. Depending on whom you believed, either Mutt or Kerrigan had been contacted by phone at the Shamrock. Would he be interested in earning ten grand for a couple of days' work? Since both Mutt and Kerrigan had previously supplemented their housebreaking incomes by helping out their neighborhood loan shark, breaking kneecaps and such, they at first assumed this would be a similar operation. Not that you ever got ten grand for kneecapping some deadbeat. And since the voice on the phone said it would take two to carry out the ten-grand tango, the brothers-in-law agreed to a meet.

"We showed both of 'em a couple pages of mug shots," Sheehan said. "Both of 'em pulled Edwards. Either they're being real cute, or we definitely make Eyeball as the payoff man for the snatch."

Eyeball, whom they claimed never to have met before, dropped a few names, convincing Mutt and Kerrigan that he represented a major mob figure. They were thrilled. This was the big time. Five-hundred-dollar kneecappings were a thing of the past.

Eyeball laid out the plan. They would wait for his call and he would tell them where and when they could snatch the children of an unnamed male who had grievously offended the major mob figure. They were to frighten the father, but inflict no serious physical damage. Then they would take the kids to a hiding place of their choice and check into the Shamrock every six hours. Eyeball would contact them there regarding what to do with the brats.

"Mutt showed me a fresh scar on his wrist. Said the little girl bit him. He wasn't happy about getting bit. He'd heard you could get rabies from little kids. He was worried."

I wondered what Mutt had done to Sarah, to pay her back. The pediatrician who examined her said she hadn't been physically abused. There were, I knew, other kinds of abuse. Nightmare threats.

The junkie bastard.

"So they lock the kids in that bathroom in the basement of the building they later tried to torch. They can scream and cry all they want down there, no one can hear. Eyeball, no fool, gives 'em spending money but he won't pay off until the gig is over. Mutt and Kerrigan don't mind, they've got enough to feed their habits, enough to hang out at the Shamrock and buy beers, which was, from what the bartender told me, a first. Once in a while they go back to the building, throw a box of doughnuts in to the kids. Then they get a phone call. Eyeball is going to take over. He wants the twins sedated and he wants them delivered. He provides the sleeping pills. Mutt and Kerrigan put the pills in the chocolate milk. I think, from what both of these creeps say, they had to force the kids to drink it. Kids are, I guess, smart enough to figure out they're being poisoned.''

''Makes a great argument for capital punishment,'' I said.

''These guys had deprived upbringings,'' Sheehan said. ''That's why they feel the compulsion to go out on the streets, break guys' kneecaps, commit arson, and terrify innocent children.''

When the twins lost consciousness Mutt and Kerrigan wrapped them in an old rug. Eyeball met them near the Shamrock, paid them off, and put the twins in the trunk of his car. Mutt thinks there may have been someone else in Eyeball's car, crouching in the backseat. He was pretty high at the time and may have been seeing things.

''Then Eyeball borrowed a ski mask from Mutt,'' Sully said. ''Must have been his disguise, he was going to meet the Eskimo.''

''Clever guy, Edwards,'' Sheehan said. ''The man of a thousand faces. So what he must have done, he follows Lew Quinn from the Columbus Park circle, makes sure he's alone. Then maybe he pulls up alongside, gives him a signal. They pull over, swap the kids from Eyeball's trunk to Quinn's. Everything is fine. Except Eyeball has second thoughts. Maybe Eyeball thinks he's been made. So he follows Quinn. The poor bastard goes to the nearest phone booth, calls you, then Eyeball pops him coming out.''

''I wonder why he changed his mind.''

''Who?''

''Eyeball, what made him decide to turn the kids over the Quinn?''

Sheehan shrugged. "Maybe he got spooked. Or figured Fitzgerald was sufficiently tenderized. Or maybe, if you believe Mutt, there was someone else in the car with Eyeball, someone else who was calling the shots."

And maybe, I thought, the cow flew over the moon.

There was a new wariness, a new caution in Lois Fitzgerald. I had called to invite myself for coffee. She was waiting inside the backdoor. As I scooted through she closed the door, setting a police lock in place. Given what she had been through, that seemed sensible. My own well-developed sense of urban paranoia made me think further precautions were in order.

"We talked about the security service," Lois said. "We both agree. I don't want rent-a-cops in this house. Lew Quinn would have been fine. You know any other Lew Quinns out there?"

"Can't say I do."

There was coffee in a Thermos jug and muffins on a plate. The radio was tuned at low volume to a golden oldies station. Jan and Dean were warbling about a dead man's curve.

Lois had her hair up in a kerchief. She kept licking her lips, which were chapped and sunburned. On her the Florida tan did not look healthy.

A small blur exploded into the kitchen.

"Uncle Jack!"

"No questions," Lois warned.

"Rory the rascal. You have fun at Disney World?"

Rory informed me that it was really awesome. Did I know that Goofy was as tall as a house? Rory had talked with him personally. I took the five-year-old into my lap and gave him a hug. The sun had brought out his freckles. The all-American boy. All he needed was a frog in his hand and a slingshot in his pocket and he could be the month of June on a Norman Rockwell calendar.

"Where's your sister?"

"Watching cartoons."

He raced back down the hall.

"They don't like to be separated for more than a few minutes," Lois explained. On the radio Questionmark & the Mysterians were counting tears.

"The psychologist helping?"

"I think so. Sarah likes her. She's going to come in every other day for a while. I don't want to take them into an office. Not just yet."

"Stay where you feel safest, Lois. Don't push it."

She had been stirring her coffee for about ten minutes. It was going to be very well stirred, that coffee. I figured, judging from her face, that Lois had lost about ten pounds. And not from dieting.

"You think it's really over, Jack?"

It was obvious what was bothering her. She was afraid the nightmare might repeat itself, that she would lose the children again. Quoting the odds wasn't going to help. She wanted a sure thing.

"They have the two kidnapers in custody. And Edwards is dead."

Lois waited, the spoon raised. Her eyes searched mine.

"I think it's over," I said. "I hope so. Have there been any phone calls?"

She shook her head quickly. "Not since we got back."

"Well, it's right there in the paper, Fitzy is back as lead counsel for the plaintiff. He makes the opening statement tomorrow. If someone wanted to get him off again, I assume they'd be using the telephone. Like before."

"I don't think I can take any more of those," Lois said. "For a while I was just plain angry. Now I'm hollowed out inside, Jack. And I'm still afraid. All the time, every minute."

"There's nothing wrong with being scared, considering what happened, but with Eyeball out of the picture, you should be okay. If I'm on the right track, he was the big worry. What he might say under cross-examination."

"You mean there's somebody *else* out there?"

The note of panic in her voice made me want to assure her that the world had returned to its normal tilt. I knew better than to lie to Lois, though. She had a built-in lie detector that matched every beat of her heart.

So I did what I could. I laid out my theory. The one where Eyeball got himself involved in a vice-related deal worth a lot of cash, enough so it had to be laundered. Either he was moving something illegal, or he was playing a game of blackmail, maybe a little of each. Whatever, it was important that Fitzy not get after him in open court. Someone, maybe his partner in the cash business, wanted to make damn sure he didn't testify.

"Whoever killed Eyeball is still out there, Lois. But since Eyeball can't hurt anyone anymore, it doesn't matter if Fitzy is back in court, doing his thing," I said, hoping with all my heart it was true. "Make any sense?"

"As much as anything else does lately. You think I'm being irrational, keeping the kids in the house?"

"No. Why take a chance? Fitzy says the trial won't go more than a week. A week inside won't hurt them."

I rolled down the hall, taking my time so they'd hear me coming. Sarah was sitting hunched, her legs folded under her butt. Holding herself very still and self-contained, with her chin on her hands. She was about a foot from the television, bathed in the flickering light. Popeye was strangling a can of spinach. Olive Oyl was tearing her hair out. Apparently this had a calming effect on Sarah, because she did not turn from the screen.

Rory said, "Sarry says hello."

She did not move.

Rory said, ''Uncle Jack, does 'pinach really give you super-power?''

''If you eat enough of it,'' I said. ''Sarah, honey, I'll see you again soon. When you feel like it I want you to tell me all about Disney World, okay?''

I thought she nodded. It was a very small nod, and possibly I imagined it.

Lois unbolted the back door. I wanted to give her a hug and a kiss, but she didn't look any more ready than her daughter. I thought about how hard it had been on her, and continued to be. Fitzy had the distraction of his work. All Lois had was a phone that hadn't rung, yet. I slipped into my down jacket, and pulled the wool cap from my pocket.

''Keep a secret?'' she said.

I nodded.

Lois reached up over the door, to an indentation in the framing. When her hand came back down it was clutching a compact revolver. Holding it carefully, she displayed a Smith & Wesson 649, stainless, with the satin finish.

Five shots, a .38 Special.

''Fitz would shit if he knew. I bought it down in Orlando. I cost me five hundred, no questions asked. I want to have something if the bastards try to break down the door, you know?''

''I know.''

''Fitz had a piece of lead pipe he picked up somewhere. 'No guns around the children,' he said.''

''You know how to use it?''

''They told me in the store. Just point and pull the trigger. I kept it in my purse and kept the purse under the pillow. Fitz thought I was worried about losing the credit cards.'' She put it back in its hiding place over the door. ''I always hated guns, Jack. I still do. Only it makes me feel like I could do something, worst comes to worst.''

''That's the idea. Just be careful.''

''You'll keep an eye on Finian? He wants to prove himself, you know.''

''I know,'' I said. ''He wants to kick him some butts.''

4

BOW TIES WERE TAKING OVER THE WORLD. THE only holdout down in front was Tom Dennet, directing the City of Boston defense. On the other side of the fence, in the gallery, I noticed that Russ White, looking mischievous and amused, wore a plaid clip-on that must have set him back at least a dollar. In the jury box there were silky new butterflies here and there, sprouting under self-conscious chins. And me without a neck ornament. I had a strong urge to go over to Jack's Joke Shop on Arlington Street and buy one of those novelty bow ties that spins like a propeller.

Move over Archibald Cox. Get out of here, Pee-Wee Herman.

Judge Otis Skittles had a voice like fingernails on slate—scratchy and brittle. He had been admitted to the Massachusetts bar at about the time Sacco and Vanzetti came to trial and had long expressed a preference for trying criminals, rather than civil lawsuits. With a backlog of more than five hundred cases, he was known to be quick with a hammer. Attorneys inclined to plod through a case dreaded Skittles, who was fully prepared to gavel them into submission, steering procedures toward a quick and concise conclusion.

Fitzy had this to say about Judge Skittles: "He's got a couple of years on Methuselah, and when he talks, dogs throughout the city start howling. But Otis is a no-bullshit guy. You do your homework, stick to the rules, you can win with Otis, the jury doesn't fuck you up. And if they do, and he's on your side, he'll give 'em such a load of hellfire they'll shrink up to the size of squirrels. And for an added bonus, he doesn't like Tom Dennet. Thinks he's smug and lazy."

Dennet, at the helm of the defense table, looked neither smug nor lazy as the trial got underway. He was all business. If he appeared at all concerned, it was when Fitzy and Milton Pridham wheeled in their secret weapon.

When he was a boy Finian X. Fitzgerald had a papier-mâché castle that was the envy of the neighborhood. Drawbridges that went up and down, a painted moat, and ramparts lined with lead soldiers. Fitzy had been the king of that castle. As an adult he retained his love of toys and models and put it to good use in many a lawsuit. The "secret weapon," not so secret to anyone familiar with his technique, was a scale model of the rooftop where Horatio Jones had died. The model was about six feet square, raised to a level ideal for jury viewing, and complete right down to the wire pigeon cages. There were even little model pigeons in each of the little cages.

Displays like that, provided by an architectural modeling firm, did not come cheap. Another reason, Fitzy confided, that he had welcomed a rich-kid attorney on the case.

"Childe Milton is not perhaps the sharpest legal mind. On the other hand, he knows how to sign checks. This can be a great talent, in and of itself. He ought to be a very popular congressman, he ever gets that far."

As for Pridham's alleged incompetence, I had only Fitzy's word for that, and my own instinctive distrust. As far as appearances went, and they are everything in the media world, Milton looked fine. Boyishly handsome, trim, serious. Everything necessary for a career in politics, with the added confidence of family wealth and the power base provided by the firm of Pridham & Briggs.

The courtroom artist for Channel 5 devoted most of her attention to Milton, giving him, in my opinion, a little more chin that he in fact possessed.

Of necessity, I planted my chair behind the last row—fire laws prohibit clogging the aisles. The last time I'd been in this courtroom I'd been right at the plaintiff's table and the mockup shown to the jury was that of the Shield, the cop hangout where I'd been accidentally shot. On the floor of the miniature club Fitzy had placed a police doll holding a tiny gun. Lying prone beneath it was another doll, leaking red ink. Me.

The civil trial of *Hawkins vs. City of Boston* had been a prolonged nightmare. But when I woke from it Finian X. Fitzgerald had persuaded the jury to award me enough money to start my life over.

I had to blink a few times to make sure I wasn't in a time loop, living it over again.

Russ White slipped out of his seat and knelt beside me as Fitzy began his opening statement.

"You think he'll pull it off?" Russ whispered.

"You can never figure a jury."

"My headline: 'Ghost of slain detective hovers over trial.' You like it?"

"Classy. Best thing since *The Turn of the Screw.*"

"My angle: 'Plaintiff attorney deprived of key witness.' "

"Meaning Eyeball?"

"The one and only. Any jury that saw Eyeball Edwards on the stand, they'd beg the judge to issue bulletproof vests. Now all Fitzgerald can rely on are the sworn depositions, Eyeball on paper. He comes through as dumb and careless, but the special effects are missing."

"He won't be there on the stand to chew the water glass?"

"Exactly. Can you see it? Eyeball turns to the jury. 'Hey, guys, wanna see by best trick?' He eats the water glass, burps. Jury cries for mercy, awards entire contents of city coffers to mother of slain youth."

"Russ, what do you know about the Bay Village connection?"

"Just what I wrote in the article. That Eyeball was on the dick patrol at the time of the bust. Relative to background, though, there's a guy here who wants to meet you. Asked me to set it up. A fellow journalist."

"Who?"

"Guy named Sylvia."

"Any relation to the boy named Sue?"

"You'll have to ask him. I dare you. His name is Peter Sylvia, he's the current publisher of the *Gay Village Banner*. Also he's the editor and the staff. He sets the type and sweeps up after."

I was unaware that the *Banner* still existed. Hadn't it died with Lester Karkis?

"Rose from the grave," Russ explained. "This guy Sylvia had been running it for Karkis, and took it over after Karkis went to the big bathhouse in the sky. Karkis never had much to do with the paper anyway, just fronted the money. Status, I assume. Got a small circulation, but everyone in the gay community reads it. Crusading for gay rights, that sort of thing."

"What's he want to see me for?"

White shrugged, "You'll have to ask him. Only thing, if he has anything interesting to relate, remember who set it up. A deal?"

I agreed to meet Peter Sylvia during the lunch recess.

Fitzy was doing what he does best: seducing a jury.

He stood over the rooftop model like a kindly schoolmaster who was puzzled and outraged at the series of events that had culminated in the violent death of an innocent boy. Using a pointer, he brought the Roxbury rooftop to life, indicating the position of the pigeon cages, the stairwell, the ramshackle shed, the brick chimney. He gave a picture of Horatio Jones to each juror. He pointed out his bereaved mother seated in the first row, who looked convincingly bereaved and frightened.

As, no doubt, she was.

"You will hear testimony describing the events that led up to the sudden and wrongful death of Horatio Jones, only son of Mrs. Ida Mae Jones, who, abandoned by her husband, succeeded in raising her son for thirteen years. In a neighborhood overrun with crime and drugs and despair, Ida Mae somehow did the impossible. She brought up a boy who excelled in school, who loved and obeyed his mother, who successfully resisted the many evil temptations of his unhappy environment. A youngster who showed such promise that scholarships had already been pledged in his name. A son who delighted in observing life and nature, an who never caused hurt to anyone in his short life . . .''

Like any good actor, Fitzy believed every line. He was firmly convinced that any administration that allowed a head case like Detective Edwards to roam the streets with a license to kill should be made to pay for the damage he caused.

As in any good play, the plot has the ring of truth.

Peter Sylvia looked a little like Al Pacino would look if Pacino had a neatly trimmed mustache and gray eyes. We had lunch in a narrow, crowded deli not far from the courthouse. Free pickles. I had a turkey club and a Sam Adams beer, bottled in Boston. It tasted like it was brewed in Pittsburgh. Sylvia had a plate of potato knishes and a Coke. As he lifted the fork to his mouth and ate the knish in neat bites, his teeth looked too white to be real. Movie-star caps.

''Three grand,'' he said, reading my mind. ''I had bad teeth when I was a kid. Horrid snaggles. Lester took pity, sent me to a dentist. The dentist was a lecherous old beast, but he gave me a reason to smile.''

Sylvia wore a soft brown leather jacket. A silk scarf, pastel green, was knotted loosely around his neck. He had rings on his fingers and, for all I knew, bells on his toes.

No rings in his ears, no keys on his belt.

''Lester was a miserable, rotten man. A gold-plated bitch. But he didn't deserve to get murdered.''

Peter Sylvia was writing a book. The book, which he had been working on for almost two years, was titled *The Life and Untimely Death of Lester Karkis*. He had approached a number of publishers with the project. So far no one was the least bit interested.

"Of course all they saw was the outline. I'm almost through with the first draft now. It's taken over my life, I'll tell you that. The *Banner* has suffered on account of it, but that can't be helped." He put a straw in the glass of Coke and drained an inch of it. "It's going to be a big, big book, if I ever find someone brave enough to publish. Big enough to shake some big apples out of the tree."

I raised my eyebrows. Sylvia showed me his movie-star teeth.

"The clue is," he said, "apples are fruits."

I tried to look confused. That was easy.

"Oh, dear, I can see I'm going to have to be blunt," Sylvia said, leaning forward. "Homos, Mr. Hawkins. Fags. Queers. Pansies."

"I thought you were a gay activist."

"Exactly. I'm gay and I'm proud to admit it. I put my name right up there on the masthead. If you have the kind of sexual orientation I do, and you're brave enough to admit it and live with it and deal with all that it implies in this society, than you're gay. If you're hiding it, living a lie, then to my way of thinking you're a fruit, or a fag, or a queer. Take your pick."

"And those are the people you're going after in this book?"

He nodded as he inhaled the rest of the Coke. The straw made a gurgling sound at the bottom of the glass.

"Lester was as gay as gay could be. Liberation was not his problem. His problem was he was greedy. He was like a vampire, living off the rest of the gay community. He owned a lot of real estate. He owned it before Bay Village became *Gay* Village. He had connections on the liquor commission, he was able to license clubs. He had important connections in Health, so they gave him permits to operate bathhouses. He made a fortune, Lester did. And he had a lot of faggy friends, a lot of them married, with families. People with Very Important Jobs, who would absolutely *die* if anyone in the straight world found out they liked to dress up in mommie's clothes. Or grope little boys. Oh, dear, I said the wrong thing. You've gone quite pale. Was it the boys? Yes, it must have been. Well, I can't help it, Lester was very wrong about that. He liked them unspoiled, you know, and *très, très* young.''

''Children,'' I said.

''Nasty little brats, most of them, runaways, or kids who never had a home. Unformed, in my opinion, and therefore unattractive. But then I never shared Lester's tastes. I like mine in the twenty-and-up range. Not *too* far up, because I can't make it with wrinklies. No, thank you, Mr. Silver Fox, even if you *do* spend all that time at health clubs, toning up your sagging fanny. Am I grossing you out? Oh, dear.''

''I can take it,'' I said, making my voice husky. ''I'm a tough guy and tough guys can take it.''

''That was *very* good. That was Bogart *exactly*. Was it *African Queen?*''

''*The Big Sleep*. Philip Marlowe,'' I said.

''I always thought he was a bit faggy, you know. Not Bogart, but Philip Marlowe. Always commenting on how handsome so-and-so was. But then I think *everyone* has a little queer streak, if you dig deep enough. Do you agree?''

''It's an interesting theory,'' I said. ''Were you there when the bathhouse got raided?''

Sylvia smiled. It was about as menacing a smile as can be gotten off when you have little bits of potato knish sticking to your movie-star teeth.

''I never went in for their sick orgy scene. You understand, I *worked* for Lester Karkis, I didn't socialize with him. Beyond being gay, and being interested in the gay movement, we had nothing in common. When I wanted to start a weekly paper I went to Lester because he was the most visible person in the community. He helped me finance *The Banner* and found the first advertisers. I did all the grunt work. And people who worked for Lester Karkis were definitely not part of his clique. He had his own parties and his special dinners and all his Very Important Friends.''

Sylvia sounded bitter and vindictive. Whether or not he had wanted to participate in the bathhouse scene was not the question. He had not been invited. I didn't think the memory of Lester Karkis was going to fare well in his book.

''You know who they were, these very important friends?''

''Some of them. The ones who got arrested, certainly. Pathetic little snobs, most of them. Terrified of doing something natural like holding your lover's hand in public. But, oh, they were eager enough behind closed doors. Dressing up—it was one long, continual costume party at Lester's house. Gauchos, drag queens, rubber fetishists, harem boys.''

Sylvia opened a package of clove cigarettes. He lit one up and made a face. It smelled, not surprisingly, like burning cloves.

''It was the harem boys who were the main attraction,'' he said, puffing on the clove stick but not inhaling. ''I thought it was positively revolting. I don't like children much, and I especially don't like them as sex objects. Nor do most normal gay men, whatever you may have heard to the contrary.''

I mentioned that at the time the scandal broke there had been some mention of drugs given to the boys, and kiddie pornography.

''Drugs, certainly. These were street urchins remember, dirty little brats. I suppose ten to fourteen years old. That was Lester's range. Living on the street as they did, most of those kids would have had drug experience. Angel dust, that's what kids like at that age. Blows their little minds. Kills a lot of brain cells. And if a bunch of creepy old men want you to dress up in harem pants and parade around at parties carrying drinks on silver salvers, well, the less brain cells the better, I suppose. Also handy if the same creepy old men want you to to engage in naughty physical activity while they take pictures.''

The turkey club must have been a bit off, because I began to feel queasy.

''You look absolutely green, darling. Don't worry, your disgust doesn't offend me. *I* was disgusted. I *saw* some of those videos they made. The boys looked absolutely drugged. Eyes like pinpoints. A very sick-making scene. Not gay at all.''

The smell of burning cloves made the air thick, hard to breathe.

''That's going to be the focus of my book. That Lester Karkis was living a lie. Pretending to be a gay activist, because there was money to be made exploiting the community. Inside he was a poor, wretched fag with a nasty kink. And he had an absolute sickness for money, for accumulating more and more of it. I think the poor man thought if he got rich enough he could make himself beautiful, or become young again.''

Sylvia stirred at the cubes in his glass, staring down thoughtfully, as if reviewing scenes frozen there in the melting ice.

''Greed, that was the key to Lester Karkis, his life. His untimely death,'' he said. He sounded as though he was quoting from his book. ''What else but greed would make him get involved with that awful business of the kiddie porn? Peddling his kinky videos to the mob for resale. Do you know how much money is involved in that scene? How much certain very sick people are willing to pay to see eleven-year-olds engage in sex?''

I said I had no idea.

''Five hundred bucks a pop is what Lester got for those cassettes. For each copy. Available in VHS or Beta for your viewing convenience. He sold hundreds and hundreds. Takes an hour to make a copy, once you have the original. Any way you look at it, that's a whole lot of money.''

Yes, indeed. Probably enough money to finance a considerable investment. An investment, say, in Cambridge real estate.

"So I take it you don't think Karkis was a suicide?"

"No way. He just wasn't the type. If there was one thing Lester knew," Sylvia said with a nasty chuckle, "it's that there is no sex after death. And with his connections, and all his money, he wasn't going to do time. Not in a prison."

"Who do you think killed him?"

"Someone who knew him. It had to be one of his secret fag friends, someone he would open the door to. Someone with a lot to lose, if Lester decided to name names. When I come up with the answer to that, I'll have an ending for my book. Speaking of the book, dear, do you think you could be any help? Speak to somebody in publishing? Someone with an open mind?"

I promised to do what I could. Everyone seemed to be working on a book. Larry Sheehan. Peter Sylvia. Everyone but me.

I had one more question, before the close air and the off sandwich drove me out of the place.

"These private parties that Karkis hosted. You ever hear about a priest being one of the special guests?"

"Dozens of them," Sylvia said. He laughed. "That was perfect, the look on your face. You see, it was a fad at the time, among that crowd. Dressing up like a clergyman, that was a favorite costume. Sort of Montgomery Clift riff. Lots of them put on your basic black, and the white collar, really camping it up. 'Oh, darling, I've been celibate for ages, let's do a mortal sin, shall we?' That sort of thing. If there'd been a real priest there, why you'd never have known. Perfect camouflage."

Outside, wheeling myself back to the courthouse, I kept bumping into Christmas. Plastic music trumpeting from storefronts. Salvation Army Santas with their cotton beards. Mobs of frantic shoppers careening like pinballs through an urban maze. There were lots of children in the crowd. Most were in their parents' tow, being dragged through the ritual of seeing the windows at Jordan Marsh and the displays on the Common. Losing one kind of innocence while enhancing another.

I wasn't in a Christmas-y mood. I was Scrooge on wheels, thinking of greed and lechery. Of sin and absolution. Of the late and unlamented Lester Karkis. Was there anyone in the world who had mourned his passing? And if so, why?

5 "SO," MEGAN SAID, "WHAT ARE YOU GOING TO confess?"

She was scooping sections out of a grapefruit and looking at me as she raised the spoon to her lips. Secret smile. I put aside Russ White's latest article on the trial. Let her have her fun. It was easy meat, taking advantage of me in the early morning.

"I did it," I said. "I killed Cock Robin."

Meg blinked her long lashes, amused. A juvenile book she had edited had just been sold to a major British publisher. A big paperback sale was in the offing. The Fitzgerald twins were safe at home, the trial was underway, and I was grousing about having to start another book. All was right with the world.

"You better hit the road, Jack, if you don't want to get your knuckles rapped with a steel-edge ruler. Or maybe they still use the rack over there in Brighton."

I clasped my hands together and bobbed my head.

"Yes, memsahib. Right away, memsahib."

If you drive the entire length of Beacon Street, through Back Bay and Brookline to the Cleveland Circle, there are more traffic lights than can possibly be counted on one cup of coffee. I know. I tried. At the circle I cranked the wheel over and went around the circuit a couple of times before picking up Beacon again and swinging south around the Chestnut Hill Reservoir. I veered north again on Lake Street. The Boston College campus was on my left and the black waters of the reservoir to the right.

Monsignor McCue operated out of a four-story gothic on the edge of the chancery grounds. Spires and towers and gingerbread trim. A huge elm, its massive trunk bearing the scars of a tree surgeon, spread bare branches over the peak of the building. Thick wire cables held the elm in place, denying the disease that had hollowed out the core of the tree. There was a certain vain-glory about it I admired, daring the wind and the pull of gravity.

The front entrance, with its steep, narrow steps and the ornate iron railings, was out of the question. I found a handicap ramp on the side and pushed into the reception area. High ceilings with elaborate corner moldings, a marble fireplace with a filigreed mantle, parquet floors. The furniture was Victorian, some of it slightly decrepit. A middle-aged priest sat in one of the thronelike chairs, presumably waiting to see the monsignor. He was reading a *Boston Globe,* open to the sports section. The expression on his face, which bore the unmistakable florid rosettes produced by heavy drinking, was not a happy one.

"Mr. Hawkins?"

A gray-haired woman entered, closing a heavy door behind her. She wore half-glasses and a conservatively cut wool suit. The long skirt did not quite manage to cover a pair of trim ankles. She looked past me to the waiting priest, her expression unflickering. To me she said, "The monsignor will see you now. This way."

She pushed open the heavy door. I followed. A thick carpet sighed under my wheels as we entered a large, *L*-shaped suite of rooms. In one of them, seated at a dining table, was Monsignor McCue. He stood as I entered. Behind him was a tall, double casement of small, leaded windows overlooking a formal winter garden.

"I was hoping you'd join me for coffee, Mr. Hawkins," he said. His tone was jovial, welcoming. Not what I'd expected.

The dining table was sheathed in crisp Irish linen. A silver coffee urn and creamer, white china cups, a tray holding fresh fruit, a basket of bread, and various jams were on display. The steam was still rising from the hot bread.

"Thank you, Helen," the monsignor said. "You might tell Father O'Hare we'll be awhile. I've no intention of rushing my coffee on his account, bless the poor man."

The secretary looked about as amused as a gila monster. She nodded and left.

"Mr. Hawkins, I consider this an honor, you stopping by to see us. I'm a great fan of your Casey books."

That explained the friendly reception. We quickly established that he should call me Jack.

"Father Duvall called not long after you spoke to Helen, to tell us of your interest in Father Sydney. Ah, and that's a very sad business, which we will not speak of until we have had our coffee and a little midmorning snack. It was Father Duvall who told me you were the J. D. Hawkins who writes the *Casey* novels."

"He mentioned you read mysteries."

"Yes," the monsignor said, rubbing his hands together. "I love a good murder."

McCue was a large, corpulent man, well over six feet and very broad in the chest. His hair was thick, close-cropped, and silvery-gray. His thick, pinkish ears stuck out like small jug handles. Gray tufts of hair sprouted from them. His eyebrows, still very black, were as large and furry as winter caterpillars. His eyes were small, blue, and shone with quick intelligence. In response to my inquiry he confessed that, yes, he had indeed played college football. Before taking orders some thirty years before he had been a starting tackle for Boston College. In a sense, he said, he had always been working or fighting for the archdiocese.

"Mostly I have to fight the weight now," he said, pouring coffee into the china cups. "I keep losing. Or rather gaining. Cream? It's very fresh, I assure you. The sugar is in lumps, as it should be. You'll find the bread is Irish soda bread, which is made in heaven, or tastes like it."

I buttered a wedge of the bread, ate some, and agreed.

"I read more than mystery novels, of course," the monsignor said, wiping his lips with a napkin that matched the tablecloth.

"For instance I read the papers. Your name has been mentioned in connection with that lawsuit, the poor colored woman."

"Ida Mae Jones."

"Lovely names those people have. Not unlike the Irish in that respect. Names that roll off the tongue. Yes. Well, in the paper it said you were at the scene of a recent crime. A detective who had the great misfortune to be shot in his own bed. And since this was the very same gentleman who accidentally shot the colored lad in Roxbury, a lad that our Father Sydney had some small contact with at the boys' mission, I can only assume your curiosity about Father Sydney is somehow connected to the lawsuit. Well, how am I doing so far?"

"Fine, Father. Only I think maybe Father Sydney had more than 'some small contact' with Horatio Jones. And with another boy, name of Spenser Eames. Black like Horatio and about the same age."

The monsignor frowned. The huge black eyebrows glowered. The blue eyes darkened a shade or two. "I believe Father Duvall mentioned the name. A troublesome boy."

"Trouble enough to get himself killed, Father. As I'm sure Father Duvall mentioned when he called to warn you I was going to make inquiries."

That amused the monsignor. He picked up another wedge of the soda bread, contemplated it with a faint smile, and dropped it back into the basket. "I don't know what we'd do without Napoleon," he said. "The man is a rock. When the first hints of Father Sydney's illness came to my attention I asked His Eminence the Archbishop to let me assign Father Duvall to the mission."

"To keep an eye on Father Sydney."

"Dear me," the monsignor laughed. "We've got it all figured out, haven't we? I might have expected that from a fellow who has a talent for contriving such deadly plots. And making your hero Casey a former Jesuit, well, that makes the books all the more attractive. Many's the time I've imagined what my life might have been had I joined the force, as my father wanted me to. That's a switch, I know, wanting the son to go on the cops instead of into the Church, but my good father, rest his soul, wanted grandchildren.''

''You were saying that Father Duvall was keeping an eye on Father Sydney.''

''Was I saying that now, Jack? Here, more coffee. Of course, you're quite correct, we did send Napoleon in for that purpoose. There had been a call or two, no definite accusations mind you. Just rumors. But we are interested in making something of the Roxbury Boy's Mission. We want to make a commitment to the neighborhood. And rumors such as those, insinuating a very grave problem, could not be left unexamined.''

''Father Sydney is a homosexual?''

One of the great black eyebrows twitched. The monsignor sighed, his huge chest falling and rising.

''Father Sydney is a Catholic, Jack. Ordained in the service of Christ. He is also a man, prone to all the earthly torments, and he has suffered grievously from one of the most heinous afflictions. A lust for the flesh of his own sex. And young flesh at that.''

''Boys, Monsignor. Twelve-year-old boys. Under the statutes of the Commonwealth, that's a felony.''

Monsignor McCue shifted his bulk, leaning back in his chair. In the garden visible through the windows behind him birds hovered over a feeder, their wings blurry in the cold December air.

''Believe me, Jack. It's worse than that as far as we're concerned. It's a crime against nature. Not being homosexual, mind you, which is not a sin; but engaging in homosexual sex, which most certainly is. Some of our Episcopal brothers are waffling on the subject, ordaining 'gay' ministers and so forth, but around here we take a very hard line.''

"Excommunication?"

That elicited a wry smile. Monsignor McCue shook his head. "To my knowledge the last priest who got excommunicated in this diocese was Father Feeney. That was a question of heresy, preaching that only Catholics could hope for eternal salvation. It was Cushing who threw him out, and then the Dago tore up the writ and let the old bastard, pardon me, Father Feeney of the Slaves of the Sacred Heart of Mary, have the sacrament again."

"The dago?"

"Cardinal Madeiros, as he was fondly referred to at the chancery. On account of his Portuguese ancestry. The point I was making, Jack, is a Catholic can't be excommunicated for his sins, not if he truly repents. Now a priest can be defrocked for behavioral problems, which is a different thing, but only after it has been proved absolutely that he is not fit to serve Christ, or offer up the Host."

"And Father Sydney repents his sins?"

"Ah, the poor man is in torment. It was all we could do to keep him from taking his own life. Which is a much greater sin, even, than the lust Father Sydney gave himself up to when he pawed, rather ineffectually I am told, at those young colored boys."

"Was Horatio Jones one of the boys he molested?"

"The other one. Spenser Eames. Evidently the Jones boy came upon the two of them on a field trip. In a backroom at the Peabody Museum. Gone in to view the dinosaur bones. Very sad. Napoleon tells me the Eames boy was a nasty little number, old beyond his years, but we consider that no excuse for Father Sydney's behavior."

"So Horatio told Father Duvall about what he'd seen at the museum?"

"He was very upset. Napoleon had to coax it out of him. The boy wouldn't tell him in so many words, but it was clear what had happened. We had Father Sydney in here immediately when we knew. The poor man had a breakdown, weeping and wailing and banging his head on the floor. I had to have two of the brothers in here to restrain him. Horrible mental strain. Complete breakdown.''

''So he's been receiving psychiatric care?''

''We take care of our own, Jack. Also, I'll tell you now, since you will undoubtedly discover it on your own, Father Sydney is very well connected in the diocese. His family has great influence in fund-raising for several of our charities. And for the college.''

There it was again. Money. Lifting up its green lizard head and blinking sullen, golden eyes. Money for Eyeball Edwards, money for Lester Karkis. Now money for Father Sydney. Of course, there needn't be any connection, where money was concerned. It was a common lizard, found under lots of different dirty rocks.

''The family,'' I said. ''They were worried about the scandal?''

The monsignor shook his great head, looking sorrowful.

''Father Sydney's family doesn't know the source of his illness, Jack. They assume he is suffering from a nervous disorder. If they suspect anything, it's that he has a drinking problem. Which indeed he does, the poor demented soul. No doubt he was under the influence of drink when he allowed himself his forbidden pleasure with that colored boy.''

I let that settle for a while, as I sipped at the coffee. It was excellent coffee. I tried some raspberry jam on the soda bread. Heavenly was no exaggeration.

''What I don't understand, Father, is why you're telling me all this.''

Monsignor McCue folded his hands across his ample belly. He seemed content, watching me nibble at the bread of his table.

''We're gambling, Jack. Throwing the dice. Trusting to providence, or rather, to your goodwill, in hopes that if you must make use of the information, you'll do so without involving the media. What I've told you about Father Sydney is definitely not something we want publicized. Neither is it a deep dark secret. Not so deep, we judge, that a man with your talent for puzzles couldn't ferret it out eventually. Then there's Father Duvall. Napoleon has many talents, but lying isn't one of them. Just between you and me and the lamppost, it has hindered the advancement of his career. Doesn't like to play the political game, Napoleon."

"Unlike yourself."

He liked that. He put back his head and laughed silently, his belly and chest vibrating with the joy of it. It is a strange thing to watch, a large man laughing heartily and making no sound. When he was done he wiped his eyes and said, "Oh, you're a card, Jack Hawkins. I knew we'd get on. Yes, you're right, I'm a game player. I have my faith and my church and if necessary I'll lie like a rug to defend them."

"Are you telling me the truth now?"

"If you like, I'll swear on the good book."

"Where have you got Father Sydney stashed?" I asked. "I'd like to talk to him."

The monsignor shifted the glance of his small blue eyes.

"I can't lie to you about that, not after you've broken bread with me," he said. "I'm just not going to tell you. He's in a safe place. Out of harm's way. He's had treatment for the booze and now he's being counseled for the other problem. More than that I cannot say. His Eminence the Archbishop forbids it. Father Sydney is out of circulation, and there he will stay until His Eminence decides otherwise."

"Father, two boys have been killed. One or maybe both were murdered. Another man died rescuing two children. Eyeball Edwards got shot. A guy named Lester Karkis, it is entirely possible he didn't commit suicide. That's a whole lot of violent death, and I think Father Sydney may know something about it."

The monsignor raised his hands and turned them palms upward. "His Eminence has spoken on this subject, Jack. Unless you carry a lot of weight in the Vatican, there is no higher appeal. Who knows, maybe His Eminence will change his mind. It's happened before. Though rarely."

I nodded. "This raspberry jam is divine," I said. "Does it come from heaven, too, like the bread? And the archbishop?"

Monsignor McCue reared back and laughed again. If you listened hard you could almost hear him.

The good monsignor wanted me to autograph copies of my books. He had all of the Casey series there, in hardcover editions, several of which looked suspiciously new. Unread, in fact. I affixed my signature to the title pages in indelible ink and thanked him for the coffee, the bread, and the entertainment.

I left him smiling. Maybe his mood would carry over to the unfortunate Father O'Hare, who entered as I left, smelling strongly of mouthwash and the sweat of fear. Outside, the hollow elm loomed over the chancery roof spires. The cables holding it upright vibrated in the wind. I decided that what kept the tree from crashing through the building was not wire, but faith, or the appearance of it.

6

FINIAN X. FITZGERALD STOOD ABOVE THE model of the rooftop where Horatio Jones had been gunned down. He had a weapon in his hands, a .38 Detective Special. Fitzy raised the gun, sighted down the short barrel, and brought it to bear on the doll that represented Horatio Jones. His eyes bulged. He blew air into his ruddy cheeks and said. "Bang!"

At least one of the jurors jumped. Tom Dennet objected for the city and Judge Skittles sustained. Not that it mattered. Fitzy had made his point.

With a grim smile he carried the weapon to the jury box, holding it in his cupped hands. He gave it first to Mrs. Escovitz, who examined the gun with undisguised loathing before passing it on to the next juror.

In the witness box, waiting patiently—he looked like he might doze off—was the ballistics expert. With one hand in his coat pocket and the other on the box rail, Fitzy resumed his questioning.

"Mr. Frank, after you examined the serial number on Detective Edward's revolver, did you then examine three .38 caliber slugs that had been turned over to you by the medical examiner?"

"Yes, sir, I did."

"And did the medical examiner inform you that the slugs had been taken from the body of a thirteen-year-old boy, Horatio Jones?"

"Yes, sir, he did."

Fitzy took an envelope from his pocket and spilled the contents into his hand. He showed the hand to the ballistics expert.

"Are these the slugs fired from Detective Edwards's gun, the slugs that entered the heart and chest of thirteen-year-old Horatio Jones?''

''Yes, sir. They are.''

Fitzy walked over the the jury box. He handed the spent slugs, misshapen and dented from smashing into Horatio Jones, still bearing traces of dried blood and tissue, to Mrs. Escovitz—who looked as though she was about to cry, or faint.

Always give them the guns, Fitzy insists. Let the jury handle the deadly weapon. Let them look at what happens to a piece of lead when it enters a human body. He'd done exactly that when he was suing the department on my behalf: When he referred to me he never failed to say ''permanently handicapped Jack Hawkins,'' just as now he never failed to remind the jury of Horatio's youth.

From the peanut gallery it appeared that Finian X. Fitzgerald was firmly in control of the case and the testimony. After entering his ballistics evidence, he called a number of witnesses, all of whom had one way or another been involved with job-performance evaluation of Detective Edwards. Most of the witnesses were either on the cops or, as in the case of the department psychiatrist, dependent on department contracts for their livelihoods.

One of their exchanges went like this:

> PLAINTIFF: So would you agree, Dr. Goldstein, that a tragic mistake was made when your evaluation of Detective Edwards was ignored by the review board?
> RESPONDENT: Well, hindsight is always twenty-twenty. But yes, in light of the several other incidents that involved the excessive use of force, I would have to agree. All the danger signals were there, as I noted in my evaluation of the detective.
> PLAINTIFF: Thank you, Dr. Goldstein. Your witness.

DEFENSE: Dr. Goldstein, would you say that psychiatry is an exact science?
RESPONDENT: No. If anything it's more of an art.
DEFENSE: That will be all. Thank you, doctor.

If City Attorney Tom Dennet had anything more clever than that up his sleeve, he was saving it for redress, or his own parade of witnesses. During a recess Fitzy was jubilant.

"We got 'em on the run," he said, putting his big arm around his assistant attorney. "Would you agree we got 'em on the run, Milty?"

Milton Pridham blushed and agreed. He looked very uncomfortable in Fitzy's friendly embrace. Beacon Hill Brahmins aren't big on Irish bear hugs. Wrinkles the artfully padded shoulders of their Brooks Brothers suits.

"We're gonna kill 'em," Fitzy said. "We're gonna wipe 'em out."

Peter Sylvia was onto something. Either that or he was taking uppers. His eyes were hidden behind tinted aviator glasses, but the rest of his face twitched with excitement. The short mustache trembled as he talked, kneeling beside my chair while we waited for Judge Skittles to return.

"I've been collating my notes, piles and piles of them. Doing a lot of simple arithmetic, putting two and two together and coming up three. Triangles, darling, that's what makes the world go round."

His movie-star caps were much on display, in gleaming white contrast to his sunlamp tan. Sylvia had traded in the leather look, duding himself up with a wide-lapel cotton jacket. He had ruined the sleeves by rolling them up in the fashion then current. His trousers, the color of creamed asparagus, were pleated at the waist and pegged at the cuff. The wide suspenders that helped hold them up were vertically striped. All he needed was a a yard of fob chain and a pair of spats and he would be equipped to do a serviceable honky imitation of Cab Calloway.

Kicking the gong around.

"All the pieces are there," he said, looking around to see that no one was listening in on our conversation. "We just have to fit 'em together, see what the big picture looks like."

"I thought you were talking about arithmetic," I said. "Two and two makes three. Or was it geometry?"

"I'm serious. There's a pattern here. I never went in for conspiracy theories—too pat. But when you mentioned priests the other day, I got to thinking. Maybe this is bigger than Lester Karkis and some creepy cop from the Vice Unit. All those Very Important Fags Lester knew. This could be high up. Somebody with enough leverage to squash a full investigation."

"I think it was J.F.K.," I said. "After he faked his assassination in Dallas he was hiding out in the back of Teddy's car at Chappaquidick. He swam away after it went over the bridge and he's been living under Boston harbor ever since. Every full moon he crawls up out of the mud and goes in for a steambath in Bay Village. He's still Catholic, of course, so he was looking for a priest to confess to."

Sylvia grinned. I was almost blinded.

"The priest," he said, "is Lee Harvey Oswald."

"I think we have the makings of a best-seller."

"You ever need a job, we can use you at the *Gay Village Banner*."

"Not if I have to wear pegged pants."

"Seriously, though, you have someone specific in mind? You mentioned was a priest ever seen at one of Lester's special parties?"

"Yeah, Spencer Tracy."

Sylvia grimaced, then patted me on the knee. I didn't feel a thing.

"Okay, we'll play it cozy. I get something juicy, I'll get in touch and we can work out a trade."

I nodded. Sylvia stood up, adjusting the pleats in his trousers. He slipped into his seat as Skittles hobbled into court. We'd had fun kidding around, but I was beginning to think maybe there *was* some sort of conspiracy in the wind. There were a couple of organizations that might be worth sniffing around. The Boston archdiocese was one. The Homicide Unit was another.

Lieutenant Detective Sullivan was down in Records, Marilyn told me. Yes, I was welcome to wait in his office. She left the frosted-glass door wide open. Just a little prudent caution, to make sure I didn't rifle his desk. I sat there in full view of the clerical staff, leafing through one of Sully's *New Yorker* magazines. Very popular among homicide detectives, right up there with *American Riflemen* and *NRA Today*.

I read the cartoons and looked in vain for any racy lingerie ads. Maybe the women who read the *New Yorker* don't wear underwear. Evidently the readership is more interested in diamonds, perfume, Mercedes Benzes, and the Wisconsin Cheese of the Month Club. But then what can you expect of people who take Pauline Kael seriously?

Sullivan entered, carrying a Styrofoam takeout carton.

"So tell me," I said, holding the magazine up, "are you one of those who take Pauline seriously?"

Sully ignored me. He sat down at his desk and opened the Styrofoam container. He took a plastic fork out and began to toss the wilted salad within. Diced carrots, yellowish broccoli, and a hard rubber disk masquerading as a tomato slice. The Styrofoam looked tastier.

"You want," I suggested, "we could go over to the Copley Bar for happy hour. They have actual food over there."

"I assume you want something, you come in here and insult my lunch."

"Just a question," I said, drawing closer to his desk, aware that the door remained open and that Marilyn had ears like radar scoops. "You have any friends high up in the Catholic Church?"

Sullivan squinted at me. He finished his mouthful of limp lettuce. He put down his fork. He crossed his fingers and said, "Yeah, me and the Pope are like this."

"So you don't have any influence in the archdiocese?"

"Let me put it this way, Jack. Last time I went to mass I was wearing knee pants. Now what prompts this sudden interest in the Church. You getting religion?"

I told him what I knew about the Roxbury Boys' Mission, Father Sydney, and my theory that the missing priest might have information pertinent to the deaths of the two boys. As I laid it out Sully got up and eased his door shut. He went back to his desk, glared at the Styrofoam salad, and flicked it into his waste basket.

"The bathhouse angle, Lester Karkis, we're looking into that. The priest, this is new information. I think I'd like to have a chat with the father, we ever find out where they have him tucked away. You got any solid information that he participated in these sick kiddy parties Karkis arranged?"

"No. But Russ White has sources who tell him Spenser Eames was well known in Bay Village. Peddling his twelve-year-old ass until he found that peddling dope was easier and more lucrative."

"Good old Russ tell you who his source was?"

I admitted he hadn't. That made Sully smile.

"It was me," he said. "I got it out of those blockheads over the Vice Unit. Who, damn it, should have reported it to Internal Affairs when they ran the original investigation on the shoot."

It was mind-boggling, Sully leaking information to the press. It was like the sphinx breaking into conversation. Unless . . .

"What are you doing, Tim?" I asked. "Trying to stir up the rubble, see what runs out?"

"Rats," he said. "That's what runs out, you stir up the rubble.

Great big rats with long ugly tails. Some of 'em even carry badges.''

As I left he had changed his mind about lunch and was fishing around in the waste bin, trying to recover his Styrofoam salad.

7

THINGS STARTED TO GO BAD LATER THAT NIGHT, after Meg and I returned from the Erlich Theatre, where we'd seen a revival of *The Petrified Forest*. We'd had a drink at the Ritz Bar afterward, just for the opportunity to rub shoulders with the rich and the elegant. I'd had a large bourbon and soda and come home feeling spunky.

"What I want to know," I said as Meg slipped off her wrap, "is where was Humphrey Bogart? I went in there expecting Bogie, I get some skinny guy from Brockton."

"It was live theatre, Jack," Megan said with a glint in her eye. "In case you didn't notice."

"Yeah? You mean those were live actors? You could have fooled me."

"You're impossible," Meg said. She kicked her shoes off and plopped down next to the fireplace, where a few embers glowed in the pile of ash. "You've got no right to complain, since you were asleep for most of the last act."

"Quid pro quo," I said. "My Latin is pretty bad. Does that apply?"

Meg shook her head sadly. "My poor mother. She's under the impression I'm marrying an intellectual, because you write books."

The telephone rang. I got over to it in time to pick up before the answering machine cut in.

"Hawkins speaking," I said. "Keep it to words of one syllable."

It was Peter Sylvia. He sounded as high as a kite, either on drugs or adrenaline.

"My first question," he said. "Will they have the courage to award the Pulitzer to a gay weekly? My second question, should I get in touch with Standish House before or after I break the story in the *Banner?* My third question, what kind of advance will Harold Standish offer for a guaranteed best-seller?"

"That's a lot of questions. What gives?"

"You're not going to believe it," he said. "But I got lucky. It was one of those coincidental things, but I found the second priest."

More than that he would not say.

"I don't know about *your* telephone, but I'm almost positive this one is tapped. Routine surveillance of a commie faggot newspaper."

I said I would be right over. Sylvia gave me the address and warned me that it was hard to find.

"I'll keep an eye out," he said. "When you think you're on the right block, honk your horn. I'll be waiting."

Megan insisted on coming. She had that look in her eye that said there was no use arguing about it.

The streets of Bay Village were coated with slush and faintly lit by neon tubes. As neighborhoods go it is small and amorphous. The old combat zone is nearby. Some of it spilled over as the Park Square renovation chewed up the area. We circled through the narrow streets several times, coming up against dead ends, or the barricade to the turnpike. I had the van in low gear, creeping up on intersections, my internal compass totally out of whack.

"Sylvia thinks there's a conspiracy," I said. "There is. A conspiracy to tear down, remove, or deface street signs."

On one of the busier streets I noticed that Karkis's old bathhouse club was still in business, under a different name. A very large and very black bouncer lounged in the doorway, wearing tight leather pants, a tight leather jacket, and a fistful of gold rings. He didn't look like the type of guy who would pass out bath towels.

We turned the corner. I tried another narrow side street, and another. Somehow we ended up back at the bathhouse.

"Nuts," I said.

"You could pull over and ask," Meg suggested.

''Only tourists do that,'' I said. ''Or someone looking for a whore.''

The whores in the area came in all three sexes. From a few yards away, cruising slowly by, it was hard to distinguish who was advertising what to whom. Spiky hairdos with sparkling highlights, red jackboots, denim cowboys, black prostitutes rigged out in huge fake furs. Transvestites tall enough to play semipro basketball. Vampires of the night, stalking not-so-innocent prey. Take your pick.

''Edgar Allen Poe was born right around here,'' Meg said. ''Imagine that.''

''The Pit and the Pudendum.''

''Honestly,'' she said, ''you are the grossest person I know.''

''Name of a club we just passed.''

''Oh.''

Sylvia had mentioned, as a landmark, a restaurant called Cheever's. Eventually Meg noticed the faint lettering in its shuttered window. I pulled up, idling, and gave the horn a beep. Fat drops of dense wet snow dissolved against the windshield.

''I think we passed through into another dimension,'' I said. ''See the signpost up ahead?''

''No,'' Meg said, staring anxiously into the dark street.

I made Twilight Zone noises. She laughed. On that night, in that place, it was a very pleasant sound.

''Earth to Peter Sylvia,'' I said, trying for another laugh. ''Come in please.''

I gave the horn a few taps. It was Megan who saw him first.

''Up the block,'' she said. ''There's a guy waving his arms.''

I used my forearm to clear the mist from the inside of the windshield.

''That's him. Lean back so I can see the sideview, I'm going to pull up.''

Megan shrank back into the seat as I peered into the mirror, pulling out into the street. Headlights filled the mirror. I jerked down on the brake lever. Meg tumbled forward, bumping her head on the dash. A black shadow zoomed by, rocking the van. It was accelerating.

"Son of a *bitch.*" I said. "You okay?"

Meg was rubbing her forehead. "Yeah," she said. "They almost clipped off the mirror, it was that close."

"Crazy bastard," I said, checking the mirror again. When I was certain no one else was coming I eased into the street.

"Okay, Sylvia, where'd you go?"

I had the wipers on, clearing the slush from the windshield. Through the blur it was obvious the corner where he'd been standing was now empty. I assumed the weather had driven him back inside, wherever that was. I tapped the horn again.

"Jack," Megan said urgently. *"Look."*

In the glare of my headlights I could just make out a ragged bundle of clothing in the middle of the street. I stopped immediately and set the emergency brake. The bundle of clothing was leaking, spreading a dark stain into the slush-coated pavement. Meg looked at me, her eyes as large as moons. The silence in the van was stifling. I cracked open the vent window and bent down to suck at the cold air. Megan made a small, frightened animal sound and then opened her door. Before I could respond she was outside.

Meg was swallowed up by the night for a few heartbeats, then reappeared in the circle of the headlights. She stood over the bundle, crouched, then jumped up quickly, putting her hands to her mouth. I put the emergency blinkers on and headed for the back of the van.

It took forever for the lift to lower me to the pavement. As I rolled through the slush toward Megan I noticed that the sidewalks were deserted. Only moments before they had been, if not teeming, at least thinly populated.

"There's so much blood, Jack," Megan said, clutching at me. "He's not moving."

"The restaurant. Go bang on the door, tell them to call an ambulance."

Peter Sylvia had been crushed, undoubtedly by the vehicle that had nearly clipped our side mirror. His body seemed to be melting into the pavement. One arm turned up at a crazy angle, fingers extended. The back of his head was a fruity pulp. I could hear Megan smashing her fists against the restaurant door, screaming for them to open up. A siren sounded in the distance, and then another, coming from a different direction.

The fat wet snowflakes kept coming down, appearing in the circle of light. They were nice snowflakes and they were trying to make a blanket for Peter Sylvia. He kept melting them with his blood. I heard Megan coming up behind me, her boots splashing. As I turned back toward her she clenched her fists and screamed.

Part of Peter Sylvia stirred. His back, twisted and broken, began to arch. His bloody head lifted from the slush, trembling violently. The face he turned toward the headlights was a mask of blood. Three holes opened in the mask. Two unseeing eyes and a row of perfect, gleaming teeth.

There was a wrenching spasm and his head fell back and did not move again.

While we waited for the sirens I tried to convince Megan that he had already been gone, that what we had had the misfortune to witness was part of a final muscle spasm. By the time the first ambulance arrived the snow was winning, making a icy shroud for the dead.

The first cops on the scene were from Area A. Suspecting the worst, they ordered the van impounded and took Meg and me into custody. I as too numbed to put up much of a fuss when they put us in separate cruisers. The last I saw of Megan for the next several hours, she was pressing the palm of her hand against the rear window of the sedan that carried her off. I was being loaded into a different backseat while a baby-faced cop tried to figure out how to fold up my wheelchair and stow it in the trunk.

The cop who was driving offered to share coffee from his Thermos. I declined.

''Hey,'' he said. ''These things happen. It was snowing, the visibility is bad. Boom, he probably came out of nowhere.''

''It was a black car. I only just glimpsed it,'' I said.

''Anything you say.''

''The victim,'' I said, ''was a guy named Sylvia.''

The cop said, ''In this neighborhood, I'm not surprised. Must be kinda tricky driving with your handicap. Maybe tough getting to the brakes, huh?''

It was not tough at all, but I was in no mood for explanations. I was thinking that Spenser ''Speedy'' Eames had been the victim of a hit-and-run. I had figured Eyeball for that one. Maybe I had figured wrong. Maybe I didn't know a goddamn thing.

Yes, I decided, my ignorance was astounding.

It wasn't until Larry Sheehan finally arrived, at about three in the morning, that I knew for sure Megan was being held in the same building. Sheehan was drenched. The only thing dry about him was the cigarette parked in the corner of his mouth, and his wit.

''What is it with you and dead bodies,'' he said, taking his soaked trenchcoat off. He dropped it over the back of a chair. Immediately water began to pool on the floor under it. ''Damn good thing you passed the breathalyzer, pal. Was it you driving or the girlfriend?''

I explained that the way the van had been modified, only I could drive it. But Sheehan knew that already. He was just prying.

''Wouldn't you know tonight would be the night I got lucky?'' he said, throwing a leg over a chair and scooting it around to face me. ''I'm at the bar in Jason's, I pick up this cute little number, tells me she's a stewardess for Eastern. I tell her great, let's take the shuttle to my place. To my immense surprise, she agrees. I put on the soft music, lower the lights, feed her a brandy that would drop a St. Bernard in its tracks, and then the fucking phone rings. Beautiful.''

Sheehan waited. His hair was slicked down, clinging to his bony skull. His eyes were deep and slightly boozy. It wasn't only the stewardess who had been drinking brandy. His thin, hatchet-shaped face creased in a smile as he waited for me to reply.

''Whatsa matter, Hawkins? You always got some wise remark.''

I was fresh out of wisdom. I had no ideas, no plans. I was just a cripple in a wheelchair, dependent on the kindness of strangers.

''Where's Megan?'' I asked. ''Is she okay?''

Sheehan studied me. I could smell his breath, and the perfume that clung to him.

''The little lady is A-okay. She's shook up. I can't say I blame her, I heard it was a real mess. They took a statement and let her go. Now she's out at the desk, making the usual threats. Your shyster lawyer friend is out there, too. All they need is you, they can have a party.''

My brain was full of static. The white noise inside my head kept short-circuiting any coherent thoughts.

''I never even saw the license plate,'' I told Sheehan. ''The car was black and fast.''

Sheehan smiled sadly and shook his head. The cigarette looked like a fang in the corner of his mouth. Maybe he was a vampire cop, stalking the walking dead. Stalking the walking, I liked that. It had rhythm. It had poetry.

''Black and fast,'' he mused. ''Hell of a description. I figured a sharp guy like you would know the serial number by now.''

''He wasn't quite dead,'' I said. ''I told Megan it was just nerves, or a muscle spasm. But he lifted up his head.''

''You poor bugger,'' Sheehan said. Smoke curled up from the white fang. His eyes were bloodshot.

''He was all smashed up. Crazy-looking.''

''Go on,'' Sheehan said. ''Get out of here. We'll go over it after you've had some sleep.''

''He looked at me,'' I said. ''Right in the eye.''

''Go on, beat it.''

It was Megan who finally came in and took me out of there.

8

I DREAMED ABOUT THE ESKIMO. IN MY DREAM I woke up and saw him standing in the corner of the darkened bedroom. He was covered with sheets of ice. Ice hat. Ice trench coat. Ice trouser legs. Shoes of ice. His eyes were open. They were not icy eyes. They were Lew Quinn's eyes and they were trying to tell me something.

What is it? I said, *What do you want?*

His mouth was frozen shut. The Eskimo could not speak or move in his icy suit of lights, but his eyes continued to implore me.

I woke up shivering.

Megan left me a note. Something about galley proofs that she absolutely had to attend to—much, much love and she would see me later, alligator.

For the first time ever I envied her for having a job to go to.

The apartment was as empty as a tomb. That suited my mood exactly. I decided there was no real point in attending the trial—Fitzy and Milton Pridham were doing fine without any help from the peanut gallery. Also I would avoid having to answer any of Russ White's questions, as he was sure to be there. I was hiding out, licking my wounds.

Too many Styrofoam cups of the Area A brew had put me off coffee. I made a pot of tea and drank most of it, sitting by the sliders and gazing out at the Charles. The river was frozen over, all but a narrow, blackish gap in the middle that stirred sluggishly, forming wavelets as Cambridge huffed and puffed her powdery gusts toward the Boston side of the world. The sailing dinghies had been pulled up on the municipal docks. They looked like frozen plastic toys. The Christmas lights strung in the bare trees along the Esplanade had been left on. In the wan daylight the faint, glowing bulbs were like luminous drops of ice. The

Hatch Shell, coated with a thin layer of snow, looked fragile and lonesome.

I turned on WGBH. Robert Lurtsema was pronouncing Bach. It sounded like he was trying to clear his throat.

"Shut up and play the music," I said to the radio. He did.

I found the second priest.

It was no good going over it again. It still didn't mean anything to me. What second priest? Assuming Father Sydney was the first, the original sinner, then who was the other? Father Duvall? Absurd. He was a watchdog, a secret policeman in the soldiers of Christ, hardly a participant. Monsignor McCue? That was a little more interesting, but still it led nowhere. McCue was covering for the chancery, clamping a lid on scandal. He was simply too large and confident of his place and purpose to risk it all by slinking around Bay Village and ducking into bathhouses, had he been so inclined.

I was left holding an empty collar, clutching at a ghost priest.

Later that afternoon Mary Kean brought me a Christmas present. Her name was Felicia.

"Megan is swimming in galleys," Mary said, after she had introduced the thin woman with brittle, shoulder-length red hair. The woman was covered in an ankle-length gray cape. Under it she wore a starched white blouse and a tweed skirt. "She said to tell you she'd be late. I'm supposed to give you a kiss, but I've got a cold, so I won't."

"How is she?"

Mary gave me a look, patted me on the arm. "Megan Drew is as tough as nails. As you well know. So do us all a favor, stop looking so damned worried."

The two women sat down on opposite ends of the couch. Mary took a box of tissues from her bag and set them on the coffee table.

"You sound like a honking goose."

"That's a B-flat," she said snuffling into a tissue. "This is a B-flat flu."

"I get it."

Mary settled herself into the couch. Felicia, whom I judged to be about forty-five, sat stiffly, her knees pressed together. She directed a prim, ethereal smile my way.

"Felicia wrote a book," Mary said.

So that was it. Another novelist. Mary Kean, dear editor that she was, had the mistaken belief that writers like to socialize with one another. This is true only in the sense that sharks like to circle together. I nodded at Felicia and waited for Mary to stop honking.

"God, what wretched weather," Mary said when she'd caught her breath. "As I was saying, Felicia wrote a book, we brought it out last year. *Slave of the Immaculate Heart*. About when she was still Sister Felicia, one of the last of the cloistered nuns. Her trials and tribulations and her eventual decision to enter the world again. Is that a fair outline, Felicia?"

Felicia nodded, her eyes distant, enigmatic.

"Lisha knows a thing or two about the Catholic Church, Jack. The Boston archdiocese in particular."

I admitted that I had recently developed an interest in the Church.

"Tell you what, Jack. You pour us a couple of glasses of white wine, we'll provide the entertainment. I myself have been doing a little research on a certain family Meg tells me you're curious about. The Owen Sydneys of Chestnut Hill and Isle Bright, Maine."

I got a bottle of wine and a bottle of Molson ale from the refrigerator, cradled both in my lap, and wheeled back in. Mary had already set out three glasses. I poured. Felicia picked hers up and held it without tasting it, nodding her thanks. A very quiet lady, ex-Sister Felicia.

Mary took out a sheaf of notes in a manila folder. She set her reading glasses on the end of her nose, sniffed, and arranged the pages on the table. Felicia held her glass of wine and waited, virtually motionless. I noticed faint splotches of brown freckles on her milky skin. Posed as she was, embracing the otherworldly stillness of the moment, she might have been painted by Wyeth, fixed forever in egg tempera.

"The money is Owen Machine Tools. Mrs. Ethel Sydney's late father. Divested in the late forties, leaving an estate now valued in the several hundreds of millions. Big bucks. Mrs. Sydney is the matriarch, takes her role very seriously indeed. Husband died young, plane crash. Before exiting he fathered three children, two girls and a boy: Theresa, Margaret, and Kurt. To say that Mrs. Sydney is a devout believer is to say that Willy Mays played a little baseball. This is a woman who *lives* her religion, with the kind of wholehearted commitment Lisha tells me is not untypical of converts. Mrs. Sydney was raised a Midwest Lutheran, but converted to Catholicism shortly after her marriage. Husband, the late Stewart Mill Sydney, was only nominally Catholic."

Mary looked up over the reading glasses to see if I was paying attention. I was.

"An interesting aside is who converted Mrs. Sydney. Who gave her instruction. I'll give you a hint; his last name starts with C."

"Caligula."

Felicia laughed. It happened very quickly and I almost didn't catch it. One clear peal of a bell, immediately muted.

"Cushing, as in Cardinal Cushing, although this was before he got the hat. A charismatic man, Cushing. You're maybe a couple years too young to remember him like I do, but the man had a great nose. A great big bulb of a thing with a character all its own. You want to make cardinal, get the hat and the throne, you first have to have a spectacular sniffer. And when it came to sniffing out money, Cushing was a bloodhound. Remember him with the Kennedys? That was politics and power and a lot of free publicity. Not to mention votes. But the Sydneys, or I should say Ethel Owen Sydney, that was very quiet money. A research library for Holy Cross. The gymnasium for a parochial school in Fall River. Mrs. Sydney thinks nothing of dropping a million or so in the collection box, when the cardinal passes it to her. This has made her very popular at the chancery. She's on her third cardinal now. He inherited the old girl, or he hopes to inherit the bulk of the Owen-Sydney fortune—for the archdiocese, of course. Every Thursday afternoon the cardinal's limo cruises over to the Chestnut Hill estate, picks her up, brings her back to the chancery. She and the cardinal kneel in the private chapel he's got over there. He hears her confession. They pray together. For penance she endows a new wing at the law school, or buys a new country for the Maryknolls."

There was another peal of the bell. Felicia covered her mouth. Over the elegant hand her eyes smiled.

"Theresa and Margaret are both Maryknoll nuns. Sister Terry is in San Salvador. Sister Peg is in Nicaragua. This is a source of great pride for Mrs. Sydney. It is a source of great revenue for the Maryknoll Sisters. Nobody will say exactly, but the scuttlebutt is that Mrs. Sydney has deposited about half of the fortune into various church coffers. We are talking well in excess of one hundred million simoleons, Jack."

"Saint Ethel of the Sacred Trust."

"Exactly. They know who she is in the Vatican, believe me. Private audience with himself, the guy with the ring and the beanie. Every Easter. Then there are the pilgrimages. Mrs. Sydney likes to travel. Her itinerary is confined to places where people were burned at the stake or where miracles have been rumored. Lourdes, Fatima. Recently she spent ten days in Ireland, hoping to see a statue of the Virgin Mary shed tears. Many people, the parish priest included, claim to have seen the statue cry. It didn't cry for Mrs. Sydney. Why should it cry? She'd just given the parish a stretch Mercedes. With a cellular phone.''

''You haven't mentioned the son. Father Sydney.''

''Patience, my child. I'm giving you deep background. You might pour a little more wine into my chalice, while you're at it.''

I poured. Felicia kept her glass back, guarding it with both hands. Maybe she thought I was trying to get her drunk and take advantage of her. It would have been easier to scale Everest on my elbows.

''What I am stressing here, for an understanding of the very enclosed world that spawned Kurt Owen Sydney, is how much his mother has given to the Church. Not only the money, but her children. The girls were in the best parochial schools from kindergarten on, virtually raised by nuns. Kurt was something of a problem child, or got that way after his father died in that plane crash. Very disturbed. Inconsolable. He was ten at the time, refused to attend classes with other students. Screaming tantrums, copious tears, very difficult. Mother Ethel, who has never been the affectionate type, begged for Cushing's advice. The cardinal provided the tutors, all seminary students. He saw no reason to force the boy, since he was a child of privilege. Also, we can assume, he saw it as an opportunity for gentle indoctrination. It will come as no surprise that Mrs. Sydney's fondest dream was that her only son enter the service of God.'' Mary paused to shuffle through her notes, fussing with her reading glasses. ''So the two biggest influences in your Kurt's life were his mother and God. It may be that he had trouble distinguishing between the two. His father, who the boy was very attached to, and who he lost at an tender age, was in heaven. This was indisputable.''

''He never had a chance.''

Mary used a tissue, tucked it away, and looked at me. ''That's the obvious conclusion, that he was railroaded into the clergy.

But he had ample opportunity to make up his own mind. After four years in a seminary he took a leave of absence. Lisha tells me this is not unusual. Often it is encouraged. Give the young man a chance to see something of the world, see if he genuinely has a calling. Apparently Kurt felt he did. Four years of Boston College, major in sociology. Graduate school at Georgetown, doctorate in theology. One year of postdoctoral work, and then he becomes a Dominican. Not, by the way, the order favored by his mother, who wanted a Jesuit. And again no rush to judgment. Kurt is not ordained as Father Sydney until he is thirty-one. He teaches for only one semester at B.C., then gets the parish posting, his own choice, we assume. A poor neighborhood in Chicago. He leaves rather suddenly after two years, spends several months in retreat. Now a curious thing happens. Mother, at the cardinal's request, funds an orphanage in that poor Chicago parish. Possibly even the cardinal didn't know the specifics of why that might be necessary, to make the gesture. Next thing for Kurt, he takes a posting in Brookline. This, we can assume, was to please his mother. We do know, from what Lisha learned, that Father Sydney was not happy in Brookline. Complained about serving as pastor to the privileged. Mommy responds by suggesting a special mission in Roxbury—also not far from Chestnut Hill as the crow flies. Convenient to the Sydney estate. Kurt agrees, indeed seems to have expressed genuine enthusiasm for the idea. Only thing, he refuses to let mother endow the boys' mission. Like all Dominicans he has taken a vow of poverty and intends to keep it in his own way. Wants to rally community support from within and decides best way to do it is to mimic the Baptist storefront, dirt poor but God-fearing. Has some initial success, then an unspecified setback. Father Napoleon Duvall joins the mission. Six months later Father Sydney takes an extended leave of absence. Reason given, ill health. Real reason, can't keep his hands off the boys."

"The mother doesn't know?"

Mary shrugged. "She doesn't want to know. Kurt has always been a sensitive type. Nerve problems. She has been told he has perhaps a slight drinking problem, exacerbated by overwork. He is undergoing therapy. Meanwhile Mrs. Sydney has insisted that the Roxbury mission be kept open, in case he should want to resume his work there, once his health is restored."

A picture of Kurt Owen Sydney was starting to take shape in my mind. A boy mourning for his father, shaped by a devout mother who appeared to love only God. The boy eventually becomes a priest tormented by his faith, never entirely certain of his direction. A soul seeking the innocence he cannot find within himself. A man struggling to resist his baser instincts, thrown again and again into temptation. Falling back into a cycle of booze, debauchery, and self-destruction, all obscured and confused by a veil of incense.

"Of particular interest," Mary said, "is the fact that all three of the Sydney heirs have entered orders that require the vow of poverty. So long as they remain in those orders, they cannot directly inherit. A cynic would conclude that it is very much in the interests of the archdiocese that Father Sydney retain his faith. If not his sanity."

"Are you a cynic?" I asked Felicia. "Is that what you think?"

Felicia looked momentarily embarrassed. No smug cynicism there.

"They're trying to protect the poor man," she said. "Some of them have good reasons, others not. I doubt very much he will ever again be put into contact with underage boys. Understand, I never met father. But I know of others like him. Probably, once he is released, he will be given a research post, light clerical duties. His doctorate is in theology, he may be encouraged to pursue that in a quiet way. Possibly, with the kind of weight has family carries, he will go to Rome. Such tastes as his are not encouraged at the Vatican, but they are more easily overlooked there."

I asked Felicia if she knew where Father Sydney was being hidden.

"I can make an educated guess," she said, looking at the hands she had folded in her lap. "Only a guess."

"Go on," Mary said. "Tell him."

"There's a place. Sort of a combined hospital and retreat," she said. She took a sip of the wine, not a small one, and leveled her eyes at me. "The priests who get sent there call it the leper colony."

Mary Kean was beaming. She tossed off the last of the wine and sighted me through the empty glass. The corners of the world softened as the winter light began to fade. Felicia waited.

"You got any idea," I said to her, "how a guy like me might go about getting in to visit the lepers?"

Felicia and Mary exchanged looks. Then Felicia nodded. "I think what we can do," she said, "we can fake it."

9

MEGAN WAS WORRIED ABOUT GETTING STRUCK by lightning. I was worried about getting stopped by the Providence cops. Felicia wasn't worried about much of anything.

"Relax," she told us. "You both look great. Very convincing."

Felicia was in the van's jumpseat, belt securely fastened, giving us a last-minute cram course on how to comport ourselves as the Reverend Father Hawkins and Sister Margaret Drew, of the Slaves of the Immaculate Heart of Mary.

"Sister *Margaret?*"

"Megan isn't a saint's name, dear. This way if Jack slips and calls you Meg it'll sound natural."

"Sister Margaret," I said, "you look sexy in black."

"Oh, shut up."

The thing about starched collars, they itch like the devil. Figure of speech. I had my hands full melding into the Providence traffic, fighting for a lane in the concrete trough that runs through the city. Providence had a lot of things going for it. The downtown was undergoing restoration, the neighborhoods were coming back, and the mayor was out of jail. It was the home of Brown University, Providence College, the Rhode Island mob, and our destination, the St. Francis Treatment Facility, a.k.a. the leper colony.

"But I don't know anything about the Slaves of the Immaculate Hearts," Megan complained. "They'll see right through me."

Felicia assured her that the Slaves were a little-known order in the western part of Massachusetts, virtually cloistered, and that no one at a Rhode Island Jesuit facility was likely to ask questions.

"If they do, just bow your head and look stricken. They'll take it for embarrassment. As one of the Slaves, you're not used to meeting new people.''

''You sure you don't want to play sister again, Felicia?''

Felicia said she was positive. For us, dressing in the glad rags of the order was simply a costume affair. For her it would be tantamount to sacrilege.

''I left the order,'' Felicia explained. ''I didn't leave the Church.''

We found the facility on an oak-lined lane adjacent to the Providence College campus. It was a massive late-Victorian building, originally constructed as a cedar-shingled resort hotel. Typical of that era, it was a sea of steeply pitched slate roofs from the eaves up. Gables, turrets and towers, all intersecting. The effect was windswept and foreboding. The rambling structure was set well back from the lane. Much of it was obscured by ragged hedges that ran higher than the ground floor. Salt air had kept the snow from gathering in the bare eaves and on the frost-scorched lawns. Here and there a white plastic candle was visible in an unshuttered window, the only tangible sign of the pending season.

''H. P. Lovecraft lived around here somewhere,'' Megan said. ''He probably walked by this place to put himself in the mood for one of his weird tales.''

''Get yourself in the mood, Sister. We're going in.''

''When the day comes,'' Meg said, ''and St. Peter wants an explanation for this, I'm blaming you.''

''Just play it like Hepburn and Tracy, my love,'' I said as we moved to the back of the van and prepared to descend. ''If you get nervous, fiddle with the rosary beads and move your lips.''

We left Felicia in the van, with instructions to start up the heater if it got chilly inside.

''Just be normal'' was her final instruction.

''Forget it,'' Megan responded, ''he's *never* been normal.''

Sister Margaret/Megan adjusted her black wool cape and pushed me up the long, curving walkway. With my shoulder hunched and my chin jutting into the collar, I thought it best to appear weak and defenseless. More an object of pity than suspicion.

Meg whispered, "If my mother could see me now, she'd hemorrhage."

As Felicia had promised, no one thought to ask for credentials. Evidently visitors were not uncommon, although we quickly got the idea they weren't encouraged. After some slight difficulty with the front steps, we entered what had been the grand foyer of the hotel. A young monk greeted us. He wore heavy brown robes, a sash with a wooden crucifix and a ring of keys. A fringe of fine brown hair surrounded the tonsure on his pate. Under his robe he had the build and the temperament of an institutional orderly, or a drill sergeant.

"I'm Brother Joseph," he said. "How may I help you?"

"Father Hawkins," I said, holding out my hand. Felicia had assured me that fellow clergymen shook hands like ordinary men. No secret handshakes. Brother Joseph's hand was strong and confident. "An old friend of mine is a, ah, *guest* here. Father Sydney. Kurt Owen Sydney."

Brother Joseph's brown eyes had been warm and friendly. Now they turned cool. Megan held the back of my wheelchair and studied the floor, most of her face obscured by the wimple.

"Oh, yes," he said guardedly. "Father Sydney. He's in the east wing, if I'm not mistaken. If you'll pardon my asking, Father, did you call him before coming down?"

The collar and the costume gave me confidence. Brother Joseph was mildly distrusting, but there was no indication that he doubted me as a priest. If he doubted me it was as a man, for the friends I kept.

"Kurt and I were at Georgetown together," I said, wheezing a little. "I hadn't heard from him in years. I got a call from a Father Duvall a few weeks ago when I had some business at the chancery. Duvall is colleague of Kurt's, I gather. Said the poor man had been having troubles. Might appreciate a visit from an old friend. The sister and I have business in Newport, and I was hoping to look in."

I coughed. Megan adjusted the shawl on my shoulders. Brother Joseph fell for it.

"Sister, please don't be offended, but we have our rules. I'll ask you to remain here. You are welcome to visit the chapel, of course."

Brother Joseph moved behind me and took over the chair. Megan backed away, hands clasped inside the folds of her habit. From under the wimple her eyes glared at me. I responded with a casual blessing. Tracy to Hepburn, over and out. She sat down in a highback chair, attempting to blend herself into the surroundings, black and white against varnished oak.

"Forgive me, Father," Brother Joseph said as he began to wheel me down a long hallway trimmed with dark wainscoting. "This is a matter of some delicacy. When you spoke with Napoleon—with Father Duvall, did he give you an idea of Father Sydney's illness?"

I coughed again and made myself wheeze. "If you're asking, do I know that Kurt disgraced himself, yes, I do. Father Duvall was vague as to the particulars. He was hopeful that therapy here might help poor Kurt overcome his . . . . problem."

"We speak openly of the problem here, Father. That is an essential part of our therapy. We call it homosexual obsession. In certain cases we encourage the afflicted to leave the clergy and adopt, if they must, the gay lifestyle. In Father Sydney's case, unfortunately, this is not a moral—or legal—option. His particular obsession is with the young. With preadolescent boys."

He wheeled me around to push me backward through the doors into the east wing.

"There were always rumors," I said quietly. "But I find it difficult to think of Kurt as a child molester."

We pushed through another, smaller, foyer. Several men sat around a card table in casual dress. None of them looked like child molesters. But then, who did? The card players nodded and waved at us as we passed through. Brother Joseph lowered his voice.

"Think of it as a compulsion," he suggested. "Father Sydney can't help himself. For a long time he used liquor as a crutch, seeking to hide the compulsion. He has undergone a long period of self-loathing. He was, for a time, a danger to himself."

I made sympathetic noises.

"Just lately, I think, we have seen some progress. He has begun to accept his condition and to deal with it accordingly."

"Can he be cured of this, ah, compulsion?"

We had entered a solarium. Winter light from the north suffused the small room. A picture window, newly installed, overlooked a barren meadow that curved gradually down to the waterfront. A shelf under the window held a variety of geraniums and paperwhites. Some were in bloom, others blighted.

"I though we might find Father Sydney here," Brother Joseph said. He placed my chair adjacent to a wicker rocker and sat down facing me. "He finds the light comforting at this time of day. Probably using the bathroom. Just as well." Speaking in a husky whisper, Brother Joseph kept his eye on the door. "As you haven't seen Kurt in some time, it might help to know a few things. If you've been up to the chancery you may have heard that when Kurt came to us the poor man was in very wretched condition. He had to be sedated and restrained. Determined to take his own life. There had been an incident with a fourteen-year-old boy. The fact that the boy evidently had considerable sexual experience—indeed may have made the initial advance—is not and should never be considered as an excuse for adult behavior. I can assure you that Father Sydney holds himself entirely responsible. This is a profane attraction he has been resisting all of his life, and it has put a terrible strain on the man. Slowly, I think, we have made some progress. The father has been encouraged to take up his studies again. We have a large collection of theology books here, and Father Sydney has been reading heavily, taking notes. The work has helped him put aside his despair. It has given him another focus.''

I asked again if there was a possibility of cure. Brother Joseph fingered the beads around his waist, giving it some thought as we waited. Beyond the frozen meadow, lines of white waves silently unfolded against the black shore.

''If it were simply that Father Sydney is homosexual, we would be trying our best to help him accept that. Of course, it would mean his leaving the clergy. There are gay organizations willing to cooperate with us—unofficially, of course. But Kurt is not a 'normal' homosexual. His attraction is to the preadolescent. The boy was fourteen but looked younger. Although Kurt struggles desperately, I'm afraid the rate of recidivism among pedophiles is very high. Normal therapy is woefully ineffective. We use group encounter, some confrontation, and in certain cases, as with Father Sydney, we have, with the permission of the client, used chemical controls. These, of course, merely dull the physical urge. They do not treat the root of the problem.''

''Saltpeter in the mashed potatoes?'' I said.

Brother Joseph smiled. ''The modern equivalent. The effect is emasculation. An enforced celibacy, which is, as I'm sure you'll agree, a contradiction in terms. There are the usual side effects. Potential liver damage, lethargy, depression. I don't think it's the answer. Merely a temporary form of penance.''

''This is all very sad,'' I wheezed. ''Very sad indeed. Is there no hope for the poor man?''

''While faith remains,'' Brother Joseph said, ''there is hope.''

''And Kurt retains his faith?''

Brother Joseph nodded. ''If he didn't,'' he said, ''I am convinced he would have taken his life some time ago. Faith, and the conviction that the truth about his behavior would destroy his mother, these are what keep Kurt Sydney alive.''

He stood up, gripping the handles of my wheelchair. We would, he suggested, seek Father Sydney in his room. Maybe the father was resting. I was surprised at the emptiness of the place and said so.

Brother Joseph steered me down a different hallway, toward a remote part of the cavernous building. "We don't get that many visitors," he explained. "The people in the east wing, where we treat our psychiatric clients, are especially reluctant to show themselves to strangers. The others, who are here for treatment of alcohol and drug abuse, are less shy. Or maybe I should say less ashamed."

As we wheeled along that empty corridor, with its doors firmly shut, I thought about Kurt Owen Sydney hiding in this ancient maze of thin-walled rooms, his mind grappling with the past, fighting the dullness of his medication and the musty stench of guilt. Suffering the clinical dissection of Brother Joseph, with his air of professionally restrained repugnance for the social leprosy he treated. With suicide forbidden, Father Sydney's only alternative was to pour over his theology books, looking for a cure. Or for forgiveness.

Brother Joseph parked me at the end of the hall, under an illuminated engraving of the Virgin Mary. Her gold-leaf halo was radiant. In her arms was a baby that looked, by a trick of the overhead light, faintly demonic.

"Father Sydney?" Brother Joseph knocked at a narrow door. The crucifix mounted there was echoed in the configuration of the door panels. "Father Sydney, you have a visitor."

There were no locks on the doors. Neither, as I immediately noticed, following Brother Joseph inside, were there bars on the windows. The room was simply furnished. A cast-iron radiator crouched against one wall, whistling faintly. A battered deal wardrobe, a straightback chair, a night table, a bed. Over the bed was another crucifix. On the bed was a blanket-covered lump.

"Kurt?" Brother Joseph said. Moving with the confidence of an orderly-keeper, he turned back the blanket.

''I can't believe it,'' he said.

Under the blanket was a row of pillows and bedding, arranged in the shape of a body. The curtains at the window stirred. I wheeled over and looked out. The ground beneath the window was blank, frozen. The brittle, broken branches of the hedge might have been damaged by a storm, or the ceaseless wind from the sea. Or a man, fleeing from himself.

Brother Joseph sat on the bed, rubbing his tonsure with the heel of his palm. He looked at me, his expression helpless.

''I don't understand,'' he said, ''Why would he leave? And where would he go?''

When I knew the answer to that, I would know who the second priest was, and why the Eskimo died.

III

REQUIEM FOR THE ESKIMO

1

TWO SIGNIFICANT THINGS HAPPENED THE NEXT day. The first was when, prior to resumption of the trial, City Counsel Tom Dennet walked over to the plaintiff's table and slipped a folded piece of paper into Fitzy's hand. On the paper was a six-figure number, high up enough so it wasn't far from being a seven-figure number, as I later learned.

Dennet stood there with his hands in his pockets, rocking back on his heels while Fitzy blinked at the figures.

"Those ain't pesos," he said. "Consult with your client. Me, I'm in the mood to blow this popsicle stand."

Ida Mae Jones was there at his place in the front row, clutching her purse, looking at Dennet with undisguised suspicion. The city attorney looked like a well-dressed snake, sleek and slippery and most definitely cold-blooded. For the last two days of testimony he had been trying to tarnish the studious, schoolboy image of the late Horatio Jones, suggesting that he had been fully capable of snatching purses and threatening arresting officers with a screwdriver. Now he was passing folded notes to her attorney, who appeared interested.

Fitzy had one question. "Payable in ninety days?"

Dennet nodded.

Fitzy and Milton Pridham left the courtroom to consult with Ida Mae Jones. I rolled over to where Russ White sat. He had a closed steno pad in his lap and was grinning hugely.

"Spill it, Russ. You look like the cat who ate the canary."

"I can't wait until I see Skittles's face when he comes in. He'll probably swallow his bow tie."

"What gives?"

"What gives is that certain very well-connected persons have decided to take the ball and go home. Dennet has been ordered to make an offer."

"They're going to *settle?* How much?"

He told me. I asked him how he knew, right to the dollar. He showed me a pair of opera glasses.

"Never go to the races without 'em," he said, snapping the case shut. "You think Mrs. Jones will go for it?"

"Be crazy not to," I said. "You never know what a jury will do."

"That's more than you got when *you* sued," White said, a twinkle in his eye. "Jealous?"

"Why should I be? I'm alive. Horatio Jones is dead."

"Yeah," White said, "so are a lot of other people."

I asked him what the hell he meant by that.

"Just a figure of speech."

Maybe. But certain names came to mind. Lester Karkis. Spenser Eames. Ernest Edwards. Peter Sylvia. And especially the Eskimo, Lew Quinn.

I got lucky, Quinn had said, *I stumbled onto something down here. An ugly situation, except it all makes beautiful sense.*

Except that none of it made sense. Not the bogus suicide of Lester Karkis, nor the shooting of Horatio Jones. Not the execution of Lew Quinn, nor the not-so-accidental death of Spenser Eames. Eyeball Edwards, hiding his genitals in death, that made no sense at all. And Peter Sylvia, run down in Bay Village—it was crazy, all of it.

"Nuts," I said.

"Pardon me?"

"Never mind."

But the lunacy was building, fogging the landscape of murder. I had been looking for rational motives, poking around for the same kind of plot structure that formed the armature for my books. As if murder were a game played by sensible rules. This was a novelist's conceit, the attempt to graft my own set of values on events way outside my control.

I had forgotten that murder was madness.

Cold, perhaps. Calculating, certainly. But the act of willfully inflicting death was like an infection, a disease that ended with insanity, if it had not begun there. Not the insanity of drooling psychosis, or of a fly-eating Renfield, but of a particular mind-set that transformed the personality into that of a killing machine, enabling an otherwise normal human being to deal out death without suffering guilt. A kind of self-willed lobotomy—except that victims of actual lobotomy tended to nonviolence.

Madness, yes. And fear.

I found the second priest, Peter Sylvia had said.

Less than an hour later the second priest had found him. A screech of wheels, a thump, then snowy silence.

In the private bathhouse orgies hosted by the late Lester Karkis, men had dressed as priests, for whatever twisted reasons. It was now reasonable to assume that one of them had smashed Peter Sylvia to the wet pavement. The same "priest" who had, in all probability, ended Eyeball Edwards's reign of blackmail with a single shot from extremely close range. A priest with a vocation for murder, administering the holy sacrament of death.

"Russ, you said 'certain well-connected persons' forced Dennet to make an offer. Can you name names?"

Russ gave me a wry grin and shook his head. "All I know is, Dennet is pissed off. He wanted to take his chance with the jury. Someone with friends in high places made a convincing argument to end it now, before Fitzgerald had a chance at redress. Testimony harmful to the reputation of the department, et cetera."

"Can you find out who put on the pressure?"

"I can try. I *am* trying."

I had a sudden urge to get out of courthouse, out of the city. I hit the hall just as Fitzy and Milton and Ida Mae Jones returned from conference. Fitzy was grinning, Milton was his usual bland Brahmin self, Ida Mae looked scared to death.

"You taking it?" I asked her.

She nodded. "Fitz say go for it. I still don't believe they'll give me that much money."

"We got 'em on the run," Fitzy gloated. "They'll be throwing the loot over their shoulders, trying to lighten up."

Milton Pridham straightened his bow tie. Soon enough he would be on camera, getting his fresh-scrubbed young face before the public. He's assisted in a highly publicized trial and won. Not bad for a guy who'd never actually practiced law. You could almost see it clicking through his brain: assistant D.A., state legislature, U.S. Congress, a serene progress toward the lucrative power niche he'd been born to inhabit. His inevitable success was written in the stars, and the checkbook.

I asked Fitzy if he had any idea who was behind the decision to make an out-of-court settlement.

He patted me on the shoulder. "Never look a gift horse," he said. Then he draped his big arm around the tiny black woman and walked her into the big white courtroom.

Route 1 North was bumper to bumper, the Friday-night rush to get out of the slush and smoke. Many of the vehicles inching through the gridlock carried ski racks. Destination: White Mountains. Object: headlong flight down a sheet of ice. As I struggled to keep the van from locking fenders, Megan rummaged through the overnight bag for a hairbrush.

Tugging snaggles out of her hair, she turned in her seat to face me. "What makes you think he'll be on the island?" she asked.

With my hand hovering over the brake lever and my eyes darting from the mirror to the mess ahead, I said, "He's got nowhere else. Can't go back to the mission, obviously. Chestnut Hill is out because mommy dearest is there, in between pilgrimages. That leaves the Isle Bright estate, or that is Brother Joseph's guess. He told me Father Sydney spoke warmly of the place. The few decent memories he has of his childhood center around summers there. And if Father Sydney isn't at Isle Bright, well, we'll have had a nice tour of Casco Bay."

"Well," Meg said doubtfully, "so long as I don't have to wear a habit."

At Danvers we cleared the sluggish traffic and got on the four wide lanes of 95. Megan fiddled with the tape deck. The Talking Heads rocked us to the traffic circle at Portsmouth, New Hampshire, where we stopped at a Hojo's for coffee. From the window seats we could look across the circle, where a huge, brightly lit state liquor store was doing a land-office business. Herding the flock of discount-booze buyers was a pack of green state trooper sedans.

"Nice game," Meg observed, as we watched the blue lights kick on every few minutes. "Bait and bust. Live free or die."

From Portsmouth we crossed the river into Maine. In another hour we were on the outskirts of Portland, a sprawling waterfront city, trading center, and homeport for the numerous islands that dotted Casco Bay. With the ferries operating on a winter daylight schedule, we took an overnight room at a squat glass Sheraton tower a few yards from the highway.

"Looks like a hatbox," Meg commented as we entered the curved facade.

The lobby was dominated by a huge Christmas tree, which reminded me that, with three days to go, I hadn't yet bought Megan a present. An oversight I intended to rectify before we caught the morning ferry to Isle Bright.

While Meg showered I looked over the plastic-embossed room-service menu. Hopeless. Finally I closed my eyes and jabbed a finger. Club sandwiches it was. With beer and a couple of après-sandwich cognacs it came to about the cost of a Broadway ticket.

"A bargain at half the price," Meg said, looking at the contents of the serving tray. "Last time I saw a little paper cup like that it had polio vaccine in it, not cranberry sauce."

"The good news is that the cognac has not been microwaved."

We turned on the tube and watched the local news. No mention of Finian X. Fitzgerald accepting a surprise out-of-court settlement in the controversial lawsuit. What was hot in Boston, Massachusetts, was not necessarily of interest to the citizens of Portland, Maine. One hundred miles and several worlds away.

"You call Tim Sullivan?" Megan asked with feigned casualness.

"Left a message on his machine. Casco Bay is just a smidge out of his jurisdiction."

"Just so someone knows where we're headed."

"I told Lois, too. In case something comes up."

"Yeah," Meg said, holding the balloon of cognac under her chin and inhaling the fumes. "As in something wicked this way comes."

I lay awake long after Megan's breathing became slow and regular. Turning it over in my head like an ephemeral Rubik's Cube. Trying to twist the damnable, infuriating puzzle into shape before it melted away into the inevitable dream of the Eskimo, the Eyeball, and the priest without a face. I thought I had it once, then lost it as the shadows of sleep pulled me down and Megan Drew's slim arms reflexively tightened around me.

2

WE BROKE FAST IN THE OLD PORT EXCHANGE, a previously scroungy section of the Portland waterfront that had been sanitized into a trendy row of high-ticket gift shops and theme restaurants. Cobblestone streets look great on postcards, but believe me, they're hell on a wheelchair. Despite my early-morning grumblings about the world being taken over by button-down Babbitts driving chariots made by the Bavarian Motor Works, breakfast was excellent.

"They may have whales on their lime-green pants and big brass safety pins on their Pendleton skirts," Meg said, "but one thing, they know how to eat well."

The warm plate of rough-cut, butter-fried Maine potatoes, sourdough toast slathered with apricot jam, and a cheddar cheese omelette improved my mood considerably. Megan, never a big eater in the morning, settled for a flaky scone, fresh-squeezed orange juice, and a mug of black coffee.

"One thing I don't get," she said. "Kurt Sydney is a Dominican. That means he's taken a vow of poverty, right?"

"Right," I agreed, forking the last of the omelette.

"So he goes out the back window on a cold day in December. How does he get from Providence, Rhode Island, to Casco Bay?"

"He can't *own* anything. That doesn't mean he can't have pocket money. Or the use of one of his mother's credit cards."

"Brother Joseph?"

I nodded. "A veritable treasure trove of information."

"Jack, the guy was sharp as a tack. How'd you fool him?"

"Brother Joseph assumed I was a spy, sent down from the chancery. I saw no reason to dissuade him."

"Okay, so much for the great imposter. But who is this *other* priest you kept mumbling about last night?"

"All I have is a theory."

Megan grinned. There was a spot of jam on her lower lip. On

her it looked delicious. ''Life is just a theory, Jack. So are you going to share this second-priest thing with me, or are you going to keep babbling it into your pillow?''

Fueled by coffee, prodded by the inquisitive intelligence of Megan Drew, I sorted things out as best I could.

It all turned on Father Kurt Owen Sydney, and whether he had ever been in attendance at the Bay Village bathhouse, as I suspected. As evidence that he had, we had Spenser ''Speedy'' Eames, who, before setting up as a drug-dealing prodigy working from Roxbury rooftops, had been one of the Bay Village street boys. Eyeball Edwards, on the dick patrol at the time of the bathhouse busts, had pursued Speedy to Roxbury—far out of his normal beat. And Speedy, from all descriptions an incorrigible, had been drawn to the mission run by Father Sydney. Could he have done so with more in mind than dealing smack to the mission kids? What if he had something on Father Sydney—his presence, say, at the bathhouse?

''You think this Speedy was blackmailing the father?''

''I'm not sure. It's one possibility. It helps make the connection between Bay Village and Roxbury. Think of Eyeball Edwards as a nasty brand of glue, binding the whole thing together.''

''But why,'' she asked, ''would Eyeball want to kill Speedy? Assuming it was Speedy he was after when he shot Horatio?''

That, I said, might be assuming a lot. Let it pass, though, for purposes of explicating the theory. Eyeball wants Speedy out of the picture. Why? Because Eyeball was in the blackmail game himself. In which case Speedy would have been competition. Or maybe, just maybe, Speedy was a danger to Eyeball's scheme. To the second priest.

''What?'' Meg said, raising her eyebrows. ''You just lost me. How'd the second priest get in there all of a sudden?''

''What if he'd been there all along? What if the second priest—who may not be a priest at all, but one of Lester Karkis's friends who dressed in a priest costume for *whatever* kinky reasons. Remember, Peter Sylvia said that putting on priestly garb was in vogue with that crowd, one of the sick games they played. What if it was this *other* so-called priest Eyeball was blackmailing? Someone wealthy enough to stake him to a multimillion dollar apartment complex. Someone worth killing for, to keep the golden goose alive.''

''Couldn't that have been Father Sydney? Why someone else?''

''No,'' I said. ''*Because Kurt Owen Sydney doesn't have wealth.* He comes from an enormously wealthy family, but he doesn't have access to big bucks. His mother does, the Church does. *He* doesn't. Even supposing he could wheedle sums now and then, keep a miniature extortionist like Speedy Eames off his back, there is just no way he can arrange financing for Eyeball's real estate.''

The way I saw it, Eyeball Edwards was in the protection racket. The second ''priest'' was his client. As an undercover agent in the dick patrol he'd had ample opportunity to scent out his prey. He'd found a rich victim, one who could be bled, and when the bathhouse bust had gone down, Eyeball had gone in there and gotten his victim out unscathed. Eyeball was in a position to make sure there was no arrest. No picture in the *Standard,* no embarrassing clips on the six o'clock news, no risk of going to prison and being disgraced for the remainder of a lifetime.

The victim would have been grateful. And Eyeball would have made him pay. And pay some more. Then, to make sure his victim remained grateful, not to mention able to continue ponying up the money, Eyeball set out to eliminate anyone who might have known his identity. Lester Karkis, for instance, staging a suicide with a misspelled note—just the kind of sloppy mistake Eyeball would make. Then Speedy, next on the list. Only instead of Speedy he hits Horatio Jones by accident—similar building in same position on a parallel street. Bad business, because it means he will eventually have to give testimony at a lawsuit trial. Finally he gets to Speedy just before the trial. The trial itself is a major cause of concern to the "victim" because God only knows what Finian X. Fitzgerald will worm out of a flake like Eyeball Edwards. There is the very real danger that he will give something away, some piece of information that will lead back to the "victim," the man Peter Sylvia identified as the second priest. Someone panics—either the "victim" or Eyeball himself—and they pull a stunt. Once again it is blackmail, snatching the twins as collateral to ensure that Fitzy will not be there in court to extract damaging information.

"Okay," Meg said. "You're making me dizzy, all this wheels-within-wheels reasoning. But what you're leading up to, this 'victim,' this guy absolutely can't afford to have his identity known, decides to call in the chips and he cancels Eyeball?"

"Right."

"And then he goes on killing? He hears Peter Sylvia is on to something, so he runs him down?"

"He's in a panic," I said. "He's done away with his strong-man—Edwards, and now he's on his own. Cleaning up loose ends. Maybe, if he's got enough leverage, he even puts pressure on the city to settle out of court."

"You're talking about someone with one hell of a lot of clout."

"Exactly. Someone who has a lot to lose. First just his reputation. Maybe now his life, they ever bring back the death penalty in this state."

"And Father Sydney knows who this guy is?"

"That's what I'm betting on. Sydney may not *know* that he knows. But he's the only one still left alive—and he's on the run, remember. He had some reason for fleeing the leper colony. I figure at the very least it's worth the drive up here to find out. Now enough theorizing. If you're not going to finish that scone, I will."

"What's the rush? The ferry doesn't leave for over an hour."

"There's something else I want to do this morning. I want to see a man about a diamond."

It was a woman we saw, and she had eyes like polished flint. At first Megan was dubious. An engagement ring was corny, old-fashioned. Then she said, well, my mother would love it. To which I responded, with no animosity toward the old girl, to hell with your mother, what do *you* think?

"I think it's sweet, Jack," she said as we window-shopped on Market Street.

"You want sweet, I'll get you a box of chocolates."

"That's not what I meant, lover. Okay, I most definitely *want* it. But they're awfully expensive, aren't they?"

"*It's* awfully expensive—you only get one. Don't worry about the money."

Easier said than done. J. D. Hawkins, impulse buyer, hadn't counted on Ms. Flint Eyes. She's been watching through the plate glass, then tracked us with twin lasers as we came into the soft, moneyed hush of the store. She had ice water flowing in platinum-plated veins, and a heart as big as a tick's eyelid. Her age I estimated at twenty going on twenty-thousand.

"Is this an engagement investment or a Christmas investment?" she asked, setting a velvet-lined tray of rings on the glass counter.

"If I wanted to invest," I said, "I'd play the ponies. This is a gift."

"I see," the saleswoman said. The tight lips and fluttering eyelids meant she didn't see at all.

After having her finger sized, Meg tried on several rings. While doing so she giggled and blushed, two things I'd never seen Megan Drew do. What she settled on was basic. A gold band with a chunk of diamond.

"But the cost," Megan whispered. "You sure?"

''Just let me make the grand gesture, okay? Diamond Jack Hawkins, mystery magnate.''

Things started going wrong when I took out my checkbook. Flint Eyes peered down, shaking her head ever so slightly.

''That's not a local bank. That is a Boston bank. This is Portland. For an investment purchase of this size, we require a local bank.''

''Lot of bad paper at Christmas?'' I asked politely, squelching a thank-you for the geography lesson.

''Exactly.''

Sounded reasonable. I fished through my wallet, extracting a charge card. Flint Eyes picked it up by the edges, as it if was coated with poison. She went to a desk, dropped the card on it, gave me a glance that would have chilled an enchilada, and picked up a telephone.

''Why don't we wait?'' Megan whispered. ''You still want to be Diamond Jack, we can do it at home.''

Flint Eyes burned a laser beam at my forehead before returning and dropping the charge card on the glass.

''The card is valid,'' she said. ''But this investment would put you five hundred and thirty-two dollars over your limit.''

After checking to make sure all of the jewelry was in place, she whisked the tray back into the display unit. Using her lacquered fingernail, she pushed the offending charge card toward me. ''We have some very nice costume jewelry,'' she said, ''if you're not ready to invest at this time.''

I was reaching for my can of Mace when Megan pulled me backward out the lobby, through the door, and into the street.

The steam was still coming out of my ears when the ferry bumped into the dock.

''I was only going to give her a little squirt,'' I explained to Megan, who was still laughing, ''to see if she was human.''

A kid wearing a long-billed cap and a green Air Force parka

came along the short line of vehicles, punching the tickets. From the bow of the ferry a wide steel plate was being lowered as the little ship nudged against the pilings, fumes rising from the diesel stack. The vessel was dented and streaked with rust. To my somewhat concerned eye it looked like something Conrad might have piloted up the Congo. I rolled down the side window.

''Destination?'' the kid asked. He had green eyes, a red face, and banana-yellow teeth. Very Christmas-y.

''Isle Bright,'' I said. ''Land of the rich, home of the brave.''

''Last on,'' he said, punching the ticket and ignoring the wise-crack, ''last off. Go left, nudgit tootha rail, and setchyer brake.''

I rolled up the window. ''I was expecting something a little larger,'' I said to Meg. ''A little more stable.''

''Relax,'' she said, sitting up high in the passenger seat to get a better view. ''It's only four miles.''

A couple of four-wheel-drive pickups raced off the ferry as soon as the steel plate hit the dock. That was it. Not a heavy traffic route. The kid who'd taken the tickets removed his cap and used it to flag the outward-bound vehicles onto the narrow, and to my way of thinking, heaving deck. As his mumble had implied, we were the last to drive aboard. After touching the fender to the welded side-rail that was the only thing between us and the deep blue sea, I set the brake and looked at Meg.

''I agree,'' she said. ''As ferries go, this is small. Toylike, in fact. On the other hand it makes three trips a day, every day, ergo it is safe.''

The steel plate crashed up into place behind us. The mooring lines were unraveled. The diesel cranked, shaking the deck, and us inside the van.

''Ergo,'' I said, clenching my teeth, ''*schmergo*.''

''This was your idea,'' Meg said. ''You knew it involved crossing water. If you ask me, it's time you got over that phobia.''

''No one asked,'' I said.

The passage was terrifying but uneventful. One enormous oil tanker tried to run us down, narrowly missing. Meg said it was at least a half a mile away and I suggested she see an eye doctor. A series of tidal waves crashed over the open bow as we headed out into the storm-tossed sea. Meg said a little spray never hurt, and that the bay was remarkably calm. When we rammed into the dock at the first island stop, going full speed, Meg insisted we'd barely kissed the pier. After a couple of cars and a pickup hurtled off at the landing we backed in full reverse, nearly capsizing.

"This is neat," Meg said, "Look at how close the islands are. You can practically reach out and touch them."

"The sea is so large, oh, Lord," I said. "And this freaking boat is so small."

At the next island everybody escaped except us.

"Like rats down the hawser," I said.

"You weren't this nervous when we went to Nantucket," Meg observed.

"That was a great big ferry. Also, it had a bar up on deck. If you face the back wall and drink steadily, you can almost forget you're surrounded by ocean."

"You never wanted to run away to sea when you were a kid?"

"They took me to the beach, I was terrified. I saw the tide coming back in, I thought it was after me personally."

"Maybe you should see a hypnotist."

"I did," I said. "I got seasick right there in his office."

Megan assured me that not more than thirty minutes has passed before we disembarked at Isle Bright. I didn't argue. If the ground hadn't been frozen and muddy, I'd have gotten out of the van and kissed it. When my nerves had stopped doing *la cucaracha* I cleared the salt spray from the windshield and looked around.

"Wow," I said.

"Double wow," Meg said. "No wonder rich people live out here."

On the map the island was shaped like a crooked finger. There was one paved road that bisected the length of it, running from the cove where the ferry docked out to Indian Point, on the eastern tip, a distance of five or six miles. The spine of the island was granite, which broke through in jagged chunks wherever the scrub fir hadn't gotten a toehold. Around us was the blue expanse of Casco Bay, with all of her islands receding into a misty distance. Each island was a rim of dark rock capped with evergreen, frosted with ice at the base and dusted with confectioner's snow on top.

We decided to drive out to Indian Point. Not that there was any choice, if we wanted to stick to the pavement. The first impression, other than the breathtaking splendor of the panoramic bay, was that the population of Isle Bright was sharply divided into two classes, lobstermen and millionaires. At a couple of the sprawling, shingled mansions, where traps were stacked next to hauled-out boats, the two classes co-existed. Mostly, though, the island residences alternated between small fishermen's cottages, obviously occupied, and huge estate houses shuttered for the winter. The typical lobsterman's yard, sloping sharply down to a craggy inlet, was strewn with traps, fishing equipment and junked automobiles. The average mansion yard, glazed with ice and crusty snow, was a barren testament to the summer lawn to come.

It made for an interesting contrast. You could imagine the island in season. The New York ad executive in his white linen shorts and the pink Lacoste shirt serving Tangueray tonics to his weekend guests, who politely ignore the stink of baitfish from the shack next door.

"Any idea where the Owen-Sydneys pitch their tent?"

"My plan is we just cruise around until we find it."

"How many people you figure live out here all winter?"

"I dunno. A hundred maybe. Ten times that in the summer. No, more you figure the servants."

"Right, the servants. You know what they say about the rich."

"They're different from you and me?"

Megan grinned and shook her head. "They've got a lot of money." The banter faded as we approached the end of the island. A natural causeway of salt-bleached granite staggered out into a deep channel of the bay. The road deteriorated, giving way to a rutted path strewn with beach gravel thrown up over the breakwater by errant waves. At the end of the bleak promontory, presumably Indian Point itself, a steel-girded tower held up a flashing white light. Blasts of wind rocked the van. White caps rippled through the channel. A fishing dragger, listing to one side, struggled against the strong tidal current, trailing a spiral of white winged gulls.

I backed the van around, reversing direction. Covering the same ground along the main road, we slowed at each driveway and inspected the roadside mailboxes.

Money. Megan had been kidding, reworking the old argument that had divided Papa Hemingway and F. Scott Fitzgerald, about whether or not wealth had a power and place beyond the counting house. I had no answer to the eternal question, beyond a certainty that money was an ample motive for murder. In the streets of Roxbury and Charlestown and Southie young men killed for piddling sums. If twenty bucks was motive enough to slice a man's throat, what would a hundred million buy?

That was how much of the Owen-Sydney fortune had been diverted into the coffers of the Church, with a sizable percentage used to retire the debts of the Boston archdiocese. A hundred million. Roll it around in your mind, it has a nice ring to it. A hundred million reasons to keep the golden goose happy, unaware of the cuckoo that had hatched in her nest.

According to Russ White, "certain well-connected persons" had pressured the city into ending the Jones trial by making a substantial out-of-court settlement. Could the "well-connected" be members of the clergy, wielding the power of the chancery?

But where did a bent vice cop fit into it? Or a skinny black kid tending pigeons on a tenement roof? Or a Bay Village entrepreneur with a penchant for harem boys? It was like trying to connect the dots on a paint-by-numbers Hieronymous Bosch.

"I think we just passed something," Meg said, startling me out of my reverie. "Back it up."

What Megan had spotted was a wrought-iron gate. A flowery black *S* had been worked into the design, entwined with a bronze cross. The gate was shut, although not locked. Beyond it a single pair of tire marks had broken through the thin crust of snow. Neatly mortised stone walls followed the curve of the drive, vanishing over a ridge.

Meg hopped out and pushed open the gate. I put the van in low gear and followed the tire tracks. My mouth was dry. The driveway dropped as we cleared the ridge. Through the scrub pine a cedar-shingled roofline was visible. Two massive fieldstone chimneys connected by a widow's walk. Beyond that, the open sea.

"Where there's smoke," I said, indicating the gray wisp that curled up from one of the chimneys.

"Not a bad little cottage," Meg said as we made the final turn down to the shore. "If it rains, they can play polo on the porch."

The porch encircled the main house, thrusting out on pilings that dropped into the water's edge. Wooden storm shutters covered all the windows on the ground floor. The shingles on the northeast face were black and curled, cracked by the weather. Long fangs of ice clung to the gutters and the porch railings. It was a great gray ark of a place, battened down for a season of storms.

Off to one side, on a bare outcropping of bedrock, was a small chapel. It had a steeply pitched roof, massive doors, and a circle of stained glass near the peak. It was shingled like the main house, although less weathered. On the great curved doors was the same wrought-iron *S* design entwined with a bronze cross. A small, unadorned wreath had been hung from the cross. Sturdy as the little building was, it looked fragile so near to the sea.

The tire tracks ended at one of the carriage-house doors. I parked there and set the brake. I switched off the motor. I could hear the hiss of the sea surging around the pilings under the main house, the dissonant squawk of gulls, and Megan breathing.

"What are you going to say," she wanted to know, "if it's him?"

"The first thing that comes into my head."

"That's what I love about you, Jack. You're always prepared."

"Semper paratus," I said. "My motto."

I unsnapped the wheel lockdowns and went to the back of the van. Megan waited while the lift shuddered me down, slapping her mittens together. The wind was cold and raw with moisture. The salt air seared my throat. The thin crust of snow in the driveway made the going hard. I let Meg help, pushing from behind.

While I waited below, Megan climbed the slab-granite steps to the entrance. The heavy knocker sounded like a gunshot as she dropped it against the door. The retort echoed from the ridge of the island, ricocheting around the cove. Meg waited, stamping her boots, snorting steam like a thoroughbred.

"Let's try the porch."

My wheels squeaked on the frozen boards. Meg held on to the back of my chair, mostly to keep her own balance on the slick surface. I wheeled close to one of the shuttered windows, squinting against the slatted darkness within. Indistinct shadows. The surf rolled in under the porch, spewing gravel in its maw. You could feel the force of the tide being absorbed by the pilings and transmitted to the deck beams. Anyone staying here in this season would be constantly reminded of exactly where the sea was, and what it might do, should the right combination of wind and wave arise. Sleep would be a fragile thing, tied to the rhythm of the sea.

"You hear that?" Meg said hoarsely, bending down to my ear.

"A violin?"

It was very faint, whatever it was, and mostly smothered by the sound of rushing water and the wind that whistled through the railing spindles.

The wind really hit us as we turned onto the main expanse of the porch. Wooden lawn furniture was stacked up against the storm shutters. Sea spray had condensed into knuckles of bluish ice along the edge of the decking. The sound of music was stronger here. Definitely a violin. Megan, cursing the cold and the wind, banged her mittens against the shutters.

"They'll find us here next spring," she said. "Poor frozen lumps coated with seaweed."

I was about to suggest we try the chapel when one of the storm doors was caught by the wind and slammed open. A tall, slender man stepped out. He wore dark woolen trousers and a baggy Irish fisherman's sweater. His hair was thin and black with streaks of gray. His flesh was pale, mottled, and unhealthy. His expression was one of profound surprise.

I rolled toward him, Megan at my side.

I said the first thing that came into my head.

"Father Sydney, I presume?"

3

THE THIN AND SCRATCHY VIOLIN WAS COMING from the black, fluted horn of an old victrola. The victrola was on a shelf that had been built into the wall near the massive fieldstone fireplace. The shelves under the victrola were filled with brittle volumes of 78-r.p.m. records, thousands of them. Pieces of smashed-up lawn furniture burned in the fireplace over a glowing bed of coals. The flickering light that suffused the shutter-darkened living room was provided by half a dozen hurricane lamps.

"The power is off for the winter," Father Sydney explained. "I suppose I'll have to have it put back on, if I decide to stay."

Megan crouched at the big fireplace, warming her hands. I positioned myself near a kerosene space heater and massaged my arms. The large room, with its low exposed beams, wide-board floor, and knotty-pine paneling, looked as if nothing has been disturbed since the summer of 1948. There were stacks and stacks of yellowed magazines, most of them long out of print. Thumbtacked to the wall were dozens of the tinted Nutting landscape photographs that had been widely reproduced in the decades prior to World War II. Most of the furniture was covered with sheets, except for a wingback leather chair the priest had dragged next to the hearth.

Father didn't seem to know what to do about us, although he appeared to be glad for our company. He fussed with uncovering another chair for Megan and insisted I maneuver myself nearer to the fireplace, because he believed the warmth to be "healthier" there, away from the space-heater fumes.

"I'd offer you a drink, but I poured all the liquor down the drain when I got here. Even dumped a pint of vanilla extract, just to be on the safe side."

"How long have you been off the stuff?" I asked.

"Six months, almost. Longest dry interval since I was, oh,

thirteen years old. The gardener used to keep a jug of rum out in his tool shack, I'd take swigs from it, then brush my teeth. Dreadful taste, toothpaste after rum. Also there was mother's sherry. That was easy enough to water. And the rye she kept for visiting clerics."

Father Sydney sat poised on the edge of the leather chair, his hollow eyes darting from me to Megan, then to the fire, where the burning lawn chair gave off a musty sea smell, popping and crackling in the flames. He had the haunted look of a man desperate to talk, or maybe confess. A not-so ancient mariner longing for a guest. His hands fluttered from the arms of the chair to his knees, then up to smooth down his hair. The priest had not shaved in a few days, which made him look unkempt and contributed to his air of ill health.

"You say you've spoken with Father Duvall? So how is old Nappy? Are the boys starting to come back? Has he got a pool table yet? He was always going on about a pool table."

When I assured him that Father Duvall had installed a pool table at last, he clapped his hands together, then leaped up to attend to the victrola. With his back to us he searched through a stack of the 78's as he talked, his voice pitched in a slight singsong.

"All those months in Providence—did you know they call it the leper colony? Yes, you must, everyone knows it—all that time, when I couldn't sleep, or I couldn't bear to think, I concentrated on remembering this victrola. What this room felt like when my father was alive. This was Daddy's—my father's—favorite place. All his Caruso records, and the popular songs. Whole stack of John McCormack songs here somewhere, the great Irish tenor. Daddy had more modern equipment in Chestnut Hill, one of the first high-fidelity systems—I think they called it 'orthophonic' in those days—but he'd never lug it up here for the summer. Always the victrola. I remember it distinctly. First he would put in a new needle—the old steel ones need to be changed every four or five records—and then he would put on *'Vesti la Giubba,'* Caruso's famous aria from *Pagliacci*. He would sit in that same chair, the big leather one by the fire, and he would close his eyes. The tears would trickle down his cheeks and I would climb up into his lap and ask him why he was crying. 'Because he sings so beautifully.' He was a lovely man, my father."

He wound up the old machine and lowered the diaphragm arm down on the record. After the dramatic buildup I was expecting Caruso. Instead it was one of Chopin's nocturnes. If you could ignore the pops and scratches, the sound was surprisingly good.

"Young Rubenstein," Father Sydney explained, returning to his father's chair. "Another of Daddy's favorites. My mother—do you know Ethel? No? She doesn't care much for music. Hurts her ears. Mother has only one interest. She wants God to speak to her, personally. He hasn't so far."

Megan, relaxing somewhat, had settled into the chair Father Sydney had uncovered for her. Between the flickering fire and the dusky glow of the hurricane lamps it was difficult to read her expression. I think she sensed that Kurt Sydney was not dangerous or violent, that if anything, we had frightened him. What he did appear to be was a man on the precarious balance point between breakdown and recovery.

It took him several tries before he succeeded in bringing a match to the cigarette that trembled in his lips.

Without going into detail I implied that we were associates of Finian X. Fitzgerald, the lawyer who had represented Ida Mae Jones in her lawsuit against the Boston Police Department. Father Sydney nodded quickly, but I'm not sure it really sank in.

"I heard somebody out on the porch, I assumed it was the police," he said, gulping at the cigarette.

"Are you expecting the police, Father?"

"If I expected anybody, it was Brother Joseph," he said, laughing nervously. "He'll be quite ticked off. I imagine. There wasn't any reason for me to go out the window like that. I could have left by the front door, only I lacked the courage to face him. Not a thing I ever had much of, courage."

I asked what had prompted his sudden departure from the treatment facility.

"Orders from headquarters," he said, laying his head back against the leather cushion. "The big enchilada. The chancellor himself."

"Monsignor McCue?"

He nodded.

"Called, said he had a suggestion." He paused to inhale deeply on the cigarette. "When the monsignor has a suggestion, you are supposed to be extremely attentive. As indeed I was. He said someone had been nosing around the chancery, wanting to interview me. Something to do with poor Horatio. It would be best if I made myself scarce. Not his words, but that was the message. So I obeyed, in my own way. Can I assume the nosy someone was you?"

"You can."

On the victrola the nocturne squeaked to a conclusion. The bulky needle arm began ticking. Father Sydney got up to attend to it. He removed the brittle old record and returned it to a folio jacket. He remained standing there by the record collection, with his arms across his chest and his hands tucked into his armpits. The daylight leaking through the storm shutters washed over him in thin zebra stripes. He swayed there, as if hearing the ghost of a melody.

"So," he said, "ask away. The monsignor will be furious, but I'm tired of lying. And hiding."

"Tell me about Horatio Jones."

"All I know about Horatio is that he was a gifted boy, remarkably curious about the world, and that he was shot and killed by an ignorant policeman, for no reason on earth."

The strangest thing about his answer was the I believed him. It didn't make sense, but that's often the way it is with a delicate thing like the truth.

"Did you know the cop involved, Detective Ernest Edwards?"

"No. I did get to know some of the detectives assigned to the Roxbury district," he said, fiddling with an album of records. "We asked them to encourage the young men on the street to come in and see us. Give the boys' club a chance. But this Edwards, I heard he was out of his territory when he went up on the roof after Horatio."

I informed him that Edwards had been a vice cop, that he had been assigned to the Male Prostitute Undercover Detail in Bay Village when the bathhouses had been raided.

"They called it," I said, "the Dick Patrol."

"Here it is," Father Sydney exclaimed. He turned, beaming, holding a record by its edges. "*'Vesti la giubba,'* on with the costume, on with the show."

"The Dick Patrol," I said, "the bathhouse operated by Lester Karkis."

Father Sydney nodded. "Yes, yes," he said, head bobbing, "you'll want to know all about that. Do you mind if I indulge myself with Mr. Caruso? I pawed through this pile for hours, and it was right here on top all the time. 'On with the show.' I think it's rather appropriate, don't you?"

He blew dust from the grooves, set it on the platter, and cranked the spring drive. When it was spinning rapidly he gently set the heavy arm in place and stood back, his hands clasped. The heavy scratches made it sound like the famous tenor was singing at the beach, accompanied by the sound of crashing surf. Still, you could hear enough to sense the power and the clarity that had made him the sensation of his age. A little man in a clown suit who had charmed the world.

"The way Daddy always explained it, the victrola was like a time machine," Father Sydney said. I got the idea the troubled priest was talking more to himself than to us. "Back in this special moment of time," he continued, spreading out his hands as he rhapsodized, "there was Enrico Caruso. He stands before this big contraption—it's like a larger victrola, really—and he sings directly into a huge megaphone, one that's almost as big as he is. This was before they had microphones, the whole thing was mechanical. Caruso sang into the megaphone, a diaphragm caught his voice and made a needle vibrate. The needle cut directly into the master record. Right into the wax. No tubes or wires or tape recorders or amplifiers. Just his voice. So in a way we're all of us connected to that moment. Caruso is still right there on the other side of the sound trumpet, on the other side of time."

He stood by the antique machine, hugging himself, until the aria ended. Then he turned and stumbled back to the big leather chair. Tears streamed down his cheeks. I didn't know if he was crying for the scratchy beauty of Caruso's song, or for the memory of his father's tears of joy.

"I'm sorry," he said, wiping his eyes with the sleeve of his sweater. "I threw away my tranks when I dumped all the booze. No more pills. I'm still very shaky. It's like waking up and finding you've been sandblasted. All those nerve endings positively *screaming* for attention."

Megan got paper tissues out of her purse.

"Thank you, dear," he said without meeting her eyes. He blew his nose, then threw the soiled tissues into the fire. "Oh, my. Memories, that's the most powerful drug of all. I feel like I've had three martinis on an empty stomach."

I waited until he'd got another cigarette going. When his chest had stopped heaving I said, "The bathhouse?"

He nodded rapidly. "Of course, yes. Why you've come. Don't worry. I'll confess all, as the saying goes. Part of my penance. Well let me see," he exhaled or signed, and seemed to shrink into the big chair. "Lester Karkis. Met him while I was a pastor in Brookline, St. Bart's. One of those social functions. Lester was representing some urban task force, or renovation group, I forget. Very foggy, you see. Very boozy days, there at St. Bart's. Hated the place. Anyhow, Lester. Charming man. Acting straight that day, or as straight as he ever acted. Wanted to argue theology, Teilhard de Chardin, all that. Well, of course, I was willing enough. He knew, you see, did Lester. All about me. Not telepathy exactly, some kind of *osmosis* power he had, able to put his roots right down into the darkest corner of your soul. Birds-of-a-feather instinct, obviously. One of Lester's terrible talents, that sixth sense of his."

As he spoke, Father Sydney looked at the fire or the floor. Now and then he would glance at me—never at Megan.

"So there I was, the latest of Lester's 'discoveries.' Absolutely adored the fact that I was a priest. Made me an especially attractive conquest."

I asked if he and Lester Karkis had been lovers. Father Sydney choked on his cigarette.

"Lester?" He coughed, cutting at the smoke with his hand. "Egad, I was then, let's see, thirty-nine years old. Way, way too old for Lester. No, I never had sex with Lester or anyone else at the bathhouse. The fact is I've only experienced what you'd call the consummate act a few times in my life. Mostly, when I was really roaring drunk and let it all hang out, it was the touchy-feely stuff. Fondling. More than that, well I just couldn't cross the line. So when it came to those disgusting orgy scenes, I was strictly a voyeur. I would pretend I was watching an amazingly realistic 3-D movie. Of course, I was always boozed to the gills before I had enough courage to go down there. No, for Lester I was simply an interesting ornament, another of the sick souls he collected. Wanted me to wear the collar, can you imagine? Of course, I refused. Then some of the younger men took to dressing up, making fun of me, I suppose. Wearing cassocks or vestments. Utterly profane."

"You're saying you never wore your priestly garb into the bathhouse, or to any or Karkis's parties?"

Father Sydney was vehement. He shook his head and banged his hands weakly against the arm of the chair. "No, no, no. Never. I was willing to besmirch myself, but never the Order. The Dominicans have been good to me. Always total forgiveness, understanding. I could *not* insult them as I insulted myself. Even as I insulted God. Lester wanted me to mock my faith, I refused him the pleasure. The only thing in my life I have never seriously doubted is the love of Jesus Christ. To Lester, that was a great joke, the pious Father Faggot who simply could not resist attending his special parties. I assume he put the others up to it, their little fad of dressing up, showing the crucifix. Oh, it was obscene, but then *everything* about that time and that place was obscene. What did a costume matter? It was all part of my pretending, my double life. When I went into that bathhouse, I was not Father Sydney. I didn't know *what* I was. But not a priest. Never, never."

Was it in the bathhouse where he'd first met Spenser Eames?

The jittering, nervous body movement stopped. Father Sydney seemed to gather a cloak of stillness about him. A kind of soiled dignity, the bare remnants of a disintegrating ego.

"Speedy," he signed. "Oh, yes. In a kind of horrible way it was Speedy's dying that woke me up. I was simply existing, going through the motions with the rest of the lepers. Taking the medication, sitting through the groups sessions, mouthing the words. But hiding inside, way back in there inside the invisible shell. Impersonating Kurt Owen Sydney, trying to respond as they expected him to respond. Inside it was like I was in a coma. I could see and hear what was going on, but it didn't touch me. Until Napoleon called with the news that Speedy was dead. Hit by a car."

"Murdered," I said. "Almost certainly."

"Yes, it occurred to me it might have been on purpose. Speedy was mixing with a very deadly crowd. The junkies and the pushers. If I thought about what would happen to Speedy—and believe me, I tried not to—I thought he would eventually get strung out. That his life would end in an overdose, or in a street fight. He had enemies in the neighborhood, territorial disputes. I knew he was dealing the stuff. Napoleon said he was bringing it into the mission. I refused to take any notice. That's the thing I always did best, turning away from whatever I didn't want to see. That was especially true with Speedy."

I said that it was unlikely that Speedy Eames had been killed in a turf war. That his death was somehow linked to Horatio Jones.

"I don't see how. Horatio was killed well over a year ago. Speedy was hit only last month."

I let it go. His reaction had seemed genuine. Unless he was a man of extraordinary acting ability, he was telling the truth—or the truth as he knew it.

"I suppose Nappy told you Speedy was a demon? Yes, I thought so. I love Napoleon dearly, although I'm well aware he loathes me, but Nappy has an exaggerated idea of good and evil, and how they are made manifest in a hell-on-earth like the streets of Roxbury. Believe me, Spenser Eames was just another kid from the streets. Much more intelligent than the average and with absolutely no moral qualms about doing whatever it took to satisfy his needs. He'd lie, steal, cheat, maybe even kill. I doubt he had a conscience, certainly not a Catholic sense of sin or guilt. But in that he was entirely human."

"Father Duvall said he was twelve going on two thousand."

The priest stroked the arms of the leather chair, his cigarette glowing. He nodded, acknowledging Duvall's assessment.

"Understand," he said. "Speedy's mother was a prostitute, and like most street hookers, an addict. Abandoned him—left him with another junkie. That woman, whose name he never knew, left him alone and untended for days on end. Finally the welfare people took him away and put him in the first of several foster homes. He was about five years old at the time. He kept running away. After a while they got tired of finding him. He lived on the streets, getting handouts from pimps, running errands. He took drugs. PCP, which they tell me is very dangerous. Eventually he started selling himself. That's when Lester found him.''

''And made him one of the bathhouse harem boys?''

Father Sydney nodded. ''Speedy was no angel, but he had that angelic face. The horrible life he'd lived didn't show. He was very beautiful. And even younger-looking than he was, which appealed to Lester. Who considered him an 'objet d'art,' as he put it.''

''And an object of abuse?''

''Without doubt. In the statutory sense and in the moral sense and, I suppose, in any damn sense you care to mention. Lester had a lot of boys like Speedy. Took them off the streets, let them crash in one of his lofts. Gave them money. Big Papa Karkis. Although he was hardly an avuncular man.''

By then my eyes had had ample time to adjust to the dim interior. I was better able to read Kurt Sydney's expression. The raw nerves he'd spoken of showed in a tic under one eye and in the way his brow wrinkled in spasms. It was as if he lacked control of his motor expressions. Not untypical symptoms of withdrawal from psychotropic and tranquilizing drugs.

The sea boiled under the porch, tearing at the gravel beach and rebounding off the rocks and pilings. I had the feeling that our presence had somehow speeded up the slow process of erosion, that the great hulking house was being undermined and would soon collapse into the cold Atlantic brine. The *Fall of the House of Sydney,* with tragic, haunting themes by Caruso.

Vesti la giubba, on with the costume, on with the show.

I asked Father Sydney how Speedy Eames had gone from the bathhouse to the Roxbury Boys' Mission.

''That was more of me kidding myself,'' he replied. He fumbled for another cigarette with trembling hands and lit it by leaning down to the fire, oblivious of the heat. ''I wanted to get him out of that hell. But at the time Speedy wasn't interested in leaving. He like the drugs, the life, the attention. To make it worse, Lester was talking about making him a 'star,' which meant using him in those dreadful videos he sold. Oh, yes, I knew about those. Believe me, even a confirmed and habitual voyeur like myself was repelled. I don't suppose it matters now, but believe it or not, I never touched Speedy while he was at the bathhouse. Then, when Lester was arrested, most of the boys he'd taken in were back on the street. That was my chance to do a good deed, rescue the boy. I went down there, sober, and suggested he come into the mission. I gave him money, enough to set up on his own in the neighborhood. Thought he'd be nearby, I could have some influence.''

''That's when get got into peddling dope?''

The priest shrugged. I notice that the shoulder of the fisherman's sweater had been singed by the fire.

''I assume so. At the time I simply didn't know. And if I thought about it at all, it was that selling envelopes of white powder was better than selling himself to Lester Karkis. Needless to say, Father Duvall didn't agree with me. To him, Speedy was a death merchant, infested with devils. And then, after the incident at the Peabody, none of it mattered.''

I asked him to describe the ''incident'' at the museum. For the first time he looked at Megan, as if hoping she would disappear. That made me wonder if she reminded him of one of his sisters, or if it was simply her sex that made him reticent.

''It was inevitable,'' he sighed. ''It has always been my pattern. In Chicago, then in Brookline. I put myself in the way of temptation and finally, eventually, I am too weak to resist the impulse. Always it has involved alcohol. I make no excuse, mind you, since I knew full well what can happen. I *chose* to drink that day, when we went to the museum. Nipping for the whole of the field trip. I must have *wanted* it to happen. Napoleon may have told you that Speedy was taunting me, tormenting me. There is some truth in that, but the fact remains: I am an adult, supposedly. At the time he was a boy of thirteen.''

The fire was getting low again. The cold was beginning to close in from the corners of the room. It was time to come to the point.

''You molested Spenser Eames? Had sex with him?''

Father Sydney covered his eyes, rubbing slowly at the bridge of his nose. In the dying of the fire I could see the fresh tears on his face.

''Almost certainly I *would* have, if Horatio hadn't stumbled in. Looking for me. To tell me all about the bird exhibit. Saw me exposed. Saw Speedy grinning at him. Ran out of the room. I ran after him, to tell him—what? I was sorry? To please keep quiet? That I would never do such a thing again? Now, I don't know. He wouldn't let me speak to him. But I could see it. In his eyes. The fear.''

That was when I knew the full extent of what was haunting Kurt Owen Sydney. Two of the children in his power had been molested. To Speedy Eames it had been a game, perhaps, one he knew well. To Horatio Jones it had been an attack on his senses, a traumatic destruction of his trust.

''And now they're both dead,'' he said woodenly. ''That's the real reason I came out to the island. I thought maybe being here again would help me think. Help me find some way to make amends. I did an awful, evil thing. God has forgiven me for that, but *I* haven't. I have to find a way to even things out, to make retribution. To do something good in the world. To balance the scale.''

I decided to change the subject, as least peripherally, and asked Father Sydney if he'd been at the bathhouse the night it was raided by the dick patrol.

"Fortunately, no. For my mother's sake. It wouldn't have made any real difference to me. As it happened, the raid coincided with one of my periods of sobriety. I hadn't been to see Lester in several weeks."

"Did you know a young man named Peter Sylvia, an associate of Karkis's?"

"Possibly. A lot of the men who came to Lester, I never knew more than the first name."

"Sylvia was the editor of Lester's broadside, the *Gay Village Banner*."

"I do remember Lester talking about him. Not exactly a warm working relationship, I gathered. It's possible I met him. I really don't remember."

"How about some of the bathhouse guests who dressed up as priests. Do you recall any names?"

"I remember mostly faces. I didn't like it, their costumes, their irreverence. They had names for me, not very flattering."

Father Sydney was drained. He appeared to be having trouble concentrating. Somewhere in his tormented memory was the image, if not the name, of the "second priest" Peter Sylvia had discovered. Of that I was convinced. In his shaky condition it was going to take awhile to find it. Pushing beyond a certain limit was not going to help. My stomach was rumbling. Given the chance to interrupt his voluntary interrogation and offer hospitality, Father Sydney accepted eagerly.

"All I brought was sliced meats and cheese and some canned food. But the stove is propane, so we can make a hot meal of it. Just let me see to this space heater, then we'll check out the kitchen."

Megan helped him refill the space heater, setting the funnel while he poured from his five-gallon jerry can. Some of the kerosene splashed. Meg was careful about wiping it up before relighting the heater.

''If you stay here, Father, you really ought to get the central heating turned on. These things are fire hazards.''

The priest was holding the can of kerosene when the porch door blew open. A woman fell into the room, pushed from behind. Daylight streamed in, putting the other figure in silhouette. Kneeling on the floor, her hands tied up behind her, was Lois Fitzgerald.

The figure in the doorway spoke.

''Merry Christmas,'' he said, ''Father Faggot.''

4 THE TWINS WERE TIED BACK TO BACK. AS THEY were shoved into the room Rory began to cry, blubbering for his mother, who lay on the floor where she had been pushed.

"Shut up," Milton Pridham said. "Or I'll shoot her. You understand, you little brat? I'll shoot your mother if you don't stop crying."

Rory stopped crying. Sarah had her eyes closed tight. She hung limp next to her brother, the clothesline cutting into her little ski parka. Her ears, sticking through her matted hair, were chafed red. Her nose was running.

Lois rolled slowly over. Her mouth was gagged. Her eyes were blank with fear.

Milton, I realized, was holding her gun. The Smith & Wesson .38 Special she'd showed me, the weapon she'd bought in Florida and kept hidden in the nook over her back door.

Father Sydney let go of the kerosene can. It made a booming sound as it hit the floor, teetered, and remained upright. Pridham swung around at the noise, crouching, the pistol extended in two hands, cop style.

"You bastards," he said. "You're all bastards."

Megan was edging away from her seat. A tongue of fire exploded from the muzzle of the .38. Carelessly aimed, it missed Megan by a few feet. The ricochet whined as the slug smacked into the fireplace.

"Sit down," he said, "and do not move."

"I know you," Father Sydney said. "I know the face."

Milton Pridham laughed. It was an ugly sound, like the high-pitched yap of a dog. "No kidding, huh? You think I'd be here if you didn't? Think we just happened to drop in? Me and the wife and the kids?"

Father Sydney tried to move toward the twins. Milton waved

the pistol toward his feet and pulled the trigger. Wood splintered as the bullet smashed into the floor. At the sound of the second shot Rory screamed. But he screamed only once and he did not cry. I nodded at him and smiled and mouthed the words "good boy."

"These are your children?" Father Sydney asked. If having a bullet strike a few inches from his feet had shaken him he didn't show it.

"Never mind whose kids they are," Milton said. "Hawkins knows. He and his snotty girlfriend. Right now, what I want is for you to walk very slowly over toward the fireplace and sit down. Keep your hands in your lap."

"You were one of the ones who dressed up," the priest said, not moving. "You were going to law school, I think Lester said."

"Do you want to go over and sit down, or shall I shoot you right where you stand? We've had a long, unpleasant ride and I've lost my patience."

Father Sydney stared at him, then walked to his chair. On the floor Lois was struggling, her arms working behind her back. Pridham bent down and put the pistol to her temple.

"Count of two," he said. "Stop moving by the count of two or I'll pull the trigger. One. Two."

Lois froze. Her eyes, like Sarah's, were squeezed shut. Pridham relaxed and stood up again. His eyes, flickering crazily behind his horn-rim glasses, seized on my left hand, which I had slipped into the storage bag on the side of my wheelchair.

"Don't even think about it," he shouted, his voice breaking. "The can of Mace, right? Ernie told me about that. He was following you out of the courthouse, and you almost Maced him. Eyeball got a kick out of that. Okay, take out the can very slowly. Now roll it across the floor to me."

I did as he said. He stooped quickly, grabbed the can, and hurled it out the door. It tumbled over the rail and into the sea. Pridham kicked the door shut. He leaned back against it, arcing the pistol back and forth, from Megan to Sydney to me. His chest pumped rapidly. He seemed to be hyperventilating.

It all started clicking into place.

Childe Milton was the second "priest," the bathhouse habitué Eyeball Edwards had picked as a blackmail victim. The bent vice cop had hooked him in the raid, then reeled him in. Pridham with his sallow cheeks and cherub's chin, must have seemed a perfect victim to lantern-jawed Edwards. Weak, wealthy in his own right, heir to a considerable fortune, connected to the corridors of power, and involved in a sordid sex scene that could ruin him or send him to jail, or at the very least make him the shame of the family. What more could a blackmailer ask?

"What happened?" I said. "Eyeball wasn't satisfied with the apartment buildings? He wanted more? Or were you just afraid of what he might say under oath?"

"Did I ask you to talk?" Milton said thickly, showing me the pistol. "Huh?"

"I understand why Lester Karkis had to be taken out, and why Speedy was killed—they both knew you, by face if not by name. What I *don't* understand," I said, "is why you volunteered for the Jones suit. It doesn't make sense."

"Shut your mouth," he said.

I shut my mouth.

"Get over here," Pridham said, pointing the .38 at Megan. "You're going to tie your boyfriend up. Come on. *Now.*"

He made her tear a lamp-cord loose and watched while she looped it around my hands.

"Tighter," he said. "Don't fuck with me, I want to see his knuckles white."

I pressed my wrists together, trying to cut off circulation and make it look good, hoping Megan would leave me room to work loose. The lashing felt discouragingly secure by the time Milton was satisfied.

"Okay," he said, "now it's your turn. Over here, Father Faggot.'' He jerked the pistol at the priest. ''Remember that name? You used to laugh when they called you that. Then you'd have another drink. Remember? Well *I* remember, it made an impression. Now take the other cord and tie her wrists together. Don't give me that holy look, okay? Remember one thing, if anything goes down, the first thing I do is shoot the brats. You want the kids zapped? Just try something funny and see what happens.''

When Megan's wrists were lashed up behind her, he relaxed somewhat. His chest slowed and his eyes did not roll quite so wildly. He sent Father Sydney back to his chair but made no move to tie him up. Either he thought he could continue to intimidate the priest with his weapon and his threats, or he had other plans. Plans that involved some freedom of movement. Or the illusion of it.

Whatever Milton Pridham had in mind, I knew I wasn't going to like it.

''I never liked you,'' he said to me. ''Snotty writer. You and Fitzy, that big dumb fuck. You think I wasn't aware of what he said about me? That 'Childe Milton' crap? Thought I was some sniveling little rich kid, too dumb to be taken into the old man's firm. Let me tell you, pal, the old man has an office waiting for me over there. Anytime I want it. I volunteered to help your show-off friend take on the city because I wanted to be there on the inside, see what kind of case he would develop. What kind of depositions he'd file. I thought it prudent to keep an eye on that moron Edwards, who messed up everything he touched. And your pal Fitzy bought it. All I had to do was tug the forelock, look confused. So tonight when the big mick comes home to an empty house, *he's* the one that's going to look confused.''

The wind had come up. It rattled the shutters. In the fireplace a gust of downdraft made the coals glow. Megan crouched sideways in her chair, facing me. One look told me she was thinking what I was thinking—that we had missed our chance. Pridham had popped off two of his five shots. Before he tied us up someone should have tried a diversion, or a rush, because he was obviously intent on silencing everyone in the room. He'd bought into the business of murder, and there was no getting out of it now. So what if a few more dead souls got added to his shopping list? Stop now and he would be indicted for murder on a scale that not even Pridham & Briggs could fix.

Young Pridham pushed himself away from the door and came toward me. His eyes were like chunks of black ice, like something alien, frozen in space.

He stopped a yard from my chair. The chromed muzzle of the .38 flickered with the reflected flames of the hurricane lamps. Pridham grinned. His face was a death mask. He had gone over to the other side and there would be no called him back.

''Just in case you've been counting bullets,'' he said, ''forget it.''

He put his left hand inside the pocket flap of his parka. When he pulled it out he was holding another gun, a make I didn't recognize. It was cheaply blued and the grip was plastic.

''Saturday night special,'' he whispered, drifting the words like a tuneless song. ''Shine your everlovin' light on me. Mrs. Fitzgerald was kind enough to show me where she kept her own gun, so I didn't even have to use mine. Wasn't that sweet of her? Even told me where her nosy writer friend had gone. Isle Bright to see a certain Father Sydney.''

He loomed in, touching Lois's .38 to the tip of my nose. I held my breath and strained at the lamp cord. If anything, pulling seemed to tighten the bonds.

''Hawkins,'' he said softly, ''you're an asshole. If you'd kept your nose out of things, none of this would have happened. It was all supposed to end with Edwards. The guy was a loser, Hawkins, like you. Made a mess of everything he touched. Couldn't even do a simple deal with your man Quinn without putting his foot in it, giving himself away. You want to know how totally devoid of intelligence Eyeball was? He actually convinced himself I wanted to have sex with him! Oh, God,'' Pridham laughed, ''if you could have seen him! Trying to direct a seduction scene in that ghastly room of his. I mean, can you imagine? I told him I'd rather die first. He started laughing that hyena laugh of his, and I thought, screw this, take your chance, *he's* going to die first.''

Something popped in the fireplace. Pridham tensed. The .38 bumped against my teeth.

''He was my first, Hawkins. And it was so easy! I pulled his gun out of the holster he kept by the bed, and do you know what that fool did? He assumed I was going to shoot him in his precious 'family jewels,' which is what he called them, like they were somehow terribly valuable. He's lying there with both hands covering himself, giving me that hairy look of his. He never even moved when I pulled the trigger.''

Pridham trembled. I could see the sweat on his hand, the nervous way his finger caressed the trigger.

''That should have been the end of it, with Edwards gone,'' he said. ''Then I noticed you conferring with Peter Sylvia, there in the courtroom. Picking his brain. As superfags go, Sylvia was okay, but he knew too many people. Vulnerable people. So what happens after he talks to you? He calls me up, asks about Father Sydney, did I happen to remember him? Very sneaky, but I knew he was putting it all together. So what could I do? It was a clean hit. I don't think he felt a thing. You *like* this, don't you, me spilling my guts?''

He let it hang, twisting the muzzle into the side of my nose. I could see his knuckles whitening as he squeezed the grip.

Megan screamed.

Milton Pridham swung around, aiming both guns at her. ''That will be *enough*.'' he shouted. ''Tell her to shut up, Father.''

Father Sydney said nothing.

Pridham lurched around a sheet-covered couch. I tried to beam a psychic push at him, make him trip and fall head first into the fireplace. No such luck. He stood there, wobbling slightly. Two-gun Milton, facing down an unarmed priest.

"On your feet, Father."

Sydney looked up at him. "If you're going to shoot me, I'd rather die in this chair."

Pridham kept the .38 aimed at the priest, and swung the Saturday night special over in Megan's direction. "The choice is, you can sit where you are and watch me shoot the girl. Or you can stand up when I say so."

Father Sydney looked at me. He looked at Megan. He stood up, hands loose at his side. Pridham backed up out of reach of those pale hands. I was trying to blink a message to Father Sydney: *Don't make a move until one of us has his hands free.*

There's a limit to how much you can express without speaking. I do think he realized I wanted him to wait. Throwing himself on Pridham wouldn't do any good, because Pridham could shoot him and wrest himself free before anyone could help.

Pridham demanded the keys to the chapel.

"It's not locked," Father Sydney said. "We never lock it."

"Isn't that nice," Pridham said. "An open sanctuary. Pretty little place. I think it'd be nice if we all go out there and get acquainted with the Lord."

I didn't like the sound of that, not at all. He had already helped Eyeball get acquainted, and Peter Sylvia, and who knows who else. Maybe he had a whole congregation somewhere, a steamy bathhouse in hell.

"You push the cripple's chair," he ordered the priest. "The rest of you, on your feet."

The wind screamed through the porch railing. Father Sydney, following instructions, had put the two children on my lap. With my hands tied up behind there was no easy way for me to keep them from slipping off, except to use my chin, pressing down on the top of Sarah's head as she buried her face in my chest. Trying to keep her there on my lap seemed extremely important at the time. I was convinced that if they fell Milton Pridham might react by pulling the trigger of the .38.

He had just the one pistol as we traversed the frigid length of the porch. In his other hand he had the can of kerosene. You didn't need to be a mind reader to figure out what was fermenting in that sick brain of his.

''Just keep moving!'' he shouted into the teeth of the wind, prodding Megan and Lois from behind. The kerosene sloshed around inside the can. I wondered how much was left. A gallon or two? Plenty.

Father Sydney pushed my wheelchair. With Pridham distracted by Lois, who stumbled and fell, slipping on the icy deck, the priest's fingers worked at the lamp cord binding my wrists. The fact that the twins were sprawled in my lap helped obscure what he was doing. Of course Pridham might have glance over at any moment, but what did we have to lose?

The water in the cove was almost black under a gray sky. The afternoon light was lengthening as the sun headed down on its short winter transit. The view across the bay was clear and vivid. The myriad islands, the frothing whitecaps, the gulls that whirled up like white leaves against the darker sky.

It was a crisp December day. Tomorrow, if it ever came, would be Christmas Eve. The children burrowed against my chest as the wind buffeted us. Milton Pridham had to shout to be heard. Not that it mattered. He was in a shouting mood and a lot of it didn't make much sense.

''This is not me!'' he screamed, jabbing the pistol at the small of Megan's back. ''I'm not here! I'm not doing this!''

Childe Milton was losing it. He had been riding a maelstrom of murder and now he was facing the eye of the whirlpool and screaming his defiance. The kerosene can banged against his leg as he staggered from the porch to the driveway.

Behind me Father Sydney slipped his fingers into the knot, loosening the bonds. My hands burned as the blood began to circulate through my wrists. As we made the bumpy transition to the frozen driveway, Father Sydney bent down and murmured, "Are the children okay?"

I nodded.

"Not to worry," he said.

Not to worry? He sounded almost cheerful. It occurred to me that the priest was just as loony as Milton Pridham; maybe the withdrawal from the psychotropics and the tranquilizers had fogged his mind.

In the driveway, behind my van, was a black Mercedes sedan. The windows were heavily tinted. Handy for hit-and-run missions, and for the interstate transportation of two abducted children and their mother. And certainly not out of place on Isle Bright.

It was uphill to the chapel. Lois, who looked to be running on empty, couldn't keep her balance. She kept slipping and falling, whacking against the thin crust of snow. Everytime Megan tried to look back toward me, Milton would scream and jab the pistol at her. The kerosene can made a hollow booming noise. Distant thunder.

The promontory where the little chapel stood was shielded somewhat by a stand of pines, out of the wind. Pridham waited until we had all gathered by the doors. Then he ordered the priest to open up.

"It's unlocked," Father Sydney said. With one last downward jerk he freed the cord from my wrists.

"I said *open it.*"

I kept my hands behind me, gripping the nest of lamp cord.

Father Sydney walked to the door. He turned back, looked toward the estate house, the bay, the looming sky. The slanting daylight directly illuminated his face. Something had relaxed. There was a peaceful tranquillity in his expression. His eyes, although darkly circled, were no longer hollow.

"Go on."

He lifted up the latch and pushed open one of the big doors.

"Everybody in," Pridham said, standing to one side. "Cold out here, let's get inside."

Father Sydney pulled me backward over the threshold, into the chapel. Inside there was an icy stillness. Voices echoed in the dark. Megan murmured something to Lois, who struggled against her gag. On my lap Rory and Sarah lay comatose. I could feel their hearts beating like little trip-hammers.

"Don't be afraid," I whispered into the tangled mass of Sarah's hair. "Everything will be okay."

When Pridham banged the door shut, the only source of light was the rosy infusion from the stained-glass window overhead. I could make out three short rows of pews, a simple altar, and the dull gleam of the communion rail.

"Light some candles," Pridham ordered Father Sydney. "Light *all* of them. No one else move."

Pridham stood by the front pew, where he had forced Megan and Lois to kneel. He kept the .38 a few inches from the back of Megan's head, looking at me to make sure I was aware. The jerry can was at his feet. Above the altar a white plaster Christ was frozen in delirious agony on an ebony cross. The painted drops of blood were as red as wine.

"You did this," Pridham said to me. "Everything that happens is because of you. You and that stupid cretin Edwards. *I* didn't want any of this to happen. It was all Edwards, his screw-ups. Shooting the wrong kid, then grabbing the two brats after I *told* him it wouldn't work, it was too dangerous. But he wouldn't listen."

Father Sydney lit a taper. Under a slim porcelain statue of the Virgin Mary was a rack of votive candles. He touched the taper to each candle. The statue began to glow softly. The children shivered against me as the flickering lights played against the steep rafters of the chapel roof. In the front pew, crouched on their knees, Megan and Lois shivered.

"Bring the taper over here."

Father Sydney obeyed, carrying the guttering candle in both hands. In its soft light he appeared years younger. I imagined him as he must have looked entering the Dominican seminary or, later, saying his first mass.

"Put it there," Pridham said, pointing with the .38.

Father Sydney put the burning candle in a holder affixed to the end of the pew. He looked at Milton Pridham, eyes blinking slowly, deliberately. Waiting. Pridham was about five feet from my wheelchair. Just out of reach if I managed to lurch forward. And if I did, there were the children, whom Pridham had cannily placed between my heart and his bullets.

Pridham looked down at the kerosene can, then at the flickering taper.

"Father," he said, "put on your vestments."

Father Sydney didn't move.

"I know they're here," Pridham said. The .38 trembled in his hand, the snub end of the chrome muzzle brushing the back of Megan's neck. "You told me all about it. How your precious mother celebrates Easter mass here. The special vestments she brought back from one of her miracle quests. Her son the holy father. Don't you *remember?* Weeping in your cups, telling us how it would kill the old lady if she ever knew how low you'd sunk? The pathetic Father Faggot, entertaining the bathhouse boys with his troubled tales. Or maybe you've blanked it out, hey? Well, it doesn't matter now, what you choose to remember."

Father Sydney spoke. "I remember everything," he said.

"Put on the vestments, Father. I want you to look the part."

I was concentrating on Tim Sullivan. On the message I'd left on his machine. If this was my story, rather than Pridham's, Casey would already be on his way. He and his sidekick Shannon would be burning up the Maine Turnpike, racing against the clock. Responding to the soft click of my word processor as the little screen glowed, filling up with words. They would arrive like the cavalry, kicking open the chapel door and dropping Milton Pridham in his tracks, just as he was about to put his awful plan into action.

But Tim Sullivan was not Detective Casey. Sheehan was not Shannon. If by some chance Fitzy got home early and immediately phoned Sully, there was a faint chance the Sullivan, remembering the message I'd left on his answering machine, might decide to check out Isle Bright. But Boston was two hours away and, more important, Pridham had come out to the island on the third and last ferry. So no one was going to arrive at the last moment to rescue us. There would be no muted bugle calls or distant sirens. There was only the faint cry of swooping gulls, and the slam of my heart battering my ribs, and the strained, choking voice of Milton Pridham, of Choate, Dartmouth, and Louisburg Square.

A red velvet curtain covered the wall to the left of the altar. Father Sydney pulled it aside. There, hanging in a shallow closet, was a white satin surplice. An abundance of gold thread was woven into the ecclesiastical symbol of the mass, exquisite hand detailing that must have cost Mrs. Ethel Owen Sydney a small fortune.

"Hurry, Father," Milton Pridham said. "We're running out of time."

He was shivering violently. I expected the .38 to go off at any moment. If he would only take it away form the back of Megan's head I was ready to make my move, futile as it might be. What did we have to lose?

"How about leaving the kids out of this," I said to him. "No need to include them, right?"

"Wrong," Pridham said. And in a flat voice devoid of emotion he told me why. He'd been there when Eyeball turned the kids over to Lew Quinn.

"The girl opened her eyes," he said matter-of-factly. "I thought she was out cold when Eyeball brought her out to the car, but she opened her eyes and looked at me. It was only a matter of time before she said something. Probably no one would believe her at first, but I couldn't take the risk. It's out of my hands now. Events must proceed."

Father Sydney slipped the surplice over his head and shook it down over his shoulders. His pale hands appeared through the voluminous sleeves. The gold thread gleamed in the candlelight.

"It was you all along," Pridham said to him. "It was you who got caught in the bathhouse. You who got blackmailed by that filthy cop. You did everything. None of this was me, do you understand? I'm not even here. I was *never* here."

He picked up the burning taper and moved to the front of the pew, facing Lois and Megan and the kids and me.

"I'll make sure," he said, slurring the words. He sounded like he'd been gargling rocks. "I'll make sure it doesn't hurt."

He aimed the .38 at Lois, his hand trembling.

As a novelist I knew what Pridham was up to. He was going to create a scene. In Pridham's scene Kurt Owen Sydney was going to play the villain. The priest was going to to be the stand-in for all of Milton Pridham's crimes. When they found the charred remains, investigators would scratch their heads and conclude that Father Sydney, a known child molester undergoing psychiatric care, had gone off his rocker and murdered witnesses who had discovered his involvement in the bathhouse scandal. The *Standard* would give it the full treatment. PSYCHO PRIEST SHOOTS FIVE, THEN SELF. CHAPEL BURNS.

There was a rumble of distant thunder. Pridham swung the .38 toward Father Sydney, who had picked up the jerry can. Pridham held the burning taper higher and tried to shout. His voice came as a husky whisper.

"What are you doing? Put that down."

Father Sydney looked at me. He smiled. He lifted the kerosene can and emptied it over his own head. The fumes were pungent and strong. His white surplice darkened as it absorbed the liquid. The rest pooled under his feet.

"You're nuts," Pridham said. He started to back away.

Father Sydney lifted his hands out from his side, as if he expected to take flight. The wet surplice flowed from his arms.

"Get away!" Milton screamed. He fired the .38. A small red hole opened in the pattern of gold threads. Father Sydney staggered, then lunged, embracing Milton and the taper he held. The white vestments burst into flame as Milton screamed. Black smoke roiled up from the flames. They both fell into the pool of kerosene at the foot of the altar. There was another thudding explosion of flame. Something wailed in the sheet of fire. It did not sound human.

Megan stood and wrenched her hands free. She saw me already wheeling the chair around with one hand, the other clutching the children. Meg grabbed Lois. The two of them stumbled down the aisle ahead of me as the air filled with dense, acrid smoke. We were all coughing and choking when Megan yanked the door open. As the wind came gusting in the air seemed to explode behind us.

We were huddled together in the van when the Isle Bright volunteer fire brigade arrived. By then the flames were leaping higher than the surrounding pines and the ice in the driveway was melting. The firemen dragged out their hoses and emptied the pumper, creating boiling clouds of steam that looked, in that weird light, like enormous pink balloons. After the tank was empty, the island volunteers, who looked happy as hell to be mucking about in black rubber boots and orange slickers, ran hoses down to the cove and eventually quenched the flames with seawater. A lot of it blew by and froze on the charred pine branches. Glistening in the spotlights, the trees looked almost beautiful, their icy boughs looming over the blackened remains of the chapel.

A light snow was falling through the night sky, cooling the last of the embers, when Fitzy arrived with Tim Sullivan. The two of them had had quite a time convincing the Portland Port Authority to send the ferry out on an unscheduled run. Sully invoked the Boston Police Department and the wrath of God. That didn't impress anyone from the Port Authority. Finally Fitzy threatened to sue, which had the desired effect.

Fitzy for once was speechless. He let Sully do the talking.

"Believe it or not, we had Pridham under surveillance," he said, running his hands through his hair as he gazed at the remains of the chapel. "Only, wouldn't you know it, we were watching the wrong Mercedes."

By then Rory was sound asleep in his mother's arms. Sarah, who refused to leave my lap, took her thumb out of her mouth just long enough to ask me one question.

"Uncle Jack," she said, in her grave and serious way. "Tell me a story, please?"

"Yes, honey."

Sarah smiled and put her thumb back in here mouth and fell instantly asleep.

It was a good beginning.

5 ONE FINE SPRING DAY IN APRIL WE PUT Lew Quinn on the train to Arlington, Virginia. The marines had room for one more good man down there. A sliver of green earth under a slim white cross. The baggage handlers at South Station were mournful as they slid the casket into the storage carriage. That had more to do with the cops looking on then any grave respect for the departed.

"I been signing off for this guy all week," Sully complained, putting a scrawl on the shipping invoice.

Releasing the remains for burial had not been easy, since the file on Quinn's death was not yet officially closed. His ex-wife, at my urging, had made the petition, and with some prodding from Fitzy, Homicide agreed to bend the rules.

Larry Sheehan took his hat off. For once he didn't have a cigarette parked in the corner of his mouth. When the compartment doors had been shut he put the hat back on. "What can I say," he said. "The Eskimo was a stand-up guy."

The air in Boston was as fresh as it ever gets. Even the carbon monoxide had a nice zing to it. Tim Sullivan was wearing a new beige spring suit and wingtips with a spit polish. From his breast pocket a white silk handkerchief bloomed. He plucked out the hanky and polished his glasses.

"I got a call from the chancery this morning," he said. "A Monsignor McCue. Wanted to know the status of our investigations. To wit, the file on the late Kurt Owen Sydney."

"What did you tell him?"

Sully slipped on his glasses. They glinted in the sun. He pulled at his left earlobe and smiled. "I had to apologize. I had to say, sorry Monsignor, we seem to have lost that particular file. Can't be found."

"I bet he was disappointed," Sheehan said.

"Yeah," Sully said laconically. "Really broke his heart."

''You lose the file on Milton Pridham, too?'' I asked.

''Couldn't,'' he said. ''Never had one.''

''What if Russ White blows the whistle?''

Sullivan shrugged. ''It's been three months,'' he said. ''He hasn't blown it yet.''

There was a squeal of steel on steel. The train bumped forward, then stopped. I knew, as they did, that there was very little chance the *Standard* would ever print Russ White's story. No one had been brought to trial. Nothing had ever been proved. The McGary chain saw no profit in taking on the law firm of Pridham & Briggs, or the archdiocese of Boston. The only way the tale would ever be published was if I worked it into one my Casey books, as fiction. I would have to change the names to protect the innocent, and the guilty, and the redeemed.

I wasn't the only one working on a book.

''How are Fitzgerald's kids doing?'' Sheehan asked. He stripped foil from a stick of gum and popped it in his mouth.

''They're doing fine,'' I said. ''No problems.''

''Great. So hey, Jack,'' Sheehan said, snapping the gum and fidgeting. ''I was wondering if I could ask you a favor.''

''Fire away.''

Grinning sheepishly, Sheehan produced a bulging manila envelope.

''It's this thing I'm tryin' to write. I guess you'd call it a memoir, huh? What it is, I talked into a tape recorder and then I had the stuff transcribed. Cost me a freakin' fortune, put my voice on paper. Could you like maybe, ah, look it over? Tell me if it stinks, or what?''

The poor bastard was actually wringing his hat. I assured him I would be happy to read it. He exhaled an invisible fog of spearmint, then jammed his hands in his pants pockets and rocked on his heels.

''I guess it must seem pretty weird to you,'' he said. ''A guy like me tryin' to express himself.''

''No,'' I said. ''There's nothing weird about it.''

Up in the girders over the track, pigeons were nesting. Tim Sullivan glanced at them warily, checking the immaculate shoulders of his new suit.

''Don't even think about it,'' he said, pointing a finger at the strutting pigeon, who cocked its head and cooed back at him.

''Listen to the guy,'' Sheehan said, laughing. ''St. Francis talking to the birdies.''

The train started to move. The Eskimo was heading south at last. The sky over the city was brand-new. The little birdies were chirping and even the winos were blinking at the sunshine and grinning. As the cars started rattling by I tried letting go of the thoughts that had been weighing me down over the last few months. Thoughts about good and bad and the large gray area in between. Thoughts about murder and self-sacrifice, about sin and redemption, about courage in the face of death. I thought about an old victrola with a magic link to the past and the static hiss that could not obscure the immortal voice of a flawless tenor.

When the last car thundered by I raised my hand and shouted, *''Vesti la giubba!''*

Larry Sheehan looked at me like I was nuts.

''What's that mean?'' he said.

''Oh, nothing,'' I said, wheeling away from the empty track. ''Just something some clown said once.''